APPLEBY'S END

APPLE

MICHAEL INNES

BY'S

END

COLLIER BOOKS, NEW YORK, N.Y.

The Macmillan Company, New York
Printed in the United States of America

APPLEBY'S END

Chapter 1

THE GUARD blew his whistle and waved his flag—how weighted with ritual have the railways in their brief century become! —and the train crawled from the little station. The guard walked alongside through the snowflakes, wistful for that jump-and-swing at an accelerating van that is the very core of the mystery of guarding trains. But the train continued to crawl. Sundry footballers in a glass box, some with legs swung high in air, stood immobile to watch its departure.

The engine tooted. In pinnacled and convoluted automatic machines, memorials of an age wildly prodigal of cast-iron, the slowly moving traveller would have found it possible to remark that the final and unremunerative penny had long since been dropped. Long ago had some fortunate child secured the last brightly wrapped wafer of chocolate; long ago had the last wax vesta released a dubious fragrance from the last cigarette—and the once flamboyant weighing machine, pathetic in its antique inability either to bellow or print, seemed yet, in its forlorn proposal to register a burden of thirty stone whispering dumbly of dealings with a race of giants before the Flood.

Just such a well-cadenced if vacuous meditation as this might the passenger, drear and bored, have constructed for himself before the guard stepped resignedly aboard, the platform dipped, points sluggishly clanked and the train was in open country once more. Sunday afternoon, which in England subtly spreads itself over the face even of inanimate nature, stretched to the flat horizon. The fields were clothed in patchy white like half-hearted penitents; here and there cattle stood steamy and dejected, burdened like their fellows in Thomas Hardy's poems with some intuitive low-down on essential despair; and now on the outskirts of a village the train trundled past a yellow brick conventicle constructed on the basis of hardly more cheery theological convictions. Inside the carriage it was cold and beginning to be foggy as well. The focus of attention was a large glass bowl rather like those used in cemeteries to protect artificial flowers, but here pendulous from the roof and sheltering gas burners of a type judged moderately progressive at the Great Exhibition of 1851. Flanking this were luggage racks of a breadth nicely calculated to cause chronic anxiety in those below. Then came photographs: a beach and promenade densely packed with holiday-makers dressed in heavy mourning; a vast railway hotel standing, Chirico-like, in a mysteriously dispopulated public square; a grove exaggeratedly bosky and vernal, bespattered with tea tables and animated by three stiffly-ranked dryads in the disguise of waitresses.

Under the photographs were the passengers. Over the faces of the passengers, or lying on their knees, or slipped to their feet, were the objects of Sabbath devotion traditional to Englishmen in the lower and middle ranks of society. There were instruments and blunt instruments, packets of weed-killer and bundles of incriminating letters. There were love nests. There were park benches over which white crosses and black circles hung mysteriously in air. There were serious offences and grave charges; there were faces, blurry and odd-angled, of judges, coroners, and detective-inspectors from Scotland Yard. Thin-lipped and driven women stood between policemen outside assize halls; persons now of notorious life lay naked on horse-hair sofas waving rattles, or dangled bootied legs over Edwardian tables.

Snow fell outside, as perhaps on half-a-dozen Sundays in the year. But every Sunday there was this sift and silt of newsprint in the domestic interiors of England. Big money lay in and behind it. In their brief elevation into objects of national curiosity these inconsiderable criminals and furtive amorists were sought out by vast organizations, groomed, glamourized and sub-edited in cliff-like buildings, multiplied and distributed with miraculous speed by powerful machines. And thence were sucked into millions of minds. It was the sucking that was really operative in the process: had the suckers not an instinct to suck it was likely that the vast organizations would find out other things to do. And so this laboriously garnered world of crime and misconduct and sensation was, in fact, a mythology—a fleeting and hebdomadal mythology called into being by the obscurely working but infinitely potent creativity of the folk. In the green Arcadian valleys Pan is dead but still a numerous Panisci lurk and follow in the parks. Armies of thieves are still littered under Mercury. The rape of Proserpine—gathering flowers, herself a fairer flower—continues still, and Dis's wagon is a borrowed limousine.

Why in these latter days should the perennial myths have so squalid an embodiment—this same splendid car in which Pluto carried off Demeter's daughter decline into Madame Bovary's patiently perambulating cab? John Appleby, himself a detective-inspector from Scotland Yard and with a weakness for cultivated reverie, had arrived at this large question when the train jerked to a halt. Twisting his neck as he sat cramped in a corner, he peered through the window. Mere dejection seemed to have occasioned this stoppage, and in mere dejection too the countryside was fading on the sight. In a field beyond the telegraph wires there stood a single gaunt tree. A tree, thought Appleby, of infinitely sinister silhouette. But this impression was of course a matter of simple projection. From the sog and wash of Sunday newspapers littering the carriage a species of miasma arose and seeped into the mind. And the mind, like a well-fed fire-engine, promptly sprayed this out again upon a waiting and neutral nature. . . .

Appleby stooped and picked up one of the abandoned papers from the floor. It opened on a youngish man, bowler-hatted, well-nourished and—surely—repulsive, standing with a truculently elevated chin before what appeared to be the shell of a burnt-out stable or hovel. Appleby glanced at caption and legend, and sighed. The Gaffer Odgers Murder. Old Gaffer Odgers had been unlovely in life, and in death he had been a faint stench as of roasted carrion. And the bowler-hatted person was Appleby himself. About eight years ago, that had been; and here was somebody writing it up for a new generation of connoisseurs. When current crime fell flat the public was very willing to be regaled from hiding places ten years deep.

It was at this point that the man sitting opposite Appleby spoke. He had lowered his book—he appeared to be not one of the hebdomadal mythologists—and was looking appraisingly at his fellow-passenger. "On the 27th of September 1825," he said, "Stephenson drove a train of thirty-four vehicles, making a gross load of about 90 tons, at a speed of from ten to fifteen miles an hour. This was on the Stockton

and Darlington railway. It is sometimes possible to feel that
our rural railway system has made little progress since."

"This is certainly a tedious journey enough." Appleby in
his turn looked curiously at the man who had addressed him.
"But trundling along is not without its charm. I'm quite content myself to leave progressive railways to the Americans."

"In America," said the stranger, "the development of the
locomotive dates from almost the same time as in England.
In 1828, on behalf of the Delaware and Hudson Canal Company, Horatio Allen ordered three locomotives from Messrs.
Foster and Rastrick, of Stourbridge. One of these, the Stourbridge Lion, was actually the first practical steam locomotive
to run in America, which it did on the 9th of August 1829."

"Most interesting." Appleby groaned inwardly. No doubt
this elderly person had an attic at home full of toy trains and
signal-boxes, and on these he would now discourse for some
considerable time. But at least he appeared to be unattracted
by popular criminology. "I see, sir," Appleby added civilly,
"that you are interested in railway history."

"Dear me, no! In fact, certainly not. I have no interest
whatever in such a subject." The elderly man raised his book
again, rather as if positively offended. Then, seemingly feeling that he had been too abrupt, he spoke once more. "I wonder if I might have the pleasure of lending you a book during
our journey? This"—he tapped the book he had been reading
—"is Dr. Bossom's recent work on the Docetists. A somewhat
diffuse exposition, I am afraid. But here"—and the stranger
rummaged in a small suitcase beside him—"is Stuttaford on
the Monophysites—an altogether more concise monograph,
if one may judge by bulk."

"You are very kind"—Appleby was somewhat at a loss—
"but I'm afraid that the subject of Heresy—"

"Is of no interest to you? Nor is it to me." The elderly
stranger was becoming quite cordial. "You would be inclined
to say that the Docetists and the Monophysites—and for that
matter the Pelagians and the Gnostic Ebionites—are to-day
subjects of very limited popular appeal?"

"Extremely limited, I should imagine."

"Exactly so." The stranger nodded emphatically. "And if
you will permit me"—he fished out a notebook—"I should

like to make a note of your opinion. And now"—he rummaged again—"here we have two romances by Anthony Hope, Spratt's *History of the Royal Society*, somebody's recent life of Dostoievsky, Swincer and Tiver on the Tyrannosaurus, a current *Turf Guide*, a volume of Livy, two pamphlets on artificial respiration—"

"I think Anthony Hope would be best." Appleby was now thoroughly mystified. Model railways had been a guess far wide of the mark. But what could one put in its place? The personal appearance of the stranger was itself puzzling. If it were possible to think of one of His Majesty's judges as reduced to obtaining his apparel from a superior second-hand shop while at the same time retaining the services of a competent valet—But Appleby shook his head. Judges don't go down in the world—or not in England. "I suppose," said Appleby boldly over the first page of Anthony Hope, "that you are a bookseller or publisher?"

"Sir," said the stranger, "I have never engaged in trade."

This was distinctly crushing. The stranger however did not intend it to be final, for he was fishing in a pocket once more and presently produced a worn morocco case. "Allow me," he continued with formality, "to offer you my card."

Appleby took the card. *Everard Raven*, he read, *Barrister-at-law*. So that was it, after all. And perhaps barristers go down in the world, even if judges don't—but not so far down as to engage in trade. On this some form of apology would no doubt be tactful. "Appleby's my name," Appleby said. "I made my guess merely on the strength of the books you have with you. The subjects are so various that I can scarcely imagine even the most catholic reader being interested in them all. Indeed, there seems to be no possible connection between any two of them."

Mr. Raven closed Dr. Bossom on the Docetists and crossed his hands comfortably over his carefully pressed waistcoat. "You are mistaken," he said. "Pardonably so, it must be confessed. For the link, although it is there, is scarcely as philosophical as I would wish. As a man of letters—for I must explain, Mr. Appleby, that I have long since given over the practice of the law in favour of literary pursuits—as a man of letters I must confess, indeed, that the link is a sadly arbitrary one. It is very much that which had to content the good Fluellen when he came to compare Macedon and Monmouth."

"A river in each," said Appleby. "And salmons in both."

Mr. Raven nodded, evidently much pleased. "I perceive that you are a student, Mr. Appleby. And the common factor among my small batch of books should now be obvious to you. The Docetists and the Monophysites may be subsumed under the common term Religion; Dostoievsky suggests Russia; the Tyrannosaurus is a Reptile; Livy treats of the history of Rome; the *Turf Guide* concerns Racing; artificial respiration is an aspect of Resuscitation; and Anthony Hope wrote about Ruritania. The link, in fact, is alphabetical. I am deep in the doggy letter, sir." Mr. Raven paused and chuckled. "What the grammarians were fond of calling *littera canina*. And hence too those floating scraps of information on Railways with which I had the pleasure of initiating our acquaintance."

"Then would I be right," asked Appleby, "if I were to have another guess and say that you are editing an encyclopædia?"

"Your guess," said Mr. Raven, "would be approximately correct. Unfortunately"—he spoke with sudden gloom—"the word 'edit' scarcely meets the case. You would do better to say 'compile.'"

"Compile?"

Mr. Raven nodded. "I write it." He lowered his voice. "I write," he said unexpectedly, "the whole damned thing."

Chapter 2

IT WAS DARK now and the journey had become interminable. The engine, while daylight lasted simply an obsolescent locomotive tugging grimy carriages across English ploughland, was now a creature, alien and dragonish, panting on some vast and laboured quest. The engine was a monster—one of Swincer and Tiver's Dinosauria, Appleby thought—with ghastly respirations striving to free itself from an engulfing

Jurassic slime. Its reeky breath, faintly luminous, flipped momentarily at the windows. Sometimes, with an indescribable eeriness, it howled against the night. The pinch of famine this, perhaps—for station by station its clanking and jerkily oscillating maw was voiding itself into the murk: more passengers were getting off than getting on. Behind the grimed glass bowl the stinking little light now shone on the dusty red of empty seats, on cigarette butts and the dottles of pipes, on banana skins and orange peel mingled and pashed with the weed-killers, the love-nests, the ephemeral renaissance of Gaffer Odgers. Only the four corners of the carriage were occupied. In one a priest, heavily-breathing and rumbling dyspeptically within, stared with glassy concentration at an open breviary. In another was a slatternly woman clutching an idiot boy. Mr. Raven, with a censorious pencil poised over Dr. Bossom, occupied a third. And in the fourth Appleby, his overcoat buttoned up to his nose, endeavoured to grapple with Anthony Hope's *The Prisoner of Zenda*. "Being the History," he read, "of Three Months in the Life of an English Gentleman." Well, perhaps the unfortunate man had attempted a cross-country journey in an English railway train.

"Boo," said the idiot boy; "boo, boo." The slatternly woman smiled gently and patted his head. "Boo, boo, boo," the idiot boy said; "boo, boo, boo."

Appleby put down his book in desperation. "About that encyclopædia," he asked. "May I enquire how long it is likely to take you, and when you hope to publish?"

"Much of it is published already." Mr. Raven took off his gold-rimmed glasses and held them some inches in front of a markedly long nose. *"The New Millennium Encyclopædia, Edited by Everard Raven, with the Assistance of Many Scholars and Men of Science."*

"But I understood you to say that you were doing it all yourself?"

"As indeed I am. Our title-page, I fear, has been conceived according to the morality of merely commercial men—"

"Boo," interrupted the idiot boy.

"—for a writer, surely, would judge the promise of an initial Millennium enough, without the otiose superaddition of novelty." Mr. Raven paused, evidently as on a well-worn joke. "And as the Scholars and Men of Science"—he tapped his suitcase—"here they are. I have at least the advantage of being able to take my collaborators about with me."

"I see. The whole affair must be rather a burdensome task."

"Assuredly it is so. Particularly as we come out in fortnightly parts. I had a message only yesterday to say that *Patagonia to Potato* would be on the bookstalls on Thursday. It really is uncommonly harassing. When one has got to *Potato* one is devilish near this confounded *littera canina*, if the truth be told. And if I cut Railways down there's sure to be a row. I shall have to omit Ruritania"—Mr. Raven shook his head dolefully—"there's no help for it. And, mind you, I doubt if anybody ever thought of putting Ruritania in an encyclopædia before."

Because the carriage was now nearly empty its temperature was dropping rapidly, and as a result moisture was condensing on the roof and falling in splashy drops. The idiot boy began to wander about in the endeavour to catch these with his tongue. The priest closed his breviary, uttered a pious ejaculation *sub voce* and produced a bag of peanuts. "But at least," said Appleby—who felt that a little cheerfulness would not be out of the way—"your doggy letter is a good distance down the alphabet. You must feel that you are nearing the end of the job."

"That's true, of course." Mr. Raven nodded without conviction. "Unfortunately after the encyclopædia there's the dictionary."

"The dictionary?"

"*The Revised and Enlarged Resurrection*. As a matter of fact, I've got some of the preliminary work on hand already."

The priest leant across the carriage. "May I," he asked gravely, "offer you a peanut?"

Appleby wriggled his numbed toes in their shoes. This now nocturnal journey was assuming a crazy quality in his mind. The train might be a Hitchcock train having its existence only on a ribbon of celluloid—in which case the priest was doubtless a beautiful female spy in disguise. Or the train might be an Emmett train lurking between the leaves of *Punch*—which would mean that it was filled with demons masquerading as farmers and retired colonels, and that the permanent way led only up the airy mountain and down the rushy glen. Not that Mr. Raven looked like a demon. Indeed, he seemed tolerably well to support Dr. Johnson's definition of a dictionary-maker as a harmless drudge. Or was there, as he looked up from Stuttaford on the Monophysites, a hint of rebellion in his eye? Appleby found it hard to tell. The engine hooted; above the priest's head the three waitresses stood at attention in their dingle; abruptly the idiot boy contrived to let down a window and there was a flurry of snowflakes and icy air.

"No, no, my lad, it won't do," said Mr. Raven benignly, and tugged at the strap. "A dirty night, Mr. Appleby. May I ask if you go far?"

"I change at Linger Junction."

"Um," said Mr. Raven and relapsed into Stuttaford. Appleby shuffled his feet, kicked Gaffer Odgers under the seat and returned to his novel. "For what relationship is there," he read, "between Ruritania and Burlesdon, between the Palace at Strelsau or the Castle of Zenda and Number 305 Park Lane, W?" The answer—it scarcely needed Scotland Yard to suggest—lay in Romantic Illegitimacy. A theme, thought Appleby, treated with rather more literary substance in Meredith's *Harry Richmond*.

"Boo," said the idiot boy.

A booksy journey. The idiot boy, of course, was straight out of Wordsworth. And it was Mr. Raven's doing. In Mr. Raven's presence everything turned booksy. It was very likely that the priest was really the late G. K. Chesterton's Father Brown.

"The Ravens," said Mr. Raven suddenly—and much as if Appleby had been speaking this fantasy aloud—"have been literary folk for generations. As you probably know."

"Oh, yes," said Appleby. "Of course."

"Which means that this sort of labour"—and Mr. Raven tapped his suitcase—"is less burdensome than it would be to a person without a tradition of letters."

"Ah," said Appleby, "tradition counts for a great deal, doesn't it?"

"Quite so. Only I must confess that I sometimes regret having undertaken these commissions. A systematic scholar, whose life is of necessity arduous, likes to have the satisfaction of feeling that his labours are on the frontiers of knowledge. But on what am I engaged here, Mr. Appleby?" And Mr. Raven tapped the suitcase once more. "A *rifacciamento*, sir; little more than a *rifacciamento*."

"Consolidation," said Appleby. "Yours must be regarded as a labour of consolidation. And of diffusion. Both, surely, very important functions of the scholar to-day." Anthony Hope, he was thinking, would be far far better than this. For it was one of Appleby's weaknesses that he was apt, out of an amiable desire to give pleasure, to involve himself in conversations of just such a ghastly insincerity as the present. "The frontiers of knowledge," he added, going the whole hog, "are important, of course. But we must not forget the welfare of the interior. The provincial cities, Mr. Raven, and the country towns. A good popular encyclopædia—"

Mr. Raven, much gratified, was fishing in his pockets once more. "Really," he said, "your image is so striking that I must be permitted to make a note of it. In moments of discouragement—"

The train, with a faint wheeze of escaping steam suggestive of more discouragement than a human being could express, drew to a halt. The slatternly woman woke up, grasped the idiot boy, and disappeared into the night as abruptly as a parachutist or a witch. The priest followed with an equal haste, as if he had some attempt at exorcism in mind. Appleby and Mr. Raven were left alone. "Yatter," said Mr. Raven.

"I beg your pardon?"

"Yatter. A ghastly little place. Yatter, Abbot's Yatter and King's Yatter. Then we come to Drool. . . . I think you said you hoped to change at Linger?"

"Yes."

"Um." Mr. Raven peered into the darkness which was again jolting leisurely by. "Inclement," he said gloomily; "really very inclement indeed."

"You think there may be some difficulty about changing at Linger?"

"But presently"—Mr. Raven spoke briskly and inconsequently, as one who avoids the premature disclosure of discomfiting intelligence—"but presently we shall be filling up." He closed Stuttaford and began to sweep crumbs, papers and peanut shells from the empty seats. "I suppose it was your aim to get to Sneak or Snarl?"

"I've booked a room at the inn at Snarl. And I certainly hope to get there to-night."

Mr. Raven shook his head. "I am very sorry to have to tell you that it can't be done. The train for Snarl never waits to make this connection."

Appleby stared at his companion aghast. "But," he said feebly, "the timetable—"

Again Mr. Raven shook his head—in commiseration, and also perhaps in some amusement at the extravagant expectations of the urban mind. "My dear sir, the timetable was printed long before Gregory Grope's grandmother fell down the well."

"I hardly see—"

"For a long time she was just missing, and her house at Sneak—a very nice house—stood empty. But when she came up with the bucket one day"—Mr. Raven was methodically stowing the Scholars and Men of Science in his suitcase— "and it was quite clear that she was dead, Gregory Grope's mother moved to Sneak from Snarl."

"Do I understand," asked Appleby resignedly, "that Gregory Grope is an engine-driver?"

"Exactly so. If I may say so, Mr. Appleby, you possess a keen power of inference. Gregory Grope drives the Snarl train, and the train of course spends the night at Snarl. But Gregory has to get home on his motor-bicycle to Sneak, and his mother is decidedly strict about late hours. It appears that it was as the consequence of a nocturnal diversion, somewhat surprising in a woman of her years, that old Mrs. Grope came to her unfortunate end. But I digress. The point is that Gregory and his train now leave Linger somewhat earlier than before. Of course you could complain to the district superintendent and I dare say something might be done about it in time.

"No doubt." The train had stopped and Appleby opened the window and looked out. Abbot's Yatter, in its aspect as a railway station, appeared to consist of an exiguous wooden scaffolding now rapidly disappearing beneath drifts of snow. As the locality was not one that he hoped to visit again the prospect of the district superintendent's eventual curbing of Mrs. Grope's matriarchal power had uncommonly small appeal. "No doubt. But perhaps you can tell me if there is an inn at Linger?"

"An inn? Dear me, no. Of course there is a waiting-room. But I think I am right in saying that it is used at present for Brettingham Scurl's Gloucester Old Spots."

"Brettingham Scurl?" said Appleby dully.

"The porter at Linger."

"Gloucester Old Spots?"

"Gloucester Old Spots. Quite a cleanly variety of pig, I have been told. Nevertheless—"

"What about King's Yatter—or Drool? Is there a pub, or somebody who might let a room?"

"Let me see," Mr. Raven frowned thoughtfully. "There is old Mrs. Ulstrup at Drool. She used to let a room. But I doubt if she does now. Not since she went out of her mind, poor old soul. Though of course you might try." Mr. Raven peered out into the darkness. "Here is King's Yatter already. Do you know the 'George' at King Yatter?"

"The 'George'?" asked Appleby hopefully.

"Fine little hotel. Incomparable Stilton and very good draught beer."

"Then I think"—said Appleby, and grabbed at his suitcase.

"My dear sir, I am sorry to say it was burnt down last year. By Hannah Hoobin's boy."

"Oh," said Appleby.

"I was on the Bench at the time. It seems that Hannah Hoobin's boy gets a great deal of erotic satisfaction from that sort of thing. I am glad to say that I was instrumental in persuading my fellow-magistrates to take an enlightened view of the case."

"Oh," said Appleby again. His disinterest in the recondite pleasures of Hannah Hoobin's boy was extreme. "I suppose it's snowing still?"

"Heavily. Ah, I told you we should be beginning to fill up." And Mr. Raven stepped back from the window to allow a newcomer to enter the compartment.

The stranger had not the appearance of one who was likely to bring gaiety to the tail-end of a Sabbath railway-journey.

He wore a somewhat threadbare suit of cypress green, a flowing and inky cloak, and a large black hat of the kind which popular illustrators used to associate with Anarchy or the Arts. His face was disposed in lines of noble melancholy on each side of a long nose. He looked abstractedly at Appleby, abstractedly at Mr. Raven, and then sat down in a corner and curved a long white hand over his eyes. The engine hooted on a rising note and the train, which appeared now to consist of one carriage only, set off at a comparatively brisk pace for Drool. It was when they had passed this station that Mr. Raven made his notable offer.

"I really think, Mr.—um—Appleby, that your best plan will be to spend the night with me. I should be extremely happy if you would do so. My place is three stops beyond Linger: Sleeps Hill, Boxer's Bottom, and then my own station, at which a conveyance will be waiting. And in the morning I think we can promise to get you across to Snarl."

This, Appleby felt, was an offer not lightly to be turned down. Whatever the domestic circumstances of the compiler of the *New Millennium* might be they could scarcely promise less in the way of hospitality than the demented Mrs. Ulstrup or Brettingham Scurl's pigs. He was about to announce his grateful acceptance when the train, which appeared to have to cope in this latter end of its journey only with the shortest laps, drew up in Linger Junction, and Mr. Raven once more popped out his head. "Not a doubt of it," he called back over his shoulder. "Gregory has gone. Ah, filling up still." And once more he stepped back to let a new passenger enter.

It was a girl this time. She had long haunches and slender flanks—she was, in fact, what old-fashioned writers would call tall and slim—and she had long eyelashes and what it was possible to think of as a long nose. Her manner was severe and composed. She sat down without glancing at her fellow-travellers, put her toes together, smoothed her skirt and brought out a book. The train was going forward slowly again—presumably as addressing itself to whatever acclivity led to Sleeps Hill—and to its regular and soporific jolting there was now added an intermittent sideways lurch and shudder. This was accompanied by rattlings, clankings, whistlings and wailings. Upon the snowstorm there had been superimposed something between a high wind and a gale.

Appleby turned to his prospective host. "Your invitation is very kind. But I would be sorry to put you—"

"Then that's settled," said Mr. Raven cheerfully. And Mr. Raven, it occurred to Appleby, was on the whole steadily cheerful. Or if he would not show up in normal surroundings as absolutely cheerful in himself yet he had, in this present melancholy setting, a large share of the quality relatively regarded. Appleby frowned at this dubiously philosophical speculation. But the gloom of all else surrounding him was indisputable. Chirico's hotel, the ranked waitresses, the holiday-makers in their overwhelming mourning: all these were becoming more sinister station by station. Nor were the new passengers at all out of key. The man with the inky cloak was staring at Appleby at once fixedly and with a vast inattention—much, Appleby thought, as one stares through a window at some distant and displeasing scene. And the girl had laid down her book and was looking at him too. The girl was really looking at *him,* but rather—surely—as if he were an oddly eroded garden ornament or a freak potato in a horticultural show. . . . "Sleeps Hill," said Mr. Raven comfortably. "And filling up."

Something long, pale and flattened had appeared against the window, like the under-belly of a sea-slug sucked hard against the side of an aquarium. Slightly above and to either side of this were what might have been two writhing caterpillars of the furry sort, and below each of these was a faint but baleful gleam of fire. The whole, in fact, was a human face engaged in some act of reconnaissance, and a moment later the door was thrown open and its owner heaved himself violently into the compartment.

It was odd, thought Appleby, that here should be another passenger with a notably long nose. And whereas the girl's nose was definitely attractive, the melancholy man's nose at least congruous with his features as a whole, and Mr. Raven's nose indisputably utilitarian in that it afforded a number of alternative resting-places for his gold-rimmed glasses, the newcomer's nose was entirely disconcerting. For the eyes, which were small and feral, were deep-set beneath beetling brows after the manner of the higher anthropoids; the forehead was low and receding; the mouth, which was large and thick-lipped, hung open in a species of rictus or fixed grimace; the figure was massive, stooped and lurching. It thus came about that the stranger's long nose achieved a sort of perpetually surprising tour-de-force in asserting a decisively human influence over what would otherwise have been an uncompromisingly simian whole.

The train had started again and was gaining speed; indeed it was going at least twice as fast as it had ever gone before. The new arrival sat in the middle of the compartment with his knees apart and his hands hanging over them in the manner of a pugilist waiting in his corner. He was breathing stertorously as if he had already fought a gruelling ten rounds. And—what was mildly disconcerting—he was glaring at Appleby with what had every appearance of being the most unbridled ferocity.

The girl was looking at Appleby too. She seemed rather taken with him. But in the most peculiar way. There was a sort of latent or smouldering passion in her glance. At the same time it was extremely impersonal. Appleby had an obscure feeling that she would not be nearly so interested in him if he were not sitting precisely as he was under the rays of a gas mantle invented in 1851. There was something unflattering about this. Appleby had a look at the cypress-suited man in the corner.

The cypress-suited man too was still staring. Not exactly through Appleby this time, but rather as if he were something phenomenal and essentially trivial with which the speculative mind must nevertheless of necessity concern itself in the effort to penetrate to a more substantial significance beyond. From under the pent-house of his large black hat the cypress-suited man was looking at Appleby like this. Appleby felt that, on the whole, he preferred the girl. It was somehow less uncomfortable to be of immediate interest in terms of optical science than to serve as a mere starting-point for some voyage into a metaphysical inane. And of course altogether preferable to either was being regarded mildly by Mr. Raven, who perceived one to be a student with a keen power of inference.

Appleby buried his chin deeper in the collar of his coat

and upbraided himself for these self-conscious musings. The sight of the truculent young Appleby in the bowler hat standing outside Gaffer Odgers' cindery hovel had begun it. After some years of being photographed in the society or close vicinity of charred bodies, driven women, blunt instruments, love nests, park benches, furtive amorists and packets of weed-killer one ought to be decidedly hardened to scrutiny. Appleby, on the contrary, was coming to feel rather morbid about it. Sometimes he wondered if it would help to grow a beard.

Rattling and clanking, buffeted by a great wind, bucketing and unbearably jolting, perpetually howling into the night, the train was now rushing dementedly down a gradient that led presumably to the abyss of Boxer's Bottom. The holiday-makers joggled on their beach, Chirico's hotel rocked as if to an earthquake, the faintly hissing light from the gas mantle flickered and flared. Conversation would scarcely have been possible—nor did any of the passengers seem inclined to communication other than by speaking looks and—in the case of the simian man—continued threatening breathings. Mr. Raven had tucked away his glasses and was swathing himself in several yards of grey woollen scarf—so carefully as to make Appleby feel a little apprehensive about the nature of the conveyance promised for the next stage of the journey. And now with a scream of brakes and an alarming hiss of escaping steam the train jolted to a halt. There was only one more stage to go.

Once more Mr. Raven put his head out, and once more withdrew it to admit a fresh passenger. This was a young man dressed in tweeds which were plainly shapeless even under an almost obliterating layer of snow. His mouth was shapeless too and held open in a twisted grin; his hair was a chaos of wavy yellow locks; his features were rugged and extremely asymmetrical; his eyes, which showed wide and amused beneath heavy brows, glinted with what was either extreme vivacity or a mild madness. And he had a long nose.

The young man shook himself like a bear, so that snow flew about the compartment. He then took a survey of those whom he had bespattered, beginning with Mr. Raven and ending with Appleby. On Appleby his glance paused; his mouth opened wider and twisted further; he appeared to be on the verge of some malicious and disconcerting announcement. Then he threw himself down on a seat, folded his arms, tossed his head backwards so that his yellow locks flew in air, and finally settled into an attitude of sardonic watchfulness such as one might mark in a man who both expects and welcomes immediate catastrophe. The train, now climbing once more, rumbled through the night with very little promise of anything of the sort.

It was odd about these people, Appleby thought. But for the fact that no one of them had uttered a word to any other, he would have supposed that there must be some degree of kinship between them. Perhaps the long nose was a consequence of the sustained in-breeding that sometimes distinguishes remote and isolated districts. Perhaps from Yatter to Linger and from Snarl to Drool this nose was the rule among people unconscious of any tie of blood. Perhaps Brettingham Scurl and Gregory Grope had it too; perhaps it was a feature still distinguishable in the unfortunate old person who came up with the bucket out of the well. . . . Appleby was aware that things were now considerably quieter in the compartment and that Mr. Raven was taking advantage of this to address him once more.

"Not more than three miles," Mr. Raven was saying cheerfully. "Unless of course anything has gone wrong at the ford. Or there are snowdrifts in Noblet's Lane. Or the axle really goes this time, or our man has been drinking again at the Arms, or Spot casts a shoe."

It sounded bad. Some sort of answering cheerfulness, however, it would be indecent not to attempt. "One can't ever bar accidents," Appleby said. "And I must repeat that it's uncommonly kind of you to ask me to stop the night."

The effect of this was notable. The cypress-suited man uttered a low moan, the girl looked startled, the simian person ground his teeth and the yellow-haired youth gave such a harsh short laugh as might be evoked in a theatre by some unexpected stroke of savage farce. At the same moment the brakes went on and everybody was on his feet in a movement so simultaneous as to be less disconcerting than irrationally terrifying. The three waitresses disappeared behind lurching and untidy tweeds; the flowing cloak of the melancholy man heaved itself like a universal darkness over the teeming holiday-makers on the beach; between Appleby and Chirico's hotel, like the foul fiend barring the way to sanctuary, was the heavily-breathing visage of the higher anthropoid. Appleby, amid a feeling of sudden obliteration beneath this long-nosed avalanche, heard Mr. Raven's voice raised in rapid introductions.

"Mr. Appleby," Mr. Raven was saying. "Mr. Appleby—whose acquaintance I have only just had the happiness of making. Mr. Appleby, this is my brother Luke, my brother Robert, my cousin Mark, my cousin Judith. Dear me, here we are."

"Appleby, did you say?" asked the melancholy man.

"Appleby?" said the girl. Her accent was wholly incredulous—as if it were self-evident that Appleby ought to be called Dobbin or Fido.

"Appleby?" said the simian man. "Well, that's very odd."

"Appleby!" exclaimed the yellow-haired youth, and gave a laugh harsher and shorter than before.

The door of the compartment was thrown open and there came a whip and howl of wind. Suddenly from the trampled floor and from beneath the seats arson and rape, thin-lipped women and blurry-faced judges, furtive amorists and Edwardian homicides spiralled upward in a crazy resurrection, flapping at the faces and curling round the limbs of the Ravens. The flurry of papers sank again; the Ravens were knee-deep in crime, were free of it, were tumbling on the platform with Appleby following.

It had been a moment of strangeness and obscure alarm. Now there was the dark, and driving snow and the rattle of the departing train.

"By the way," said Appleby, "what is the name of this sta—"

He stopped, his question already answered. Straight before him, sufficiently lit by the yellow rays of a hanging lantern, was a boldly lettered board. He read the inscription

---

APPLEBY'S END

Chapter 3

THE INKY cloak of Luke Raven flapped in the gale like a backcloth to chaos; snowflakes in epicycle and nutation, in precession and varying ellipse played a mad astronomy about him; he grabbed his hat, raised his melancholy face and yelled to the welkin. "Heyhoe!" yelled Luke Raven.

"Heyhoe, Heyhoe!" Mark Raven, his yellow hair streaming like a bright exhalation in the night, joined in the call. "Heyhoe-oh!"

"Heyhoe, *Hey*-hoe, *HEY*-hoe, Hey-*HOE*-OH!" Robert Raven who was rotating warily on his heel much as if he expected the whirling snowflakes to stab him in the back, joined with a positively Bacchic frenzy in the chorus. And even Everard Raven, that mild-mannered and learnedly-preoccupied man, was calling "Heyhoe!" into the darkness with surprising vigour. Only the girl Judith remained silent; after a minute's pause she plodded some paces down the platform, up-ended a suit-case, sat on it, and contemplated her family and their chance companion in a gloomy repose. Appleby, who found himself watching this young person with a good deal of attention, stamped his feet—or rather attempted to, with a soft crunch of snow as the only result. Was it the proper thing for all passengers to join in this queer ululation upon reaching Appleby's End—or was it a rite peculiar to Ravens? And what about an Appleby—was he not in something of a special case? These reflections were interrupted by the arrival on the platform of a creature having much the appearance of a giant weather-bound tortoise. Judith was the first of the Ravens to see the new arrival. "Heyhoe," she said, "where the deuce have you been?"

Heyhoe came to a halt—a process involving so slight a loss of momentum as hardly to be perceptible to the naked eye. It was to be hoped, Appleby felt, that Spot—the quadruped upon whom all now depended—had notions of locomotion somewhat more vigorous than his driver.

"Been?" said Heyhoe. "I mun eat my dinner."

Heyhoe was so strikingly reminiscent of Caliban that this was an altogether appropriate opening line. The forehead was low and receding; the eyes were small, feral and deep-set beneath beetling brows; the mouth hung open in a species of rictus or fixed grimace. Heyhoe, in fact, was remarkably like Robert Raven—without the nose. He was further distinguished by being to an incredible degree stooped and bowed to earth; it was this, together with a long, scrawny neck emerging from a multiple series of cloaks like Mr. Tony Weller's in the old prints, that gave the tortoise-like effect. "I mun eat my dinner," Heyhoe repeated with finality, and began to circle slowly round the platform collecting bags and suitcases. Of these he presently bestowed such an astonishing number about his person that when he finally crawled off down the platform the appearance presented was very much that of a pile of inanimate objects mysteriously endowed with spontaneous if microscopic locomotion. The rest of the party —it might have been more natural to say of the cortège— followed. Snow was coming down in an obliterating way. It was colder than it commonly is when snow is falling.

Even at Heyhoe's pace they were soon out of the station— which appeared to consist, indeed, of a few planks by way of platform and of a shelter which might have afforded adequate cover to the hardier type of Great St. Bernard dog. The railway company, it would appear, long before opening up this district to the advances of civilization, had altogether lost confidence in its task.

They passed through a wicket and now seemed to be standing nowhere in particular, except that before them loomed a vague dark mass, somewhat taller than it was broad, uncertainly elevated upon wheels, and approximately answering—though on a somewhat smaller scale—to Appleby's notion of a stage-coach. It seemed hardly possible that any single quadruped could budge it under the best conditions, let alone on country lanes some six inches deep in snow. The Ravens however viewed what was plainly their family conveyance without apprehension, and Everard Raven bustled forward in the most cheerful way. "Heyhoe," he said, did you remember the footwarmer? There ought to be just room inside for all."

Heyhoe shook his head. "You mun have potatoes," he said with satisfaction.

"Potatoes, Heyhoe? What d'you mean by that?"

Very deliberately Heyhoe took an ancient carriage-lamp from its socket, opened a creaking door and shone the dull light into the interior. "You mun have potatoes," he repeated. "And the hens mun have corn and the cow mun have cake. And Spot mun have his bottle of hay."

They all peered inside, aghast. A superabundance of sacks, each heavy and unwieldly to an extreme, gave the interior more the appearance of a market wain than of a carriage suitable for the reception of six fatigued gentlefolk. Everard Raven shook his head. "Room for Judith," he said. "But for the rest of us it looks like the box."

"And the boot." The ferocious Robert was patting Spot amiably on the haunches, and in the light of the remaining lamp Appleby discerned with some relief that this vital factor in the evening's proceedings was a brute of enormous proportions. "Perhaps some of us had better walk." Robert as he made this reasonable proposal turning round with a gesture infinitely threatening and violent. He glared at Appleby with spine-chilling ferocity. "But it would be a shame if we didn't manage to get Mr. Appleby inside too."

A man of weaker nerve might have suspected the Ravens' carriage of being an ingenious lethal contrivance—so incongruous were Robert's speech and demeanour. Appleby's protestations, however, were made solely on the score of politeness, and they were overborne by enthusiastic commands and injunctions from which only Heyhoe abstained.

"Quite right," said Judith. "Plenty of room for Mr. Appleby. Push him in."

"Certainly," said Luke. "Everard's friend must unquestionably have the advantage of the conveyance. Heyhoe, assist the gentleman to a seat."

"Push them in," shouted Mark. "Push in Judith, push in the befriended stranger." He gave a shove at one of the sacks. "Potato pie. Cattle cake collops. Down with the lid."

"A rug," said Everard. "Only three miles—if we have luck at the ford. Heyhoe reasonably sober, I should say. Noblet's

Lane, though. Mustn't mind the bumps. Worry about the axle. But soft fall in the snow."

There was a moment of much confusion at the end of which Appleby found himself in darkness, in a confined space, and in some doubt as to which adjacent protuberances were potatoes and cattle cake and which Judith Raven. These difficulties, sufficiently harassing under conditions of relative stability, were presently increased by the carriage's giving a violent lurch and then settling down into a wobbling motion discomposing to the stomach and centripetal in mechanical effect. Appleby felt something pressing heavily on his head. This proved to be the roof. He was, in fact, perched up on the bottle of hay.

"If you remain up there when we get in the lane you will break your neck." Miss Raven offered this information in the most impersonal way. "And if you come down you will find some six inches of seat between me and that sack. You will probably judge social embarrassment preferable to a dislocated cervical vertebra."

This was scarcely what could be called a come-hither attitude; nor on the other hand was it positively frosty. Appleby made a noise which he hoped was indicative of mild jollity and easy good fellowship. "I'll see what can be done," he said, and slid cautiously down the side of the bottle. Judith gave a little on the one side and the hay gave a little more on the other. But it was an extremely tight fit. The carriage began to wobble in a particularly agonizing way, and it was just possible to hear Heyhoe cursing on the box. "I believe," said Appleby, "that it was Dr. Johnson who held few pleasures to exceed that of driving through the country in a post-chaise with a pretty woman."

There was a moment's silence. "I should say," said Judith, "that you weight about eleven stone six."

"Well, yes—I do."

"And you must be just on five foot eleven. Which suggests you are in pretty good condition—for a don."

"A don!" Whether because of this arbitrary attribution to the academic profession or because of Miss Raven's concentration upon the appraisal of the mere physical and ponderable man, Appleby felt distinctly offended.

"Only a don would bring out a pedantic thing like that

about Dr. Johnson. Besides, cousin Everard is always picking up dons. Not, of course"—Judith was suddenly polite—"that we're not very pleased that he should have picked up you."

"Thank you. But I'm not a don. I'm a policeman."

"A policeman? Do you mean a *detective?*" There was a silence during which Appleby received the impression that his companion was rapidly thinking. "Shades of great-uncle Ranulph! No wonder Everard nobbled you. He's always harking back to the disreputable family past."

"He hasn't mentioned your great-uncle Ranulph. Was he someone who had to be—well—detected by a detective?"

"Certainly not." It was Judith who was offended now. "Do you mean to say you've never heard of Ranulph Raven?"

Appleby, who had been considerately supporting some of his eleven stone six on his toes, shifted his position and found that he was now quite frankly sitting on his companion. "Ranulph Raven?" he said, a shade wildly. "I seem to remember a Pre-Raphaelite painter—"

"That was his cousin."

"And a bishop who said something witty about Matthew Arnold—"

"Ranulph's younger brother."

Appleby made some attempt to change his posture anew. The attempt, being something like that of a small boy who makes an abortive effort to wriggle from the lap of a displeasing relative, merely made things additionally awkward. "A poet," he suggested hopefully. "Who was in the Foreign Office and wrote triolets and madrigals."

"Another brother—and the grandfather of Mark and myself. Ranulph Raven had any number of younger brothers. He also had three sons, all of whom you've met: Everard, Luke and Robert. Mark and I are the children of their first cousin: what are called first cousins once removed. That's why we say 'cousin' to them although they're enormously older. Are you uncomfortable, or just restless?"

"No, I'm not uncomfortable." Appleby found himself choosing his words with care. "But as it does appear to be necessary that one of us should sit on the other, I think it might be better—"

"Ranulph was a novelist."

"Good lord!—yes. Stupid of me. And enormously prolific. A sort of second Wilkie Collins. But, as I was saying—"

"Mr. Appleby, if I saw any prospect of sitting on *your* knee I would certainly prefer it to your sitting on mine. But it's too late for such a major upheaval. Unless we shout to Heyhoe and make him stop."

"I think perhaps we'd better do that. I'd be quite pleased to get out and walk." Appleby paused on this, conscious that it was not the happiest of remarks. "I mean—"

"Perhaps we could manage a shift round, after all. If you get your shoulders over there"—and Appleby felt his shoulders seized and given a vigorous shove—"and *these*"—his knees were gripped—"*down here*—" There followed several seconds of contortion, during which Appleby received a lively if confused impression of the graces of Miss Raven's person. Then he found himself planted square on a seat and his companion tucked into some vacant corner on the floor. She gave a final wriggle of her thighs somewhere near his ankles. "Anatomy," she said from out of the darkness, "is a species of knowledge useful in a tight place." And she laughed —softly but, Appleby thought, with an undertone of her wild, yellow-haired brother.

"Useful, no doubt—and altogether essential to a sculptor."

"However do you know that?" Judith's voice was quite startled. "What do you know about us all?"

"Singularly little." Appleby was wondering whether it was to his credit that he was now regretting having ceased to be dandled on the knees of an attractive girl. "But from the particularly inhuman way you look at one I could tell that it was art. And from the muscular force at your disposal in pushing people round I should judge that it is less likely to be just paint brushes than a hefty mallet and chisel. After all, I told you I'm a detective. You remember that Sherlock Holmes used to offer chance acquaintances similar treats."

"Glyptic work does take a certain amount of punch." Judith spoke with a shade of complacency. "Really nice girls just mess about with clay, or dabble in oil where their grandmothers dabbled in watercolour. Incidentally, Leonardo da Vinci thought of it in the same feeble fashion. He called painting a liberal art, because you just sit and poke at a canvas in a gentlemanlike way. And he called sculpture a servile art, just because there's honest sweat in it."

"Donnish," said Appleby.

"What's that you say?"

"I said that you too have your Dr. Johnson."

"I'm only making polite conversation. But perhaps you would prefer mute communion?" Judith chuckled maliciously in her corner. "Shall I give your legs a dumb squeeze?"

"Not at all." Appleby spoke hastily. "I mean I'm most interested in what you say—about Ranulph Raven. A Victorian novelist. And enormously prolific."

"Ah—you've noticed Heyhoe."

"I beg your pardon?" Appleby, whose wits were somewhat frayed by the rigours of his journey, took this for a merely random remark.

"Just like cousin Robert, isn't he? And most of the servents are legacies like that, I believe. And the only legacies Ranulph left. You'd expect all these novels to have turned into a little capital, wouldn't you? Not like madrigals and triolets. Naturally there wasn't any cash in *them*. And we all seem to take to activities of that sort. Sculpture, for instance; there isn't a bean in that. Which is why we all sponge on cousin Everard and his encyclopædias and things."

Appleby felt mildly uncomfortable—partly because he turned out to be sitting on a broken spring, and partly because he was learning rather more about the Ravens than was necessary. "I think," he said, "that you are a distinctly bald young woman."

Judith gave a startling yelp of laughter. "Judith Raven," she said. "The *Venus calva*."

"I merely mean that you give a markedly unvarnished picture of your family."

"And why not? Pictures should be unvarnished. You can go on touching them up until you varnish them: didn't you know? Not that the Ravens need touching up; we're a classical group already. And I might as well tell you what you're bound to find out anyway, seeing that you've decided to come snooping round."

"Snooping round!" Appleby was horrified. "My dear Miss Raven, I assure you that only the merest accident—"

"Nonsense. It's perfectly clear that you put yourself cunningly in Everard's way." Judith Raven again paused for what seemed to be rapid calculation. "And a good thing too. I've felt for a long time that the whole business ought to be cleared up."

"The whole business?" Appleby felt slightly dazed. "Do I understand that you suppose me to have come down to clear up some family mystery?"

"It's as plain as a pikestaff. Only you'll have the devil of a business. You see, it's not so much a matter of clearing up the present as the past. Or so it seems to me. And at Long Dream there's a lot of the past lying about. There must be something like eighty tons of it in my studio alone."

"Long Dream?"

"That's the name of our place. The village has disappeared long ago. Generations of Ravens picked it bare. And Ranulph polished off the skeleton." Judith paused on this dark saying. "We're Long Dream Manor."

"I see. And are you the lady of the manor?"

"No. Aunt Clarissa is that—Ranulph's half-brother's daughter."

The carriage was now moving more slowly and with a jarring motion, as if Spot were being cautiously edged downhill. Appleby contrived to get one arm round a sack of potatoes and to ease himself a little off the broken spring. It was because she had herself become aware of this discomfort, it occurred to him, that Judith had decided on and achieved that nightmarish change of places. "I am afraid," he said, "that I find your family confusing. And I have every intention that it shall remain so. My business is in a place called Snarl. In Long Dream Manor and its inhabitants I take no interest whatever."

"Oh, you'll soon find your way about. There's a very helpful family tree in the hall. With Ravens legitimate and illegitimate perched all over it. And, mind you, they can be dangerous birds." Judith paused. From outside there came a sinister murmur, as if Heyhoe were quarrelling with one of his employers on the box. "And isn't it strange," Judith said, "about our station being called Appleby's End?"

"A curious coincidence."

"Just that."

Appleby peered into the darkness, obscurely disturbed. Had there been some odd shade of compunction in this mysteriously attractive young woman's voice?

Chapter 4

WITH A bump and a lurch the carriage came to a stop. Some stray article of stores—it felt like a heavy, sharp-cornered tin—hit Appleby on the head and a nobbly sack tumbled over on his chest. It was evident that the whole Raven equipage had tilted over at an uncertain angle. A window had dropped open, and snowflakes and curses drifted in from the dark.

"Would you say it was the axle?" asked Appleby. "Or just Spot casting a shoe?"

"Neither. It's the ford. We're stuck in it."

"Good Lord! Are you sure?"

Judith laughed what was now a thoroughly wicked laugh. "I am sitting," she said, "in several inches of water. And from this, as your professional training will tell you, there is the inference—"

"Can't you get up? Let me try to give you a hand." Appleby groped cautiously in the darkness and found himself clutching what seemed to be a bare arm. "Now, then—"

"But that's the nape of my neck!" Judith's protest was vigorous. "Don't you know about the man who picked up one of his children like that?"

"I know nothing about him. Is the ford sometimes deep enough—"

"The child was killed instantly. The man was fearfully distressed. And he had to explain it to the doctor. 'Doctor,' he said, 'all I did was this.' And he turned and picked up another of his children—"

"Be quiet," said Appleby. He himself now felt water up to his knees, and he was not all disposed to sit back and listen to macabre stories. "I think I can just get my head out of that window."

With considerable effort he did so, and was rewarded with

a series of unexpectedly clear observations. For the moon, as if unable to restrain its curiosity in this nocturnal tragi-comedy, had burst through the clouds and now hung, idle and gaping, over a snow-covered landscape through which wound a turbulent stream lined with gaunt trees. In the middle of the stream stood the carriage; the level of the water had risen above the hubs, and in front had almost covered the empty and down-trailing shafts. At this last appearance Appleby stared for a moment in mute astonishment; then he twisted his head and looked backwards at the bank. The figures of three Ravens were discernible. All were shouting and one of them—who must surely be Robert—was prancing up and down, waving his arms. And what they were yelling was clearly distinguishable. "*Hey*-hoe," yelled the abandoned Ravens: "Hey-*HOE-OH!*"

Appleby looked the other way. On the farther side were Spot and Heyhoe himself—the former tethered to a tree; the latter apparently sitting on a stump and contemplating the scene with calm. Appleby twisted back into the carriage. "Heyhoe," he said, "seems to have cut the traces and got away with Spot. They're on the farther side."

"The horrid scoundrel!" Judith was justifiably indignant at this deplorable lack of fidelity in a family retainer and blood-relation. "What's he doing about it now?"

"I rather think he's filling his pipe."

"The disgusting old man! I hope Spot kicks him. But can you see the others?"

"Yes, they're on the other bank and in a considerable state of excitement—not at all like Heyhoe. Though I don't know that at the moment they're being any more useful." Appleby spoke somewhat tartly. "Yelling like mad, all three of them."

"Three of them!" Judith was dismayed. "But there ought to be four. Three old ones: Everard, Luke and Robert; and one young one: Mark. Do stick your head out again and see."

Appleby did as he was bid. There was certainly a Raven missing. He was about to turn back and confirm this disconcerting intelligence when a voice spoke as if from the heavens above. "My dear sir," said the voice—which was a hoarse and melancholy one. "My dear sir, we owe you our apologies for this deplorable misadventure. And may I trust that my cousin is not wholly submerged?"

Unbelievingly and with considerable physical agony Appleby directed his gaze upwards. A great oak with wide spreading branches overhung the stream and the carriage, and perched in this was what appeared to be a vast bird with folded black wings and cypress green under-plumage. "I was on the boot," Luke Raven said. As his perch was precarious he spoke laboriously but evidently feeling that courtesy required some adequate explanation of his predicament." And I was swept off by this branch just before the carriage stuck. I should be obliged if you would order Heyhoe to take some appropriate action. Let him fetch ropes. Let him bring a ladder. Let him call Colonel Jolys' keeper, or young Shrubsole, or the lads from Murcott's farm."

"Heyhoe is lighting his pipe," Appleby said.

"I understand that Everard has no objection to Heyhoe smoking—when in the open air and not actually on his box. But at the moment the recreation is altogether untimely. Let him mount Spot and bring assistance from Willow Farm. Let him rouse the road-mender at the end of Noblet's Lane. Or the Sturrock family at Great Tew. Let him—" At this point Luke Raven's admirable plans for calling out the surrounding lower orders were interrupted by a rending noise and a resounding splash.

"Whatever's that?" Judith's voice came apprehensively from inside the carriage.

"I'm afraid it's Luke falling into the stream. He was up a tree."

"Up a tree?"

"A most reliable looking oak. But something went wrong. I'm watching him; I think he's going to be all right. Yes, he's wading now. And the bank's quite easy. He's ashore."

"Which side?"

"Heyhoe's. He's talking to Heyhoe. Heyhoe has produced a bottle. I think your cousin may be said to be upbraiding him."

"I should jolly well think so. Isn't the water rising? It's up to—to nearly my arm-pits." For the first time Judith sounded really disturbed.

"I think it is." Appleby, though beginning to feel that the situation was not without positive danger, spoke cheerfully. "And these windows are unfortunately a bit on the small side. We must get a door open, and edge out one or two of these confounded sacks. Then we'll be able to move; and perhaps they'll serve as a sort of stepping-stones to the shallower water. Or we can get on the roof and wait till Heyhoe's stirred to action. Here we go." Appleby managed to wrench open a door; the current caught the bottom of it and flung it ajar; he made a big effort and pitched out first one and then another unwieldy sack. "And up you get." He hauled Judith to her feet and then—rather more because he felt at odds with inanimate nature than for any immediate need— he shoved out two further sacks. They stood up in the almost empty carriage with a sense of being kings of infinite space. "The potatoes won't come to any harm, but about the cake for the cow I don't at all know. And as for the books on reptiles and religion and resuscitation and all the other *litterae caninae*—"

"I don't know what you're talking about." Appleby had an impression that Judith, who must be soaked to the skin from the waist down, was settling her hat at a correct angle on her head. "Do we wade or swim?"

"Wade, I hope." Suddenly he lurched against the side of the carriage. "Good Lord! I do believe—"

He was right. Lightened of its load, the whole unwieldy conveyance had risen like an ark upon the waters. For a few seconds it spun as if it were a great top, so that they had to clutch each other and finally collapsed on opposite seats. By the time they were on their feet again the carriage was moving with the current and gaining momentum rapidly; a few seconds more and the stream was bearing it at a far brisker pace than Spot could have achieved. Momentarily the Ravens on the bank could be heard shouting with even greater vehemence. Then their cries died away.

"Swim," said Appleby soberly. "It's only a few yards. But there's an altogether surprising volume of water coming down."

"Better wait." For a moment Judith took charge. "There's a sharp bend. We'll probably be washed on the bank. Here it is."

The moon had disappeared again and they could judge of their situation only from the movement of their queer craft. It had tilted sharply on its side, so that the open door banged to; but now it had returned to an even keel and its motion was difficult to judge. They waited for some seconds. "It certainly hasn't grounded," Appleby said. "What happens after the bend?"

"Oh, then you come into the river."

"The river!"

"The Dream. It gets quite broad here. Hullo, here's the moon."

Once more Appleby peered out. They had made better speed than he had guessed, and the prospect around him was extremely disconcerting. Instead of a narrow and turbulent stream with banks only a few yards distant on either hand there was now a great expanse of water, smooth, slow-moving, and argent under the moon. "It's absolutely grotesque!" Appleby said. "We might be on the Volga."

"Of course there isn't much of it like this. It narrows again about a mile down." Judith was looking calmly out of the other window. "Why don't we sink?"

"Heaven knows. But the sooner you and I stop being inside passengers the better. It's either swim straight away or climb to the roof. If the first, get some of your clothes off; if the second, not."

"We'll try the roof. Swing the door open and see if we can climb by that." Judith Raven was perfectly collected in this strange situation. "And as for clothes, a wet skirt's likely to be a nuisance in any case." With surprising speed she divested her self of this garment. "You first."

Without great difficulty Appleby got on the roof and hauled Judith up. They lay for a moment panting heavily—and their panting brought home to them how utterly still was everything around. Not a lap or ripple of sound came from the fantastic forepeak of their vessel, and all about them was the oddly noticeable silence that belongs to falling snow. "I say," said Appleby, "do you think your people are still hollering at each other across that ford?"

"Sure to be. But we've got right away from them—and all chance of dinner. I think it's rather restful—like the cinema before they invented all that nasty noise." Judith laughed softly. "By the way—did Dr. Johnson say anything useful about traveling like this?"

"It's more the sort of thing favoured by Shelley. Fantastic

voyages in unlikely craft. Occasionally we shall meet a serpent or an eagle. And most of the voyage will be through a system of underground caverns. These tell us much about the psychotic condition of the poet." Appleby was staring warily ahead down the glimmering river. "And I may say that you yourself are quite in the picture—providing we regard you as a personification of Hope, or Art, or Liberty. Only you ought to be dressed in something filmy and transpicuous."

"I don't think I like Shelley as much as Dr. Johnson. And my dress is not at the moment a suitable subject for conversation." Judith stretched out her silk-clad legs in a sort of ironic exhibitionism. Then, finding this rather chilly, she hunched her knees up to her chin and clasped them in her arms. "Now if this were August," she said, "it would be altogether romantic. I should look back and dream of my wonderful policeman. Our delights, I should recall, were dolphinlike. But his conduct was irreproachable and his conversation uniformly improving." She sneezed violently. "As it is, I would swap you without a moment's hesitation for a bowl of hot soup."

"And if the temptation came, I don't say I wouldn't part with you for a decent cigarette." Appleby fumbled in an inside pocket. "Hullo, here are some, as a matter of fact. And quite dry. Matches too."

They smoked—and for two people who had met only an hour before felt most companionably inclined. The glow from her burning cigarette outlined Judith's nose. Was it indeed by some millimeters too long? Undoubtedly she was a creature beautifully made—and for Appleby there was particular attraction in some enigmatic quality to her mind. She was looking at him now with a concentration that might—as in the railway carriage—be æsthetic and speak of her profession. The problem, conceivably, was how to modify the ears or relate the forehead to the plane of the jaw. Or was it some entirely different speculation that now occupied her mind?

The river was narrowing again. Now etched in moonlight, and now altogether shadowy and obscure, there floated by on either hand delicate alders and stout, gesticulating elms. Willows, pollarded and rime-covered, overhung the river like frozen cascades; and presently a line of poplars, aloof and towering, cast great bars of shadow obliquely across the water on which snow still softly fell. The carriage as it floated smoothly through this wintry nocturne rotated slowly on its axis, so that the whole scene was like a chill kaleidoscope in white and black and silver and grey. Appleby found it increasingly difficult to look out for snags in the water. "If this roundabout-business gains momentum," he said, "we shall presently be spinning like flies on a top. A pity there seems to be nobody abroad at this hour. We should become a legend that would cling about the countryside for generations, don't you think?"

Judith shook her head. "Quite enough legends already." She waved her hand in a gesture embracing both banks. "All this is the Raven country still, you know."

"Is it, indeed?" said Appleby—in the respectful tones in which the English commonly acknowledge such territorial statements. "Then you can't all be so overwhelming a burden on your cousin Everard's resources."

"My dear man, I don't mean we *own* it. All Everard has left is a chunk of park and a couple of hummocky farms. I mean this is the country Ranulph wrote about. Hardy's Wessex, Trollope's Barsetshire, Ranulph Raven's Dream country. See?"

"I see. And did Ranulph create the legends, or just find them lying about?"

"It rather seems as if he grubbed them up. Anything with lurid possibilities that happened within twenty miles about he would ferret out and add knobs to."

"What a dismal trade." Appleby spoke with distaste. "Did Ranulph write about nothing but crimes?"

"Anything melodramatic served. Long-lost heirs and missing wills and Eastern drugs and somnambulism—stuff hopelessly *vieux jeu* now, but it went down well enough at the time. Particularly somnambulism. It's unbelieveable the number of queer things that happen in sleep in Ranulph's world. And he liked the supernatural—or the supernatural and water. For instance, I remember one story called *The Spectral Hound*. It's about some great brute that's suspected of having rabies and is hanged. Everybody sees it hanged in a barn. But its ghost turns up at night and haunts the place, and presently all the other dogs round about go rabid too. Well, a ghostly bow-wow handing round hydrophobia is a bit too steep, so they investigate and discover that the creature had been buried in a dung-hill. The warmth and ferment had revived it."

"Resuscitation. Your cousin Everard should make a note of it. But I don't think it sounds a very entertaining story."

"Oh, I don't know." Judith seemed inclined to stick up for the family genius. "That sort of thing depends very much on how it's told." She threw away her cigarette. "But I think this tell-me-a-story idea is falling a bit flat. I vote we swim. There's a five-mile walk in front of us already."

"And through what appears to be completely empty country. Doesn't anybody live round here?" Appleby found himself speaking rather as if the paucity of the rural population was a personal grievance. "Were they all despatched by the mad dogs?" His glance returned from the snow-covered countryside to the riverbank. "By Jove, we're drifting straight inshore."

The river had widened again at a broad bend, and towards the outer perimeter of this, where the bank was low and the water probably deep, the current was steadily driving them. It looked as if in a few seconds a jump would be possible. "Come on," said Appleby, "we'll make that dinner yet." He pulled Judith to her feet, so that they stood unsteadily on the curved roof of the carriage. "When I say jump, jump."

"Don't be silly. I shall jump when I think it's a good idea myself." Judith was taking off her shoes. "And if it's me who falls in—"

They both jumped to safety. Appleby, rolling over and sitting up in the snow, was in time to see the Raven carriage veering out towards mid-stream. Then he turned to Judith; she was standing on one leg, slipping on a shoe again. "Look here," he said, "where the deuce is your coat?"

"Left it on board. Too heavy and flappy to risk jumping in."

Appleby took off his overcoat. "Here," he said, "put it on."

Judith shook her head. "If you turn out to be the chivalrous type of policeman I shall bite."

"Put it on."

"Nonsense. Once I get walking briskly—"

"Do you think that I propose to be found roaming the

countryside with a—a disrobed girl? Put it on and let's tramp, for the Lord's sake. Why I didn't choose Brettingham What's-his-name's pigs—"

They tramped—uncertainly up a long snow-covered selion through plough-land. They climbed a gate and were in what was probably a green-bottomed lane between hawthorn hedges. They trudged down this. "Take it back about the pigs," Judith said. "Take it back and I'll give you some chocolate."

They munched chocolate. "I suppose you can find your way?" Appleby said.

"Of course. At least, I think so. The country certainly is oddly unfamiliar by moonlight."

"Will it be better in the dark? For there isn't going to be much more moon. But at least there's going to be no shortage of snow." Appleby halted suddenly. "On the other hand, there's rather an absence of hedge."

Judith stopped. "What do you mean?"

"Aren't we meant to be walking between hedges? Well, they've gone." Cautiously Appleby explored a dozen paces around them. "Clean vanished. We're standing in the middle of nothing."

"Oh dear! We must have got out on the down."

"No doubt. There's a perceptible slope. Would you like to slither or climb?"

"Better slither. More shelter down below—and most of the lanes are on the low ground. I've no doubt we'll come to a cottage presently, and they'll put us right."

They slithered. "Murcott's Farm," said Appleby darkly. "Or young Shrubsole, or the Sturrock family at Great Tew." The snow was driving suffocatingly against them; it was like poking their noses into a strangely icy feather-bed.

"I don't know what you're talking about." Judith expended breath that would have been better kept to contend with the elements. "I think this is a perfectly idiotic exploit. Gosh!— there's a house. Down there on your left."

Again Appleby explored—and the effort took him through a snow-drift. "There's a fence," he reported, "—which is something. But it's not a house. It's a hay-stack. I suppose that means there must be a house of sorts near. We'll follow the fence."

But Judith didn't budge. "I say," she said, "—I've been told that hay-stacks are most frightfully snug. Escaping prisoners always sleep in them."

"No doubt. But we're not escaping prisoners. Come along."

"One takes off one's wet clothes and burrows in. At first it's extremely prickly. But presently a delicious warmth—"

"I don't believe a word of it."

"—a delicious warmth steals through one's every limb. Come on. Let's try." Judith was climbing the fence.

Appleby followed. He had the impression that Judith was discarding further garments and he played his last card. There'll be rats," he said.

"Rats."

"Yes—rats. Place teeming with them."

"And I said Rats." Judith was laughing in the darkness. "I believe you consider it improper. No doubt a policeman—" She stopped suddenly. "But I can't get *in!*" she cried indignantly. "It's like a brick wall."

"Naturally. Think of the weight. You could get in only near the top. So put that coat on like a good girl and—"

"But I've found a ladder!" Judith was triumphant. "And I've no doubt the rats will stick to the lower storeys. I'm climbing." Her voice came from somewhere above his head. "Shall I draw it up after me?"

"Leave it where it is," Appleby said.

Chapter 5

WERE THE Assistant-Commissioner to hear of all this Appleby's End would be an affair of a shattered reputation. But of the merits of hay there could be no doubt. The escaping prisoners were entirely right. For some time Appleby had been deliciously warm. Had he even, perhaps, been asleep? He rubbed his eyes.

Not that it would really do to settle in for the night. Their predicament next morning would be highly ridiculous, for they would have to emerge from their burrow and confront a zealous countryside already preparing to comb the downs and drag the river. Moreover—and Appleby looked at the luminous dial of his watch—although their adventures appeared to have occupied æons of time and compassed a considerable area of the earth, the home of the Ravens could not really be very remote, and the night was still comparatively young. Some species of dinner or supper remained a possibility, as did a night's repose between sheets securely walled off, for a time, from this impetuous girl. "We'll start again in an hour," Appleby said into the darkness. "Quite likely there'll be a bit of moon again by then."

"I'm not going."

"I think we'd better. It would be awkward to wait till daylight and be found by the bull."

There was a rustle in the hay. "The bull?"

"Somewhere in this field. I've heard it snuffling round. And listen! There it is bellowing somewhere near the other side." It was certainly true that through the falling snow a dull lowing could be heard.

"I don't call that a bellow. It's a moo." Judith Raven's voice was faintly uncertain.

"It's the sort of subdued noise," Appleby said, "that bulls make at night."

"What utter rot." Judith was now thoroughly alarmed. "You're simply preying on my irrational fears."

"Perhaps. But during the next sixty minutes"—Appleby spoke dispassionately—"your irrational fears will grow. In the end they'll be positively nightmarish. And then we'll quit. Meantime you can tell me another story—just to distract your mind."

"I don't want to tell you a story. I'm sleepy." Judith suddenly spoke in a massively sleepy voice. "Very snug."

"Then tell me what on earth should put it into your head that I was proposing to investigate the mouldering skeletons in the Raven family cupboards."

"Don't know what you're talking about. Comfy now."

"And I'll tell you about a Spanish sculptor—an anarchist—who built a time-bomb into a colossal group representing the Triumph of Benevolent Autarchy."

"I don't believe it."

"And I don't believe your cupboards have any skeletons at

all. Except of mice and bats and spiders—if spiders have skeletons."

"Our cupboards *have* got skeletons."

"They have not."

"Very well. Listen." In Judith Raven's voice, Appleby thought, there was an odd hint as of sudden resolution. "I was born on the thirtieth of July, nineteen hundred and dash."

"What do you mean—and dash?"

"Isn't that the way stories begin? Ranulph's always did. Nineteen hundred and dash, in the village of dash in dash-shire."

"But this isn't one of Ranulph's stories. It appears to be your own."

"As a matter of fact, it's a bit of both: Ranulph's story and mine. Although I'm not thirty—"

"I'd be surprised if you were twenty-two."

"—and Ranulph died in 1898. There's a real date for you. Shall I go on?"

"If you really have a story to tell—which I altogether doubt —for goodness sake do."

"You must understand"— Judith Raven's voice as she began her story took on a measured narrative tone—"that my brother Mark and I have lived at Dream ever since we were children. Our parents were dead, you see, and there was only grandfather Herbert, and he lived there too. He had grown tired of the Foreign Office, or perhaps they had turned him out because he was old, so he lived on his nephew Everard, Ranulph's eldest son, and still did madrigals and things after breakfast. Of course he was ever so much younger than his brother Ranulph. There was the bishop and several sisters and other brothers in between. I rather liked grandfather Herbert. He was dirty but terribly distinguished. I used to do him in plasticine—the grey kind, so the dirt wouldn't show.

"Well, Mark and I were kids, and Ranulph, of course, had died twenty or thirty years before, and nobody thought of him—or so you would think. Certainly nobody bought his books anymore, and he'd blewed all he ever made out of them, and there were heaps of Georgian and Victorian Ravens who had been distinguished in weightier jobs than romance-writing—so why should anyone bother? You can't even see his remains at Dream unless you go poking about bookcases and cupboards and bureaus; whereas the Ravens who painted and the Ravens who sculpted and the Ravens who collected rocks and fossils and stuffed animals and mediæval armour have all left their possessions lying quite obtrusively about—as I shall do in my turn, I suppose. Well, that was how it was. So it was quite a time before Mark and I found out there really was a Ranulph Raven legend—what you might call a popular legend. The first we heard of it was from the blind old man who came tap-tapping over the bridge with a stick."

"Ah," interrupted Appleby. "And delivered a Black Spot. And was later ridden down by horsemen in the night. I do think when you start spinning a yarn you should keep off *Treasure Island*."

"He was very old and he came tapping over the bridge below the long meadow—which means that he must have come from somewhere round about Great Tew. There was a man working in the ditch, and the blind man must have heard him, for he called out to him and they talked. And then the man who was ditching gave a shout and a wave at us where we were playing Indians or something in the grass, and we ran up to see what it was about. The blind man leant over a gate and talked to us—or rather talked in our direction in a cunning, fearful sort of voice. He was a horrible old blind man, and it was very horrid—more so because the man who was ditching for some reason climbed out and went away.

" 'Come here, young lady and gentleman,' he said; 'come here, my dears, and let me talk to you.' It was just like the beginning of something sinister in a story. And so, in a sense, it was."

Appleby rustled in his hay. "You're not a bad hand at this. Only atmosphere and pace a little lacking. The great art, I've been told, is to get both at once."

" 'Master Raven, young sir,' he said, 'and Miss Raven, my young lady'—so we knew the ditcher had told who we were— 'very proud of your famous grandfather you must be, my dears.' Well, of course Herbert was our Raven grandfather, and we were well enough up in that sort of thing to know nobody could call Herbert famous. Madrigals just don't take you all that way. So we guessed the nasty old person had got things mixed and probably meant our great-uncle the bishop, or his kinsman the Pre-Raphaelite, or one of the others. As for great-uncle Ranulph, he just somehow didn't come into our heads.

"The blind man rambled away, and offered us a bag of sweets he seemed to have brought on purpose, and Mark had to hold on to them though they looked very nasty, because he was afraid the man would hear if he chucked them in the ditch. We wished we'd had the dogs with us.

" 'And great scholars you must be,' the blind man said, 'with all these grand book-learned folk in your family. Latin you'll have learnt, and Hebrew, and French too it's not unlikely. Bless your sweet, well-educated heads.' Mind you, I don't say he said just that. I'm no good at dialect, and he's beginning to sound like an Irishman, which he wasn't. But that was the general effect."

Judith Raven paused. Far away in the night the sound of a motor engine could be heard, labouring up a hill. The note dropped with a change of gear and the sound ebbed rapidly away.

"Quite so," said Appleby. "After twelve years or so you can't be expected to give the police a verbatim report. Go on."

"And then he sheered off that, as if he was scared of something, and he rambled for a bit and yet somehow we couldn't get away. It was as if we knew there was something really odd to come; we were rather like the Wedding Guest before the Ancient Mariner told him of the albatross, you may say. And then he got back to our supposed learning. 'You'll have read all your dear grandfather's fine books, I don't doubt,' he said. I doubt if either of us had read anything of Ranulph's; and, as I've said, Ranulph wasn't in either of our heads, anyway. But Mark made a sudden grab at my arm, which I knew was instead of that loopy great laugh of his—"

"Did he have that as a boy?"

"Mark has always been exactly like Mark. And he said, 'Oh yes. We read them all through once a year aloud. That and the novels of his friend, Sir Walter Scott.'

" 'So there couldn't,' said the blind man, 'be a story of his put in print and you not know it?'

" 'Dear me, no,' Mark said. 'We know the whole lot as well as we know our Bibles.'

" 'That's two good children,' said the blind man, and he gave a relieved sort of sigh. 'Always be at your Bibles, the same as I am.' And he rolled his eyeballs—which looked awful—up to heaven in what was evidently meant to be a pious way. 'And now,' he said—and he leant forward as if to make a clutch at us, and there was something eager and ghastly in his voice—'and now, will you tell me this: did your dear grandfather ever write down the story of the blind lad that killed his brother?'

"It was a nasty shock, even though, of course, we couldn't make head or tail of it. And I suppose we just stared at him for a bit, and then he spoke again and his voice was trembling. 'Did he?' he asked. 'The blind lad who hated his brother for what he'd taken from him—and knew he always *would* hate him?'

"I was scared and I think Mark was scared too. But scare just puts the devil in Mark. 'Yes, of course,' he said—as loud as if the blind man were deaf as well. 'That's one of the most famous stories grandfather ever wrote.' "

Judith Raven broke off and there was a moment's silence. "Now tell me," she said. "How would you expect the blind man to react?"

Appleby, who found he had been listening with a good deal of attention, answered at once. "I should expect him to show panic or alarm."

"But he didn't. What came over his face was the most unmistakable and ghastly disappointment. 'Then a curse on him and on you!' he cried. And without another word he turned round and went tap-tapping back across the bridge. We never saw him again."

"I see. And *is* there a Ranulph Raven story about—"

"There is not. We found out afterwards that there isn't, as it happens a single blind person in the whole Ranulph *oeuvre*."

"Well, well! By the way, this doesn't happen to be true?"

"My dear man, it's merely the beginning of something I happen to have decided to tell you about. So just go on listening. By the way, is it still snowing? I'm all cuddled up in the dark."

Appleby peered out. The snow had stopped falling and overhead, where the moon rode high, the clouds could be seen as clearing; already it was possible to see the contours of the downs and to interpret something of their nearer surroundings. "No more snow," he said—and continued to stare across the uncertain countryside, perplexed.

For what was to be made of this queer tale—pitched at him, whether through impulse or calculation, by this decidedly intelligent girl as if to crown an evening's queer adventures? The incident described had happened long ago; and when it happened its dominant feature had been the cropping up of something already remote in time. But if anything was clear about Ranulph Raven it was this: that his oblivion was now as complete as his success had once been extensive. He was not even one of those prolific writers, for the most part long unread, whose fame yet survives in two or three familiar titles. Ranulph had left no *Moonstone*—nor even an *Uncle Silas*. Literary immortality he had none. How then could his legend haunt a countryside, as Judith had declared—and his name stir fears and passions in an old, blind man?

Appleby roused himself. "In half an hour we shall be strolling gently home," he said. "Go on with your yarn."

"That was the first time I heard of the Ranulph legend. And in a way it was the last—or the last for a long time. For though I discovered quite a lot more about it not much more *happened* while we were kids. It became a matter of historical investigation, you might say. Mark and I made a game of it. We discovered that the—the ramifications had been pretty extensive.

"Apparently that sort of thing does occur. Legends about literary folk and other queer fish often circulate in the districts where they've lived, and are even carried about the country. Tramps carry stories just as chapmen used to carry ballads and broadsheets. Everard says that Branwell Brontë is a legendary figure quite far west into Lancashire and north right up to Northumberland."

To Judith Raven's voice, disembodied in the darkness, it was pleasant to listen. And if she were something kept in a glass case one would be willing to contemplate her almost indefinitely. Indeed to all the senses, whether in isolation or combination, the reports she would yield could be nothing but satisfactory—in an extreme. "Northumberland?" said Appleby absently. "You surprise me. I never heard of that sort of folklore before."

"Not many policemen have—except, perhaps, the quite uncultivated and ordinary ones." Judith laughed in the darkness. "It's only among the simple that such stories run. And of course it is surprising. Particularly about Ranulph, because with him it's really *queer*. You see, he had the reputation of being a sort of Sibyl."

"Sibyls were girls."

"I know they were, silly. Do you know the Sistine Chapel? I like the Delphic Sibyl best. But not so much as Jonah. Jonah's lovelier even than Adam, if you ask me." Judith's pleasant voice was suddenly grave and beautiful—and the effect of this was to suggest some increasing dissatisfaction with the mysterious narrative upon which she was engaged. "Why did Michelangelo make Jonah like that? I thought he was an old man with a beard."

The clouds were clearing rapidly and behind them was the cold glitter of Orion and the Bear. *Now lies the earth all Danae to the stars.* . . . "Judith," Appleby said—for obscurely some decision had come to him—"Judith, if you must tell a story, tell it and don't interrupt with a lot of culture-patter."

"Though fancy a sculptor wasting time on all that paint! But some of those nude youths—"

"Look here, I'm the next thing to a nude youth myself and most horribly prickled. Who ever heard of talking about Michelangelo in a haystack? Get back to Ranulph."

"I don't see that Ranulph is any more appropriate, for the matter of that. But, as I was saying, Ranulph had a reputation among the rude peasantry for having possessed prophetic powers. That's what Mark and I found out. For instance, we found out from Everard's old housekeeper—who's dead now—that in Ranulph's time people used to come and consult him about the future, just as if he were an old woman with ear-rings sitting in a tent."

"I see. And did he, in fact, make this special talent of his available to all comers?"

"He was affable and conversable—that's what the house-keeper said. Actually I think he just supposed it a chance to suck up copy—or material, if that sounds less journalistic. You see, his method, as I've told you, was to worm people's stories out of them and then splash them over with his own bright colours. It doesn't really seem promising to me. So few people have stories worth speaking of, after all. I'm sure I haven't. A woman without a past and without a future, whom no novelist could muscle in on." Judith's voice was muffled and Appleby had the impression that she was scrambling into a garment. "But perhaps people who are anxious enough about the future to consult the local squire as if he were a black and midnight hag are likelier to have had a past worth writing up. Though I don't exactly see why."

"It wasn't their past and it wasn't their future either—except now and then." Appleby, suddenly incisive, had scrambled from his burrow and was sitting in the icy air, staring across what was now again a moon and snow blanched country. "Yours is a forty-year-old story or more—but uncommonly fascinating, I'm bound to say. And, very likely, you would have supplied Ranulph with excellent copy, despite your blameless past and empty future. You're quite sure it will be empty, by the way?"

"I shall have one or two one-man shows." Judith Raven too had emerged. "Friends will praise the stuff in sixpenny papers. And before I settle down to my later spinsterhood at Dream there will be several love-affairs with practised but chronically inept intellectuals, and perhaps an episode of farcical but painful bewilderment with a dumb and passionate D. H. Lawrencian yeoman. Or possibly all that is just girlish fantasy."

"I suspect it is. In fact, your actual future is going to be quite different, I should say. Still, there's the point."

"What point?"

"There's what Ranulph was interested in—and what explains your blind, tappity-tappity companion of childhood. Of course people's pasts aren't of much utility to manufacturers of sensational fiction—nor their actual futures either. But their fantasies are."

"I don't understand." Judith was visible now, a slim silhouette against a silver-grey infinity. "Or do you mean . . . ?"

"Yes! That was what Ranulph in his snooping round must have developed a technique for eliciting. Perhaps he just took tea with the women and poured beer down the men—that and had rather a subtle way of leading them on. He made stories out of people's day-dreams—out of good, current Victorian day-dreams. No wonder his books sold in their time. Of course he had his flair for writing up and heightening actual sensations too—putting the knobs on as you expressed it. But he had a taproot on all the eccentric and lurid and scandalous things people *saw* themselves doing. And sometimes, of course—and perhaps years later— *they would really do them*, or something tolerably like. And there it would all be already in one of Ranulph Raven's stories."

"So the blind man—"

"Even among illiterate people"—Appleby went on unheeding—"this would sometimes seep out—and the result would be a popular notion that his stories were really a species of prophetic books, crammed with the future. Occasionally, no doubt, people would recall letting slip their less presentable projects to Ranulph. But they'd keep quiet about it. And—yes—now you see the explanation of your blind man. As a lad he cherished a nasty plan to liquidate his brother. He continued to cherish it. But he remembered having let it out to Ranulph. And he had heard the legend and how Ranulph's stories were all mixed up with actual events. So he had a fear—probably pretty baseless—that it would be risky to commit a crime certain cardinal features of which might have been put into a book donkeys' years before. Hence his fury on being told by your brother that there *was* such a yarn of Ranulph's. If he had been *scared* that would mean he was afraid the published story might lead to the detection of something *he had once done*. But he wasn't scared; he was disappointed and angry. He was disappointed and angry because he judged that in the circumstances it would be unsafe—now, years later—*to go ahead*."

"I must say you have quite the professional touch." There was a rustling and Appleby saw that Judith had slithered down the ladder and was standing in clear moonlight below. "A calculating machine couldn't do better," she called up mockingly. "One just slips in the facts at one side and out comes the solution at the other. Not even a handle to turn or a lever to pull. Can you jump? Or would it upset the delicate mechanisms?"

Appleby jumped. "Don't you think it a likely explanation?" he asked as he scrambled to his feet.

"I rather think it is. But it means that the blind man whom Mark and I met when we were kids was meditating putting into effect against his brother some murderous plan he had been cherishing for thirty or forty years. That's pretty stiff."

"I would call it extremely nasty." Appleby took Judith's arm and helped her over the fence. "Listen," he said. "It so happens that I want to know whether this story of yours is all fibs. Yes or no?"

"No." She looked at him doubtfully, her brow puckered. "The whole story of the blind man is gospel. Why?"

"Because for some reason you don't seem very proud of it." Appleby hesitated. "In fact you seem less pleased with it every time we look at each other."

"What rot." Judith was stuffing her battered hat viciously in a pocket. "It's just that the Ranulph business is tiresome, I suppose."

"But the Ranulph business is surely all past history now." "Is it? Well, yes—I suppose it is." They trudged on in silence. Suddenly Judith stopped in her tracks. "Appleby's End!" she said. "Surely they couldn't—"

"Whatever are you talking about?"

"Nothing." Judith Raven plunged forward again, ankle-deep in snow. "Nothing at all."

Chapter 6

THERE WAS clear moonlight now and the only trouble was the snowdrifts; in places these were deep and they floundered. But Judith had found her bearings again and led the way confidently uphill to where a great elm stood dimly silhouetted against the sky. Here was a lane and they went ahead steadily.

Midwinter and midnight lay about them; their clothes were

for the most part soaked in river water; a thin and biting wind blew. But the landscape, softened and withdrawn beneath the snow, was as beautiful as it was still and cold. The Comic Spirit, hitherto so decisively in charge of the wanderers, slipped quietly away and Poetry, stealthy of approach as always, dominated and enfolded the scene. It was mysterious —the more so as their proceedings were now directed to so rational a goal. Bacon, eggs and coffee were the forces beckoning them on. But they followed as to a trumpet of silver.

Appleby's trousers clung wetly to his legs. *"Sed iacet,"* he chanted,

> *"Sed iacet aggeribus niveis informis et alto*
> *Terra gelu. . . . "*

"Is that the beginning of the story about the Spanish anarchist sculptor?" Judith, her wet hair flattened round her head like a boy, was glancing at him with an obscure new wariness in the moonlight.

"No, we haven't got to that yet. Still some of this Raven business to clear up. What about a race?"

"Not in this overcoat."

"I'll carry it."

"I thought I was wearing it to satisfy your sense of decorum."

"Ready, get set—"

They raced wildly through the snow and fetched up at a bend in the lane, panting. Judith once more huddled into the overcoat. "We might even," she said, "be home before the family. They would all go ploutering round, you know, knocking up the countryside and saying we must be searched for. I'm surprised we haven't met strings of angry rural bobbies already. Is 'bobbies' disrespectful?"

"It's not really so many hours since we drifted away from the ford. Your man Heyhoe would scarcely have crawled the length of his own shadow. Not that there isn't a likelihood of our being searched for by now. Do you know, I once or twice thought I saw lanterns moving when we were up in that haystack? But about those Raven skeletons."

Appleby paused. Pertinacity is among the attributes that the human male instinctively supposes the female to prize. Conceivably it was this, rather than any sharply awakened interest in remoter Ravens, that was now inducing him to pursue the shadowy Ranulph mystery.

"The facts, so far, are these: Ranulph Raven went about collecting other people's skeletons and storing them in his own cupboards at Dream. Every now and then he would select a likely one, clothe it in abundant and flamboyant flesh of his own manufacture, and—lo and behold—there was a new Raven sensational novel or story. A great deal of labour in the way of invention was saved, and there wasn't much danger in the matter of libel for the simple reason that the skeletons he collected were fantasy skeletons: the awful things people would *like* to do. Perhaps he had some abnormal hypnotic power. He wormed his way into the confidence of the rector's wife until she whispered to him how she loved to imagine herself pushing the doctor's lady down a well."

"For that matter," Judith interrupted, "not long ago there was an old woman called Mrs. Grope—"

"I know, I know. And I know too about Hannah Hoobin's boy. Am I not a detective? And these are just the sort of affairs Ranulph would like were he alive to-day. But Ranulph never saw the twentieth century. These queer activities of his go back from forty to eighty years. It's past history, as I said before. So what did you mean by saying or believing that I had come down to clear up a family mystery? Explain yourself. And briefly. For presently we must have another race."

"No more races."

"Another long race. I find it necessary to make sure that you don't catch pneumonia. Do you think I want to explain to the local coroner how the deceased and I went burrowing in a haystack?"

"I think you would do it austerely and well. Not a blush would be brought to the cheek of the young person. And if it's *you* who gets the pneumonia I'll do a memorial to you to be set up in the yard of Scotland Yard—if Scotland Yard has a yard. It will be called Object."

"Object?"

"All my carvings are called Object now. It seems to be the thing. Would you mind the—" Judith broke off. "What's your Christian name?"

"John."

"Would you mind the John Appleby Memorial being called

Object? It *could* be called *Objet trouvé*. But that would mean something I'd found lying about and thought interesting—which seems a bit mingy for a Memorial. Perhaps—"

"You told me that you had felt for some time that the whole business ought to be cleared up. You believed, or affected to believe, that I had come to do the job. I'm rather curious to know why. But of course you can make a secret of it if you like. Possibly it was just a nervous joke."

Judith stopped short. "It was nothing of the sort. You know very well I'm not the sort of person to entertain strangers with nervous jokes. *Or* to believe in bulls—"

"Look out!" Appleby made a dive at his companion, lifted her in air and dropped her over the fence; then he vaulted over himself. "By Jove," he said, "that was a narrow shave. Did you see him?"

"See what?" Judith picked herself up, a good deal bewildered.

"The bull, of course. And didn't you feel its hot breath down the nape of your neck?"

"I think you're ghastly." Judith climbed back over the fence. "I think you're the absolute End. What is the absolute End? Mr. Appleby's End." Momentarily she clutched his hand. "What nonsense."

"Listen." Appleby was trudging ahead again. "What's really ghastly is the night I'm having. Carriages float away beneath me. Girls conceal me in haystacks. The delusive hospitality of your cousin mocks me across vast frozen distances like the banquets of the Barmicide. The local peasantry are ridiculously hunting me with hurricane lanterns. And my only consolation—"

"Rubbish."

"—one of my only consolations is the possibility of satisfying a little harmless intellectual curiosity. And perhaps you're curious yourself. Well, feed the machine. Slip in a few more of the facts."

"Look here, it's a bit thick." The self-possessed Judith Raven was unaccountably confused. "I mean, it's becoming a false position—"

"Just what *do* you mean?"

"That it's embarrassing talking this rot about Ranulph's ghost. You'll laugh at it." Judith was assured again. "But the fact is this: that every now and then Ranulph's ghost pops up and does something rather ineffective by way of vindicating Ranulph's character as a seer."

"Am I laughing?"

"Apparently not. But I expect your intellectual curiosity has abruptly ceased."

"I don't think it has. For instance, here's a question. That blind-man business ten or twelve years ago: did you or your brother tell anybody about it?"

They were skirting a plantation and the moonlight lay in chequered pools about them. Judith glanced doubtfully at Appleby. "We're sure to have told everybody. Why?"

"That's what we call a routine enquiry. Now tell me about the operations of Ranulph's ghost."

"Very well. But the trouble is—" Judith broke off, halted and stared into the darkness of the plantation on their right hand. The little, cold wind had died. Everything was utterly still.

"Mr. Appleby—John—didn't you hear a shout—or a cry?"

The tops of the pine-trees, snow powdered, faded uncertainly into the heavens. But each tree cast a dark cone of shadow across the path. And this—the fact that it was the shadow rather than the substance that had outline and definition—imparted something eerie and problematical to the scene.

Appleby looked curiously at Judith. "A shout is likely enough. I thought I saw those moving lights again only a couple of minutes ago. How far are we from your home now?"

"Not more than a mile. So if there are shouts and lights it may just be fuss over Heyhoe and Spot and the others. But I suppose *they* are quite likely to have got going a fuss about *us*. Luke would have all sorts of plans ready in no time for finding the bodies, and getting a cart to bring them in. All that's just his line. All the same, what I thought I heard—" Judith listened again and then shook her head. "If they are hunting," she said, "let's dodge them. We'll turn into the wood at the bottom of this hill and take the bridle-path. That brings us straight into the stables. What was I telling you?"

"What the trouble was."

"Yes, of course. The trouble about the doings of Ranulph's ghost is this: they're so ineffective that it would take an expert in Ranulph to know there were any doings at all." Suddenly Judith's accent had become whole-hearted and decided. "That's the bother. Ranulph's ghost squeaks and gibbers for all it's worth. But nobody hears, because the world is too much occupied with all sorts of loud noises of its own." And Judith as she gave this obscure explanation kicked at the snow in front of her.

"But ghosts nearly always are ineffective. Not story-book ghosts, but scientific ghosts—the kind real people really persuade themselves they've seen. Ineffectiveness is their hallmark." Appleby spoke absently; the country dropped away on their left, and was widely visible under a moon over which small clouds were drifting; as he gazed across it he could have imagined that it was itself peopled by ineffective but gigantic spectres—so strange was the procession of faint cloud-shadows over the snow. "I should be most surprised to hear that Ranulph's ghost had effected anything really startling. By the way, are *you* a Ranulph expert?"

"I've done what we told the blind man we'd done then: read him all through. There's something rather fascinating about the extreme badness of Ranulph's prose. Facetious and polysyllabic—and clearly he thought it just the cat's whiskers. An awful warning, I should say, to cultivated persons who believe themselves to have a talent for writing in a popular and condescending way. And yet he was in fact very widely read—for his matter, I suppose. And I believe you've hit on the truth of that. His stories are just like the rubbishing adventures one sometimes invents for oneself when bored. Though with the erotic bits left out—or just hinted in a sentence of uncharacteristic spareness and restraint."

Appleby laughed. "His great-niece—isn't that what you are?—has rather a nice sense of words herself. But they keep on leading her away from the point. I think you said that Ranulph went in for the supernatural in his tales?"

"Quite a lot—but in the stupid way in which it always turns out to be a mistake. Grandfather's ghost is universally believed to stalk about the cellarage, and then in the last chapter it turns out to be one of the footmen stealing port.

Fancy having a big, devoted public and getting away with that."

"Just fancy. But the question seems to be: what is Ranulph —or his ghost—getting away with now." Appleby looked soberly at Judith. "Are you suggesting that the ghost tries to arrange things so that some of his hoary old stories start coming true—forty years on?"

"Something like that. And here's an example. There's a story of Ranulph's called *The Coach of Cacus*. As you're fond of quoting Latin you'll remember that Cacus—"

"Was the son of Vulcan, and a cattle thief. He confused people of my profession who might be around by hauling cattle about backwards by their tails."

"Quite so. And this was just one of Ranulph's stupider, pot-boiling stories, which appeared first in something called the *Household Magazine* in 1887, and later in the second series of his *Tales: Chiefly Imaginative or Grotesque*."

"Good Lord!"

"Everard's title, actually; those two volumes were posthumously collected, and he's literary executor. A bit of a flop, I think they were, for Ranulph's public died before him. Anyway, this yarn is about a coachman who got away with something nasty by harnessing his horse head-first into the shafts and making it back away through the snow or mud or something. Tracks appearing to lead in the wrong direction and throwing people off the scent. Cacus-business, in fact. What do you think of that?"

"Singularly little, I'm afraid. The carriage wouldn't go straight, and anyone knowing horses would only have to glance at the tracks—"

"This is where we turn off." Judith had stopped and now pointed to a stile on the farther side of the snow-filled ditch. Beyond was a narrow ribbon of path, gleaming white, which disappeared through a plantation of young, thickly planted pines. "Not our land," she said. "But the owner doesn't mind. Dreadful that he should plant this stuff instead of real trees. Soon the whole countryside will be looking like some ghastly bit of Scotland. Or Alaska, in weather like this." Judith shook her head darkly over this squirearchal sentiment, and was for a moment very much a child repeating the wisdom of her elders. "Come on. There are several dips that are sure to be full of drifted snow. But it's a short cut and we'll dodge the anxious searchers. Or shall we?"

Even as they negotiated a narrow plank over the ditch there had come an unmistakable shout from somewhere ahead, and this was answered by another shout from further away. "Dr. Livingstone," Appleby said as he helped Judith over the stile, "before Stanley appears through the jungle and discovers us, perhaps you could—"

"It happened to Heyhoe."

"Heyhoe?"

"Last winter. In snow just like this. He'd gone into the local pub one night when he was supposed to be doing something else. He left Spot and his cart outside. And when he came out the brute was harnessed in the wrong way around, just as in *The Coach of Cacus*. The ghost of Ranulph, you see, amusing himself by playing variations on his own old story. And Heyhoe was so tight—the disgusting old man!—that he couldn't make out what had happened. So he tried to drive through the village—*damn!"*

Judith had abruptly plunged knee-deep in soft snow. It was clear that they were confronted with the first of the dips. Appleby hauled her out and they struggled to the farther side. "Nothing like keeping up the evening's fun to the very end," he said. "But your ghost story disappoints me. Very evidently the thing was a practical joke by someone who knew Ranulph's Cacus yarn. Your brother, most likely. I have a notion that the idea of Heyhoe's trying to drive the preposterous Spot home would appeal to him."

"It appealed to him enormously. But Mark didn't do it, all the same. He's not much of a Ranulph fan and he didn't even know *The Coach of Cacus*."

"Sure?"

"Quite sure. Mark and I have an agreement not to tell lies to each other. It's extraordinarily convenient."

"No doubt." Not far away, it seemed to Appleby, there were voices; and once, most certainly, a lantern had glimmered through the trees. The long *tête-à-tête*—or better, perhaps, *pas-à-deux*—with Judith Raven was about to come to an end. "No doubt—though you might find it less convenient if you had to extend it to other people. But just who played the joke doesn't much matter. Perhaps it was your cousin Everard, relaxing after the aridities of the *New Millennium*. Or your cousin Luke, relaxing from I'm not sure what."

"Luke is much possessed with death."

"I might have guessed it was that. Or perhaps the visually-intimidating but mildly-spoken Robert—"

"Of course it was a joke. And, by itself, tolerably funny, no doubt. But the point is that it's only one of a number of incidents. I think that's the word. Incidents not funny, usually slightly sinister, but always extremely . . . ineffective. The horse-business has been much the most noticeable. And they've all hitched on to the Ranulph *opera*."

"I see." There were voices nearer now, and Appleby gazed ahead. The moon was unobscured and brilliant; the narrow path through the silent, dark pines was a spotless ribbon of dead white, leading them almost hypnotically on; immediately before them it appeared to slope downwards gently and then curve round to the left. "I see. But, even if ineffective, these incidents seem to have been on your mind. And you call them sinister. There's really something about them that upsets or scares you?"

"Scares me? Rubbish!" Judith Raven tossed her head contemptuously as they swung round the bend in the path. "That blind-man affair years ago may have scared me. But I was a kid then. Now—" Judith's voice died into a queer gasp; she swayed and her knees crumpled beneath her; and Appleby caught her as she fell. He glanced ahead; where he had seen her stare, transfixed. There, dead in their path, ghastly on its carpet of moon-drenched snow, its eyes wide and glaring, lay—impossible to mistake—Heyhoe's head. For a moment Appleby too felt dizzy. There were lights, voices about them, and men running forward, heavy-footed and panting from among the pines.

Chapter 7

MISS CLARISSA RAVEN poured coffee from battered but beautiful Queen Anne silver. "A great loss," she said. "Sugar, Mr. Appleby? For Spot, that is to say."

"Dead?" said Mark Raven. He leant across the vast table, fork in hand and secured a slice of ham with something of the controlled violence of a man who harpoons a whale. "Heyhoe dead? Hell."

"Hell?" Luke Raven, who had satisfied his appetite, was standing before the great carved fireplace within which a large green log reluctantly smouldered. "This place is too cold for hell." Luke's domestic conversation, it was already apparent, largely consisted of the gloomier utterances of the poets. "Hell is murky," said Luke Raven—inconsequently but with considerable rhetorical effect. He folded his arms across his chest and glowered at his kinsfolk as if through some mephitic mist.

"Plenty of coffee." Miss Clarissa's voice, although intended to be matter-of-fact merely, held hints both of triumph and surprise. She sat at the head of the table and her silver hair and pale complexion merged themselves with the jugs and basins. "Rainbird always rises to an occasion. I'm very glad it wasn't Rainbird. Rainbird!"

"Yes, marm." Rainbird was a battered old person in a boiled shirt, much like a butler in a whisky advertisement who has been left for a long time out in the wet. "Yes, marm," said Rainbird.

"I'm glad it wasn't you. Disorganisation inside the house is much more trying than outside."

"Thank you, marm."

"Spot will feel it very much—and, indeed, it will be most inconvenient. Consider the funeral. There is *only* Spot. And Spot is so old that really only Heyhoe could manage him. So it would appear—"

"That Heyhoe should have stayed alive long enough to drive to his own obsequies." Mark Raven laughed vigorously

61

as he offered this witticism. But his eyes, Appleby noticed, seldom left the face of his sister Judith, who sat silent and pale before an unbroached boiled egg.

Clarissa frowned. "I was about to say that it would appear necessary to send to Yatter for one of those hearse things. With plate-glass all round and a mute perched at each corner."

"Hardly at each corner," Everard Raven, who had been sitting in what appeared to be mild stupefaction, was stirred to speech. "Possibly on the box—"

"Look here." Mark interrupted suddenly and seriously. "Is there something *queer* about Heyhoe's death? I don't like the feel of all this a bit. I didn't like the manner of the people who brought him back. What's it all about?"

Judith spoke for the first time. "His head," she said; "his head was lying on the snow." She stared in front of her. "On the snow," she repeated in an expressionless voice.

"No, no." Robert Raven, scowling ferociously, put down his coffee cup and walked round the table. "You've got it wrong, my dear." He put a hand gently on Judith's shoulder. "The poor old chap's body's up there in his room. And his head's on his shoulders, all right. And it always was, if you ask me. Pretty shrewd was old Heyhoe, don't you think?"

Judith stirred and shivered; then, wanly, she smiled. "Am I being a fool?" she asked. "Did I just see things? We came round a corner and I thought I saw—"

"Snowdrift." Robert picked up an egg-spoon and took the top off Judith's egg. "Big dips in that bridle-path. He was buried up to the neck in snow—and quite dead when you saw him. Naturally it gave you a bit of a turn. Particularly after your odd wanderings—not to speak of sailings. Mr. Appleby carried you home. Do you know that you had straws in your hair? Just as if you were a distraught heroine."

Suddenly Judith laughed. "Oh, Robert, it was hay! Mr. Appleby and I had been tumbling in the hay."

"Tumbling in the hay?" Clarissa looked placidly surprised. "Was not that rather unseasonable, child?" She turned a misdoubting eye on Appleby. "And, indeed, rather—"

"Clarissa," said Everard hastily, "the events of the evening are still distinctly confused. But we are extremely grateful to our guest for having looked after Judith so well. And now I think it would be wise if we all went to bed. There is no denying that a certain amount of awkwardness awaits us in the morning. So a good night's sleep will be just the thing."

"Awkwardness?" Clarissa turned anxiously to Rainbird. "Rainbird, there are plenty of eggs, and so forth? Coffee-beans, even—and something for luncheon?"

"Oh, yes, marm. At least a dozen eggs. Coffee I'm rather doubtful of, marm, but there's still a little tea in the last chest. Potatoes is going to be our trouble, marm. Cook had arranged with Heyhoe—with the late Heyhoe, as I should say, marm—"

"Let cook prepare abundance of cabbage. Everard, there will be no awkwardness—not until we have to think about that funeral. Perhaps Billy Bidewell or Peggy Pitches had better be sent over with a note to the vicar's in the morning. He must have a very good idea of what to do with the dead."

"Potatoes?" said Everard. "Did I hear somebody say something about potatoes? *Patagonia to Potato* is going to be out on Thursday. And the doggy letter still a chaos! Really, this could not have happened more unfortunately. And I fear, Clarissa, that you do not quite apprehend what I mean by awkwardness. The awkwardness will be with the police, and people of that sort."

"No doubt there will be policemen." Clarissa peered into an empty coffee-pot. "But Rainbird is perfectly competent to entertain them in the servants' hall. Judith, why are you making faces at me?"

"Because of Mr. Appleby, aunt Clarissa. Mr. Appleby is a policeman."

"Is he, indeed?" Clarissa was not at all disconcerted. "Now-adays there are so many interesting careers, are there not? But I was referring to the local constabulary. And I shall suggest that cook make a nourishing cabbage soup. If there aren't enough cabbages Heyhoe must go over and fetch some from the Hall farm."

"Heyhoe," said Luke, "doth inherit the vasty hall of death."

"Dear me, yes—how stupid of me! That is what this is all about. And will somebody tell me, by the way, why the police should be interested in Heyhoe's death? Now, if it had been Rainbird—"

Everard coughed. "My dear, it appears to be the general opinion that it is impossible to bury oneself up to the neck in a snowdrift. Only some species of avalanche would produce such an effect. It would seem, therefore, that somebody must have deliberately dug the unfortunate old man in."

Clarissa looked at her kinsman in mild surprise. "Everard, do you mean that Heyhoe has been *murdered?*"

"It rather looks as if it must be called that."

"Then I think it ought to be investigated. If such things are allowed to occur nobody is in the least safe. It might happen to Rainbird! Rainbird, you had better not venture far from the house until there is a thaw."

"Very good, marm."

"No doubt it is Hannah Hoobin's boy. Only last month he stole a turkey from the Murcotts. Everard, I told you it was a mistake to keep him out of gaol. First the Murcott's turkey —a remarkably fine one, Mrs. Murcott says—and now this. Judith, why should you give that hysterical laugh?"

"I'm only yawning—by way of preparing to go to bed." Judith had got rather unsteadily to her feet. "Rainbird, Mr. Appleby has been most kind to me. Do see that he has soap as well as towels, or towels as well as soap."

"Very good, Miss Judith."

"Good night, everybody. Aunt Clarissa, come along."

The two ladies of Dream Manor were gone; Robert saw them out of the long room; Mark's eyes, Appleby noted, again never left his sister until the door closed behind her.

Everard moved towards the fireplace. "As I say, I think we ought to be off too. Or shall we have a cigar? The *New Millennium* people send down a box every time we tick off a letter. Remarkably attentive they are—in little matters of that sort. Mark, be a good fellow and fetch them in."

Mark left the room with alacrity and appeared to be away rather a long time. Rainbird moved softly about clearing the table, or rather making such redispositions as he appeared to think requisite for breakfast. Every now and then he murmured "Heyhoe," softly; but Appleby, after listening carefully, decided that this was a mere ejaculation, made without reference to the dead coachman. Presently Mark returned; he looked relieved—perhaps only because he had succeeded in finding the cigars. Everard opened the box with an air, disclosing the largest Romeo and Juliettas that a leisured smoker could wish to see. It looked as if at least an hour's further confabulation with the Raven menfolk lay ahead.

Appleby, forlorn in borrowed clothes, considered the prospect without enthusiasm. But at least it would give Rainbird ample time to add soap to the towels or towels to the soap. And now Everard remembered that Clarissa might find the cigar-smoke oppressive in the morning, and that it would be better to move to the library. So they all left the dining-room—a large apartment hung with innumerable oil paintings which the light was inadequate to distinguish—and passed across what was already familiar to Appleby as an excruciatingly draughty hall. Robert Raven padded as if through a zone in which skill in unarmed combat might at any moment be required; Luke's lips moved in an inaudible threnody; Everard, who had put on a faded rose-pink jacket salvaged from some wine club of his youth, toddled ahead like a careworn cockatoo; and Mark contrived to stand aside and view the whole procession with his most *louche* grin.

The hall of Dream manor, as well as being draughty, was long, narrow, and sadly disproportioned as the result of the injudicious addition of a pretentious Regency staircase. But what made it really odd was the Mongolians. For each Mongolian had a glass case to himself, and these were disposed in a quincunx pattern all over the available floor space. There is something markedly disconcerting in a miniature Madame Tussaud's deposited in a country gentleman's hall, and where there has been loving concentration on the more inscrutable Oriental types this effect is accentuated. The Mongolians—they had been collected by Ranulph's third brother, Adolphus, a person of some talent who had joined the Romish communion and become a bishop *in partibus*, but who was later converted on his death-bed to the religious system of the Zend-Avesta—the Mongolians eminently possessed that creepy half-life which all waxworks share, and which analysis shows to proceed from our conviction that they are uneasily aware of their own mere waxiness. The Mongolians, then—tirelessly exacting this obscure psychological manœuvre—stood dotted about the hall and Everard, threading his way between them, explained to Appleby that they were arranged according to the best ethnological knowledge of the eighteen-eighties. "A landmark," he said. "In its day our uncle Adolphus's collection was something of a landmark in its own field. Pray notice the ferocious countenance of the Kurd. And only a few years ago (this one is a Tartar, and I think the force of the expression *to catch a Tartar* will immediately come home to you), only a few years ago the whole thing was wanted by a museum. In Idaho, I think, or perhaps it was Oregon. Only there was a hitch at the last moment."

"They didn't," said Luke, "see their way to *pay*."

"And here we are." Rather hastily Everard threw open a door. "How pleasant to see an excellent fire."

The library fire was really not at all bad. But any cheerfulness which this might have imparted to the room was countered by the noticeable absence of some ten or fifteen thousand books. The library, that is to say, was lined with shelving from floor to ceiling, but, with the exception of islanded volumes and groups of volumes here and there, the shelves harboured nothing but dust, empty cigar boxes and tobacco tins, pipes, carpet slippers, fragments of dog biscuit, some foils, a fencing mask, ink bottles and a small model horse, hinged at the tail and opening so as to display the muscular system and internal economy of the animal. But if the Muses as most classically conceived had taken flight from Dream they lingered as patronesses of the most oppressively permanent of the plastic arts. Ranged round the room were some dozen life-size figures and groups in gleaming white marble. The Rape of Europa was immediately distinguishable —Europa being in high spirits and needing only a frilly skirt to present the appearance of a bareback rider in a circus. A companion piece, in which a bull and a glossy lady were yet more inextricably entangled both with each other and with two astoundingly contorted young men, Appleby identified provisionally as a Punishment of Dirce. He was looking round with some apprehension for a Pasaphaë when Everard Raven patted him amiably into a chair.

"Ah," said Everard, "I see you are looking at poor uncle Theodore's work. Most of it, of course, is in Judith's studio, but the choicer pieces were brought in here. The youth clasping what Mark insists is a beer-barrel is Genius guarding the Secret of the Tomb. Theodore's *chef d'oeuvre*, however, is generally taken to be the one opposite the fireplace. It is called Struggle between a She-Bear and a Man of the Old

Stone Age. A bear was brought specially from Russia and accommodated, it is said, in the butler's pantry. And the Old Stone Age Man was inspected and approved by Charles Darwin." Everard paused and unexpectedly chuckled. "Of course this sort of thing is not exactly in a modern taste. I myself prefer Judith every time. Indeed a few years ago we explored the possibility of selling Theodore up. But there were unexpected difficulties."

Mark struck a match and lit Appleby's cigar. "You see, we left it too late. Until recently these things could be put in vast machines and ground into powder for making a very superior sort of bathroom tiles. But now it appears that they use sour milk. Books, on the other hand, always have their price. We have found that a folio volume of eighteenth-century sermons is a reasonably good breakfast all round. And the works of Voltaire in full calf it isn't easy to eat one's way through under a month."

"Mark," said Everard, "is referring to the fact that the library has been—um—in part dispersed. We have kept a working library upstairs in the Scriptorium. But the books down here were not of much interest to any present members of the family. It seemed a pity, therefore, to—ah—keep them idle."

Mark flung himself into an ancient sofa. "So we passed 'em through the larder. Mr. Appleby is at present in process of digesting a volume of Dodsley's Miscellany or a badly cropped copy of Dryden's Fables."

Everard Raven looked mildly pained. "Mark," he said, "when I was a boy I was taught that gentlemen don't talk money after dinner. And even if that good habit has fallen into desuetude—"

The conversation of Mark Raven, it seemed to Appleby, was in even poorer taste than the marble statuary of his great-uncle Theodore. Perhaps the Heyhoe affair had got this odd young man badly rattled. Anyway, a change of subject would be all to the good. "I don't suppose," asked Appleby, "that any word has come in about the carriage yet?"

Everard shook his head. "Nothing at all. And I am afraid that it will have gone over Tew Weir and that the battering will be the end of it."

"A great loss," said Mark. "For Spot, that is to say."

"The carriage was in very poor repair." Robert Raven, whose features under the influence of warmth and cigar-smoke were beginning to lose the extremity of ferocity which had hitherto distinguished them, seemed to put this as a comforting suggestion to Everard. "It would have fallen to pieces of its own accord, in time."

"Which," said Mark, "goes for Heyhoe too."

"Time?" Luke Raven, who had been leaning against the mantelpiece and gazing in a melancholy way at what was evidently Theodore's idea of the Rape of the Sabines, came forward like an actor who has been presented with his cue. "Time with a Gift of Tears," said Luke. "And Grief with a Glass that ran."

"There were potatoes." Everard's voice held a harassed note. "And cake for the cow. Billy Bidewell must be asked how long cows will go without cake."

"Pleasure, with Pain for leaven," said Luke.

"When one comes to think of it, of course, the carriage would be of little use without Heyhoe—"

"Summer, with Flowers that fell."

"—or Heyhoe without the carriage. But it is extremely distressing, all the same. I can see that Judith has had quite a shock—"

"Remembrance, fallen from Heaven."

"—and that Clarissa, too, is upset. The events of the evening have been—"

"Madness risen from Hell."

Mark Raven gave a yell of laughter. "One to the poet!" he cried. "Luke has hit the nail on the head. Somebody grabs a half-witted old coachman, yanks him along to a snowdrift, buries him up to the neck and leaves him to the operation of the laws of thermo-dynamics. Everard says it is extremely distressing. Luke says—"

"Swinburne," said Luke with gloomy modesty.

"Swinburne says it is Madness risen from Hell. Let Mr. Appleby, who is entirely unprejudiced in the matter, decide which is right."

Appleby remained silent. It was clear that the Ravens enjoyed desultory conversation among themselves and were capable of keeping it up indefinitely. No need to interrupt. And there was—surely there was—much about them that required a little quiet thinking out. Were they really birds as queer as they now seemed to be to a strayed policeman at the end of a long day first of massive monotony and latterly of fantastic incident? And where had they all been between the serio-comic episode of the ford and the ghastly discovery of Heyhoe? Appleby frowned. Where had he himself been? Floating down a river in an ancient carriage and in the company of an unaccountable girl—a ludicrous performance which circumstances had decreed should now in all probability, become a front-page story. Inspector Appleby, what happened when visibility became so poor that you could momentarily proceed no further? We climbed into a haystack. Into a haystack, Inspector? A haystack. And, I suppose, fell asleep there? I'm afraid I really don't know; perhaps so; certainly not for very long. . . . Decidedly it sounded silly. And *had* he conceivably been asleep? Had Judith been asleep?

The Old Stone Age Man—whose gaze passed, most improbably, just wide of the She-Bear's left ear—squinnied at Appleby with all the cunning suspicion of the primeval forest. Dirce, on his right hand, looked as if she might at any moment perform a further somersault on her bull and land him a well-directed whirret on the ear. The Mongolians in the hall, mildly disconcerting though they were, had nothing of the restlessness of Theodore's marmorean creations. Nor, in their multiplicity of faded barbaric garments, did they look anything like so chilly. . . .

Heyhoe. Only the graceless young Mark, so far, had really faced up to the nastiness of that icy end.

Chapter 8

THERE EXISTED, Appleby reflected, a highly esteemed school of prose fiction which represented the rural inhabitants of the British Isles as possessed by a ferocity and general nastiness to which the Kurd and the Tartar of the late Bishop Adolphus could scarcely hope to measure up. Was this, then, a regular winter sport, unsuspected in the metropolis? At stated seasons did the simple peasantry delight in stamping their senior brethren into compacted snow? The effect as of some horrid decapitation had certainly been striking; was it an example of the lingering art of the folk? Or—since this macabre fantasy was surely baseless—what rational purpose could be served by such a deed? Was it within the bounds of possibility that—? Appleby, here beginning to frame some professional question, found that his thoughts on the whole matter led nowhere. Just nowhere—unless conceivably to the late Ranulph Raven?

Why had Judith told him all that rigmarole, ending with the story of the preposterous harnessing of Spot? Probably just because she had felt that way, and with no ulterior motive whatever. Appleby shifted his gaze from the Old Stone Age Man to a rapturous Sabine lady, and suddenly quite a new idea started into his head. He turned to Everard. "I suppose," he said, "that Heyhoe was a fairly elderly man—older than any of you?"

Perhaps because they had been talking of something quite different, perhaps because the question had an odd turn to it, all the Ravens looked mildly surprised. "Heyhoe?" said Everard. "Dear me, yes. Old as the hills, poor chap. Must have been a stable lad about the place when I was a baby in arms. About a contemporary of Rainbird's, I should say. Wouldn't you, Robert?"

"Rainbird and Heyhoe," said Robert carefully, "were both born some years before any of us."

Which brings us back, thought Appleby, to Ranulph. Judith has already built up Ranulph as such a legendary figure in my mind that it is hard to realize that three of his sons are here in the room with me. And a fourth has been dug out of the snow. And a fifth—it now almost appears—is pottering round arranging a breakfast table across the hall. In fact the Dream Manor household is eminently a family affair. But if Heyhoe—

"Heyhoe," said Everard. "How right Mr. Appleby is to recur to him. You know, we must get all that clear. What happened to each of us after our—em—dispersal at the ford? The jotting down of a note or two would not, to my mind, be by any means amiss."

"Ask Mr. Appleby," said Mark. "It's just his line. Judith tells us he's a policeman."

Everard frowned. "I certainly heard Judith make some obscure joke. But I hardly suppose—"

"It's quite true." Appleby, who was becoming very sleepy, endeavoured to give his features an adequate expression of mild apology. "I am a detective-inspector from Scotland Yard, and on my way to enquire into some troublesome affair at a place called Snarl. As I explained to Mr. Raven when he was good enough to bring me along, I hope to get over there to-morrow morning. The death of your coachman is, of course, no business of mine whatever, and I haven't the remotest intention of taking down notes about it."

Mark Raven jerked up his chin with a movement that sent the yellow hair tossing above his forehead. "Then why did you ask whether Heyhoe was older—"

"If I may say so, these are uncommonly good cigars."

Everard beamed. "As I think I remarked, the *New Millennium* people are most enlightened in matters of that sort. It comes of one or two of their directors being of decent family, no doubt. I'm sorry to say the *Enlarged Resurrection* folk don't sound nearly so promising." Everard shook his head and looked gloomy again—almost as gloomy as Luke. "And of course we must not worry Mr. Appleby with Heyhoe. His profession is purely—um—fortuitous and coincidental. Any further reference to it, my dear Mark, will be uncivil. We shall piece the matter out as best we can to-morrow morning and give an account of it to our own local police. Robert, I think Mr. Appleby might be interested in the group at the far end of the room. It is called Nausicaä and her Maidens Washing, and is estimated to weigh seventeen tons."

Appleby doubted if he had any substantial interest left except bed. It would, of course, be satisfactory to know whether among the voluminous writings of Ranulph Raven there was anything prophetic of Heyhoe's displeasing end. But on that Judith was the authority, and he would himself, no doubt, be off to Snarl on quite a different matter before Judith was up and about again. Everard too must know a good deal about the body of his father's writing; had he too the impression that the ghost of Ranulph haunted Dream? On this a little fishing might be done while consuming the last third of the *New Millennium* people's cigar.

But at the moment Robert Raven held the field. Standing before Nausicaä and her Maidens Washing, and eyeing their nicely rounded contours much as if disposed to bite out great collops of gleaming marble flesh, he was discoursing mildly on the harmless if expensive nature of his late uncle's pursuit. "Of course he did very little actual carving himself. Nineteenth century sculptors didn't. At least one *scarpellino* was employed chipping away full time. Among the benefits of the growth of science, you know, is this: that it gives the Theodores—talented, second-rate men—something more or less useful to do. His sort of fair-to-medium intellectual energy is drained off elsewhere. Science and pseudo-science. To-day Theodore would be a professor of economics in some hole in Wales."

"Science?" said Everard. "Well, I don't know. But certainly there's a terrible lot of *it*. I ought to be getting on with Science. Devilish near, by the time one's got to Religion."

Luke too had placed himself in front of Nausicaä—whose innocent exhibition of *les tetons et les fesses* he seemed to view without even the faint carnal curiosity which the art of Theodore seemed alone calculated to arouse. "Science?" said Luke. "Consider the rocket gun and the time-bomb. Science has done nothing but sharpen the fangs of the sabre-toothed tiger." And Luke, who appeared to vary quotation with epigram, walked gloomily away.

"But," said Appleby, "there is such a thing as specific inclination or talent, after all. Your uncle Theodore might have been a professor of economics in Wales or elsewhere. But your father, surely, would never have been other than the kind of writer he was."

"The kind of writer he was?" Everard was amiably discursive. "Now, what kind *was* he, would you say? I don't know that we've ever as a family got that fixed. You see, Ravens have never done anything in what you would call a popular way—or not as a rule. I suppose the *New Millennium might* be called popular"—and Everard looked momentarily rueful, as was proper in a scholar who yearned to labour on the frontiers of knowledge—"but anything of the sort has always been the exception with us. Even this stuff of Theodore's was regarded as utterly refined in its day. Chaste was, I believe, the word commonly applied to it."

"Do you hear that?" Mark Raven interrogated the most nubile of Nausicaä's Maidens, and enforced the question with a resounding spank. *"Le mot juste,* if ever there was one." He shook a finger warningly. "No, no, my girl—it won't do."

"I do not say"—Everard eyed his young cousin meditatively —"that there is not a marked strain of coarseness which sometimes appears in our family. But almost without exception we have been earnest. Our dear father, therefore, was always something of a puzzle. Was he earnest? Did he endeavour to impart real literary quality to his work, or did he consciously write down? We just don't know. Although I myself edited a collected edition of his work for publication shortly after his death—and it cannot be described as a success, I am sorry to say—I really formed no very clear idea on the matter. Now, Roger was an interesting man. A first cousin of papa's, and a most distinguished Latinist. A little collection of translations from Horace and Martial which he put out was extremely well received. Jowett of Balliol was delighted with it."

"Is that so?" said Appleby. Disinterest in the highly-coloured writings of papa was quite clearly the ruling attitude at Dream. Roger, Theodore and Adolphus had been earnest, and were preferred. Were the present generations earnest too? Everard plainly worked like a slave. Judith with a mallet in her hand was no doubt as earnest as Theodore had ever been. It was Luke's line to be burdened with a melancholy temperament— which was presumably a way of being earnest without the necessity of buckling to. Mark was somewhat enigmatic; Robert wholly so; and Clarissa was seriously resolved that Rainbird at least should remain unburied in the snow. This was about the sum total of Appleby's knowledge of the Ravens so far—and as he grew sleepier he became increasingly prone to the delusion that he had known them through uncounted years. He decided to have another shot. "I gathered from Miss Judith," he said, "that she was very well up in Ranulph Raven's works. Indeed, I almost felt that they were on her mind."

"Judith's mind?" said Mark. "You would maintain Judith has a mind? She certainly has a temper, and sometimes she has wit, and occasionally she has designs. Beware of Judith, Mr. Appleby, when she's by way of having designs. But a mind? Cousin Robert has the family mind and rather resents it. That's why he looks so *farouche*. Pray observe the ferocious countenance of the Kurd."

But Appleby was not going to be beaten so easily. "Miss Judith," he repeated, "seems to have Ranulph Raven's books on her mind. Thinks them uncanny. Something of that sort. Something about that horse. Spot, isn't he? And one of Ranulph Raven's stories. I didn't quite understand it. But she seemed to think there was something queer."

"Spot?" said Mark. "Oh, that! Well, I suppose she felt the necessity of entertaining you with something. Did she tell you about the blind man when we were kids?"

"Yes; she told me about that."

Everard took the cigar from his mouth and looked at Appleby in mild surprise. "That old family story! I haven't heard it mentioned for years. And yet it was an uncommonly strange affair which we never got to the bottom of. There was of course an element of what they now call *rapportage* in papa's work. He picked up material from the countryfolk round about in rather odd ways, and as a result he seems to have gained something of a preternatural character in their regard. But whether the blind man had really committed some crime and believed papa to have wormed it out of him and put it in a book we shall clearly never know. If I remember aright it was some little time before the children came out with the story, and we judged it best to take no action. I trust we were right. Robert, would you say that we were right?"

"Probably not." Robert Raven had retreated a few paces and was now approaching Dirce's bull with the finely controlled bellicosity of a figure in a Hemingway tauromachy. "But it's an old story, as you say. What Judith must have on her mind is the business of *The Coach of Cacus*, and the other affairs of that sort. Luke's tombstone, for instance."

This was bewildering. "Your brother," Appleby asked politely, "has a tombstone?"

"A Christmas present." It was Mark who broke in. "Somebody sent Luke a tombstone—and what could better hit his taste? Did you ever read Richardson's *Clarissa?* The lady takes several volumes to die. And she keeps a coffin in her bedroom and calls it the 'dread receptacle.' " Mark gave his sudden, harsh whoop of laughter. "Well, Luke has a tombstone just like that—thanks to an unknown donor. My notion is that he always longed for one, and so he sent it to himself —like Gub-Gub."

"Gub-Gub?" said Appleby.

"Gub-Gub was Doctor Dolittle's pig."

"Really, Mark"—Everard Raven held up a protesting hand —"if Mr. Appleby must be told these grotesque and confusing things is it sensible to mix them up with *Clarissa* and Doctor Dolittle's pig—particularly when Luke's tombstone is mixed up with a book already?" He turned apologetically to Appleby. "I don't suppose you happen ever to have read my father's *Paxton's Destined Hour?* It's about somebody called Paxton who is strolling past the sort of place where they make tombstones when his eye is suddenly caught by his own name. He finds he is reading his own tombstone, complete with the date of his death—"

Appleby frowned. "But I've read a story like that. And certainly not by your father."

"Quite so, quite so." Everard looked embarrassed. "But these things do happen. You will find, for instance, that Conrad's *Inn of the Witches* is very much the same story as Wilkie Collins's *A Terribly Strange Bed.*"

"Everard," Mark said, "if Mr. Appleby must be told these grotesque and confusing things—"

"The short of it is this." Robert pitched his cigar end into the fire and turned round with an air of firmly winding up matters for the night. "There's this story of my father's in which Paxton, having seen the date of his own death inscribed on a tombstone—a mystery never accounted for, if I remember aright—waits in mounting apprehension for that particular date to come along. He shuts himself up in an attic. He won't see anyone, just in case he's a homicidal maniac. He won't eat anything, just in case the food has been accidentally or purposely poisoned. Then at last, at the end of twenty-four hours of agonized apprehension, he hears the hall clock chime out midnight below. He rushes triumphantly from his attic, trips in the dark, tumbles downstairs and breaks his neck. The clock was just two minutes fast. What d'you think of that?"

Appleby took a last puff at his cigar and looked across the derelict library to where Luke, a dark green blob against Genius guarding the Secret of the Tomb, was plainly sunk in sombre meditation on the furthest processes of vermiculation and decay. "I don't think it at all bad. Much better than Cacus. And the story I remember was different: something about a runaway horse."

"The unfortunate hero did his own running away in this case. Well, that's the story. Paxton had his destined hour. And so with Luke. Only Luke didn't just *see* a tombstone. Somebody sent him one by rail. Complete with date of death. The reference to *Paxton's Destined Hour* was obvious."

Appleby was regarding the melancholy Luke with fresh interest. "And how did your brother feel about it?"

"To start with he went round telling everybody. And that was awkward. For some little reporter creature on our local paper got hold of the story, and it looked as if Luke was going to be thoroughly pestered. Fortunately Everard's solicitor, who is a family friend, was here at the time and stopped any fuss. After that Luke began rather to hug the thing."

"I see. May it be said to account for his present—well, rather elegiac mood?"

"I should hardly say so. Luke is commonly like that. But as the date approached—what you might call *Luke's Destined Hour—*"

"You mean the date's *past?*" As he asked this question Appleby was quite unable to keep a thoroughly professional disappointment out of his voice. "It's all over?"

"Dear me, yes. How long ago was it, Everard? Six months, I should say. The appointed day"—Robert spoke drily, yet with a certain compassion—"must have been not without its discomfort for a man of naturally morbid mind."

Mark Raven lounged forward towards the fireplace. "We did what we could," he said. "Offered to fit up one of the attics. Sent for a fellow from Yatter to check up on the clocks—"

"Be quiet, Mark. If Mr. Appleby is to be burdened with family history he needn't have family humour piled on as well. The date came, I say, and of course nothing happened.

We scarcely know whether Luke was really disturbed. Anyway, the day just passed."

"How very flat." Appleby remembered that Judith was impressed by the ineffectiveness of the ghostly Ranulph's proceedings. "But of course you would not regard it quite in that light."

"Luke still has the tombstone. He says that only a little alteration will be necessary, and it will do later on." Everard shook his head sadly. "The dear fellow feels the need of economy, no doubt."

"But surely not in tombstones." Mark was lighting a line of bedroom candles near the library door. "We can all have the most whopping monuments, if we choose. And I think I'll have Nausicaä. Has it ever occurred to you, by the way, that Theodore has got her wrong? She and her girl friends ought to be washing King Alcinous' vests and pants. But here they are, just washing themselves. A chaster conception, no doubt."

"I seem to recall," said Everard, "that Homer when he tells the story of Odysseus' arrival on Sheria—"

Appleby moved resolutely towards the door. "Nothing like a candle," he said to Mark, "to light you to bed. Which is mine?"

"—and the subject of a lost play by Sophocles." Everard's voice, comfortably instructive, drifted across the room. "When I come to Sophocles—and Sophocles is deuced near when one is beginning to think of Science—I shall be able to mention cousin Roger's conjecture that certain Sophoclean fragments— But, dear me, how late it is—or early, perhaps one ought to say! We must really be getting Mr. Appleby off to bed. And Billy Bidewell must be told to make some arrangement about getting him to Snarl in the morning. I hope, my dear sir"—and Everard came toddling across the room— "that you will come back to us when your—um—business is transacted. We are all most sorry that you should have been harassed by the untoward course of our affairs. I would like to have leisure to show you my Scriptorium. And Judith, I am sure, would be anxious to have your opinion on her work. Luke, too, would enjoy your conversation. This evening, I fear, he has been in somewhat taciturn mood." And Everard murmuring these vague and amiable courtesies, fished ineffectively among the candlesticks. "I believe Rainbird has forgotten an extra one. No—here it is. Pray be careful of the draught as Mark opens the door."

They passed out into the hall. The Tartar and the Kurd and all their kin, infinitely reposeful after the Baroque contortions of Theodore, stood uncertainly revealed in the light of the five candles. Everard paused to expatiate on a figure with drooping moustaches and a nastily curved sword; then, mercifully, proceeded to climb the dilapidated Regency staircase. They passed down a succession of corridors, some straight and businesslike, some winding and with undulating floors. A large place, Appleby reflected, which had plainly come into being by a process of accretion over several centuries. And here—at last—was his bedroom. A few further polite expressions and he was alone.

The room, irregularly shaped and large, was panelled in dark wood to the ceiling. Two oil lamps gave a soft, yellow light to which a faintly flickering counterpoint was added by candles burning unsteadily on the mantlepiece. Below this glowed quite a brave fire, and before the fire a Persian cat lay stretched. The bed was a four-poster, formidable with massive tester and faded hangings. The sheets were a fine linen, lavendered. A folded slip of paper lay on the pillow.

Appleby walked across to the bed and sat down. The sheet of note-paper, a clear blue, was curiously compelling where it lay—a focal point around which the whole shadowy room stood disposed. An obscurely fateful slip of paper. He picked it up and unfolded it slowly; then he carried it to the nearest lamp.

DEAR MR. APPLEBY,

There is nothing corresponding to the death of Heyhoe in Ranulph Raven's works. You are in his room, by the way, and everything he published is in the bookcase near the door. My aunt Clarissa would, I think, have me say that the biscuits in the tin, though few, are fresh; and that the cat is because of the mice. The safety-razor is Mark's; he will sleep late. The soap was shocking and something honest from the kitchens has been substituted.

Yours sincerely,
JUDITH RAVEN

Appleby read this through, frowning. Then he perched it on the dressing-table and read it through again as he undressed. Presently he turned it over; there was a single sooty smudge on the back. He was looking at this rather wide-eyed when there came a tap at the door and the ancient manservant Rainbird entered.

"I hope everything is as you would wish, sir?"

"Dear me, yes. It's very kind of you to have lit a fire at such an unearthly hour."

Rainbird's gaze travelled slowly to the fireplace. Then he stooped and picked up an empty water-jug. "We always endeavour to make Mr. Everard's guests comfortable, sir. Is there anything else that I could get you?"

"No, thank you—nothing at all."

"Then good-night, sir. Or good morning, as I ought to say."

The door closed softly on Rainbird. Appleby slipped into pyjamas—Mark's, no doubt—and walked over to the fire. For a moment he warmed his hands before it, gazing into the flame. The day had assuredly been something of an Odyssey and had ended—where? Was it indeed Nausicaä's Scheria— or was it the Circean Aeaea? Might it be Ithaca itself? And at least was there not something truly Homeric in this: that the princess in her own person had kindled the traveller's evening fire?

Appleby extinguished the lights and tumbled into the late Ranulph Raven's bed.

Chapter 9

BILLY BIDEWELL, promoted by the calamitous events of the preceding night to the overlordship of Spot, was blessedly unsuggestive of any connection, illegitimate or otherwise, with his employer's family. He was a fat boy with a face as round as a full moon and as ruddy as a pippin; his expression was markedly unreflective; a low, short whistle on a single note, emitted at fairly regular three-minute intervals, he appeared to regard as a sufficient vehicle of communication with the external world. Appleby, whose few hours of sleep had been filled with nightmarish wanderings among Tartars and Kurds, and who now, wrapped in an enormous leopard-skin rug, was perched somewhat uncomfortably on a board thrown across the sides of a farm wagon, found him a decidedly restful companion. The air was crisp; the sun, still low on the horizon, was red and ever so faintly warm; its level beams sparkled on the snow. Spot stepped almost silently along the lane; the wheels crunched cheerfully behind; from here and there came barnyard noises; in front lay Snarl and whatever conundrum the county constabulary were thinking to pose. Long Dream and the unlikely proceedings of Ranulph Raven's ghost should have been fading rapidly from Appleby's mind. But professional instinct is strong—particularly in face of an ideal opportunity for Pumping the Servants. "Very sad about Heyhoe," Appleby said.

"Ur," said Billy Bidewell.

"Quite shocking," said Appleby.

Billy Bidewell whistled. Then, unexpectedly, he broke into speech. "It might ha' been worser," he said. "Happen it might ha' been worser by far. They might ha' set Spot and they only set Heyhoe. So who cares?" And Billy directed at the rump of the ungainly brute ambling before him what must have been intended as a glance of affectionate regard.

"Set?" asked Appleby. "Isn't that what you do with turnips?"

"Ur," said Billy—and added with a sudden, rich and unnerving satisfaction, "they set Heyhoe in the snow."

"Yes," said Appleby. To expatiate on the deplorable nature of Heyhoe's end was clearly not the right line. "They set him, all right. But who's they? That's the question."

Billy Bidewell turned his round face to Appleby. It was covered with a large, vague surprise. "They?" he said. "Why, who would it be, mister? Them as were through with 'un. Them as had had enough 'un. Mr. Everard and Mr. Robert, to be sure. And Mr. Luke and—"

Appleby stared aghast at this terrible youth. "You mean to tell me you believe that all these people set upon Heyhoe and—"

"—and Mr. Mark and Miss Judith. And happen Miss Clarissa too."

"It may interest you to know," said Appleby indignantly, "that I was with Miss Judith myself the whole time."

"Ur," said Billy, with profound but obscure expressiveness.

Appleby began to wish that the rural centre of Snarl would heave in sight. But Spot was walking in a measured way along an interminably winding lane. High banks were on either side and it was not possible to form any clear estimate of what progress was being made. Billy had returned to his whistling, but some shade of thought appeared now to have gathered on his brow. And presently he spoke. "Where?" he said.

"What do you mean by where?" asked Appleby severely.

"Where was you and Miss Judith all that time, of course."

Billy's simplicity was—or appeared to be—too massive to admit of the notion of insolence. Appleby, therefore, felt constrained to a reasonably informative reply. "After the accident to the carriage she and I were separated from the others and had a good deal of difficulty in making our way back to Dream."

"Ur."

"When you speak of setting Heyhoe—" began Appleby.

"Rainbird do say you were in haystack."

"Certainly." In this awkward matter, it appeared to Appleby, there was everything to be said for a confident tone. "It came on to snow very hard, and we had to take shelter by a haystack for a time."

"Rainbird," said Billy relentlessly, "Rainbird did say *in* haystack."

"Quite so. Surprisingly warm."

"Ur," said Billy. "Ur, ur!" And he turned to stare at Appleby with unaffected admiration and awe."

"My good fellow"—a touch of feudal distance, Appleby thought, might usefully be given to the conversation—"what should put it in your head that your master and his brothers could possibly have anything to do with the death of Heyhoe?"

"Carriage were gone, weren't it?" Billy's normally slow speech had turned even slower, as if it had occurred to him that Appleby, despite a masterful way with him in haystacks, was not in full enjoyment of his faculties. " 'Carriage be gone,' they'd say. 'And in cart Billy Bidewell do manage Spot as well as Heyhoe.' And then: 'Here be snowdrift,' they'd say. 'Let uns set t'old devil in.'" And Billy nodded his head—sagely and with evident approval of this drastically conceived act of liquidation.

"Do you expect to be set in yourself one day—say when Spot is finally put out to grass? Or that you and Spot will be set in together?" This part of England, Appleby was almost coming to believe, had its own peculiar customs out-rivalling those of darkest Africa.

"Ur," said Billy Bidewell.

"And can you tell me why they should choose just that rather noticeable way of dispatching Heyhoe? Why should not Mr. Everard and Mr. Robert and Mr. Luke have pitched him in the river?"

"Because Ravens 'ud do nowt like other folk. And maybe because of the story."

"*The story?*" Appleby sat up so abruptly that the reins jerked in Billy's hands and Spot paused from his labours and looked round reproachfully. "You mean one of Ranulph Raven's stories?"

"*Ur!*" Billy offered his favourite ejaculation seemingly by way of a contemptuous negative. "One of Gammer Bidewell's stories, in course."

"Gammer Bidewell? Do you mean a relation of yours?"

"Grandmother. Her tale of the howling and hollering head."

Billy announced this with considerable gusto. Perhaps, Appleby thought, making one's flesh creep was an appetite which all Fat Boys share with their immortal prototype in *Pickwick*. "A tale of a fearful maid," added Billy—this time with a rolling and inexpressible relish. "And how she came on a howling and hollering head."

"Well," said Appleby, "—how did she?"

"This fearful maid, as young and tender as any in the parish, was walking through squire's ash spinney." Billy's voice had risen a pitch, presumably in imitation of Grandmother Bidewell. "It was Spring and the stinkweed was rife in the ditches, ruddocks were like little leaping flames in every hedge, from across the meadow the bawcock and the blubberbird—"

"Leave them out," said Appleby. "Drop the stinkweed and keep to the maid."

"Well"—Billy was rather put to a stand by this—"she came

round a bend and there was the head. Lying on the ground, it was, just as if tumbled there by a scythe. And it rolled its eyes and foamed at the mouth and the maid was trembling like the aspen and then the head hollered and howled like the souls of all the damned. It was the head of squire himself and it lay there in a little clearing among the ash trees and squinnied at that fearful maid. And her wits left her, poor tender peat, and she never spoke again. But sometimes she would holler and howl just as squire's head had done. And squire was offended at that, and turned her and hers out of parish.

Apppleby stared at Billy Bidewell. "You mean the *same* squire—the one who had lost his head?"

"He had no more lost his head than I have." And Billy tapped his round and innocent cheek with great satisfaction. "It was all the doing of a great doctor famous in those days. A mint of strange cures, he had. He would shut you up with the cows—"

"Dear me," interrupted Appleby. "Beddowes did that. A very well-known physician about the beginning of last century."

"There!" said Billy in triumph. "If that isn't to show that Gammer Bidewell's stories were truer nor parson's by a long way. But another of the cures, and the one he was trying on squire, was the earth bath. And an ash spinney, he believed, was the sovereign place for that. So squire was set there regular by valet. Only this time valet had forgot and tarried too late in pub."

"I see. In fact, a perfectly rational story. Just another case of the footman stealing port."

"Gammer Bidewell said nowt of footman." Billy looked perplexed. "But it do be terrible to think of that fearful maid."

The cart had turned a corner and between Spot's leisurely-bobbing ears there appeared first a church tower and then the straggling vista of a village street. Snarl was achieved at last. Appleby began to divest himself of the leopard skin rug, which had obscurely impressed him as a particularly incongruous habiliment for a detective-inspector from Scotland Yard. Under this was an excessively black and enveloping greatcoat of Luke Raven's—and this too after a moment's deliberation Appleby discarded. In the suit of Mark Raven's shapeless tweeds which stood next revealed it might be possible to make a more or less colourable appearance, and when Appleby had filled a pipe with his last scrap of dry tobacco he felt tolerably equipped for return to the normal world of police investigation. "Billy," he said, "about that story of the squire's head: would many people know it round about these parts?"

"Ur." Billy delivered himself of his most emphatic negative. "Gammer never told that story to nowt but me."

"I don't see how you can know that."

"She said she never told it to nowt but me. She kept it for I because I did so like to be thinking of that fearful maid."

"Then," said Appleby, "it doesn't seem as if Mr. Raven or his brothers could know of it."

Billy Bidewell shook his head darkly. "They know of most things. They say Mr. Everard has got all the knowledge in all the world all writ out on little slips of paper in his room. And what could be more freakish than that? Nowt—but setting Heyhoe because of the old story. And it do be terrible"— ghoulishly Billy reiterated his master theme—"to think of that fearful maid." Then a new thought seemed to strike him. "Mister," he said, "you must know a powerful deal about maids."

Appleby looked at Billy Bidewell in astonishment—and realized that a shadowy haystack was hovering before this dreadful youth's inward eye. "Billy," he said firmly, "I think you had best stop here. I'll walk to the inn."

The exterior of the Farmers' Arms was chiefly distinguished by an enormous escutcheon upon which lions, leopards and griffons ramped and rambled in surprising profusion. In a community in which the aged were so picturesquely disposed of as Heyhoe it seemed not impossible that the yeomanry gave themselves to raising such exotic cattle—nevertheless Appleby regarded it with fleeting surprise as he passed inside and was shown to a flyblown room in which were closeted a military man in pepper-and-salt and a uniformed officer of police. These proved to be Colonel Pike, the chief constable of the county, and Inspector Mutlow from Yatter. Before the inspector was a large notebook, and before the chief constable were several glasses of port. These respective possessions they contemplated with an equal gloom, and this contemplation—somewhat intensified—they now transferred to Appleby.

"Awkward business this," said Colonel Pike. "Have a port." He looked critically at the line of glasses before him and with a stubby forefinger suddenly advanced one out of the ranks. "Any port in a storm," said Colonel Pike—and looked balefully at his subordinate.

Inspector Mutlow made a toadying noise in his throat—indicative of mirth at once irresistible and respectfully restrained. "An awkward business," said Inspector Mutlow.

Appleby looked from one to the other. "I haven't been told anything about it," he said. "Or only that it's rather odd. What's happened?"

"Happened?" Colonel Pike frowned. "Mutlow, what *has* happened?"

"Quite so, sir. What *has* happened? Very nicely put."

"Man's an ass," said Colonel Pike. "Might be useful as a damned dictaphone, but doesn't earn his feed in the police. Though for that matter nothing much *has* happened. Simply that Mulberry's fussed over it. Wouldn't have expected it of him. About dam' all. And must have us bring a feller down from London." Colonel Pike looked at Appleby with convinced distaste.

"Well, sir"—the misprized Mutlow ventured upon a tone of mild reproach—"there *is* a boy missing."

"Rubbish—half-witted boy—nothing more."

"Would that," Appleby asked, "be Hannah Hoobin's boy?"

The two men stared in astonishment. "Well I'm blessed," said Colonel Pike. He looked appraisingly at Appleby. "Not a friend of Mulberry's, by any chance? He has some deuced odd ones."

Appleby shook his head. "I don't know Mulberry," he said politely.

Colonel Pike drowned what was evident outrage in a swig of port. "I'm talking of Sir Mulberry Farmer. Lord Lieutenant. Big man down here. Old friend, too. Wouldn't have asked them to send you down else." Colonel Pike looked from Appleby to Mutlow and his expression of disgust deepened. He looked from Mutlow to Appleby and it became appraising once more. "Think I'll take you over to luncheon with him. You seem perfectly presentable."

"Thank you very much," Appleby said.

"Mutlow, you can go away. No further use for you. No—

stop. Give Mr. Appleby your appreciation of the situation. Avoid prolixity, incoherence and irrelevant detail."

"Very good, sir." Mutlow put his hand in a pocket much as if to reach for a stiletto—in which case, thought Appleby, justifiable homicide would be the only decent verdict. But all that emerged was a large handkerchief with which the harassed inspector proceeded to mop his brow. "It's an affair of statues, like," he said.

"Of statues?"

"And a waxwork," interjected Colonel Pike.

"A *waxwork!*" Appleby sat up very straight.

"Dictaphone habit catchin'," said Colonel Pike.

"And seems to me," continued the inspector, "all to have come of Sir Mulberry's getting a litter of pigs."

"Gloucester Old Spots," said Colonel Pike.

"Ah," said Appleby. "From Brettingham Scurl at Linger, no doubt."

This was a great success. Colonel Pike set down his port glass and stared at Appleby much as if he were in the presence of the Preternatural. Then he relieved his feelings on Mutlow. "Mutlow," he said, "how matters *seem* to you must often be admitted as of considerable psychological interest. But its relevance to police investigation is invariably *nil*. Proceed."

"Sir Mulberry got this litter of pigs a good time back, and one of the pigs was a male pig—"

"Man means a boar," said Colonel Pike.

"Thank you, sir; that would be the technical word, no doubt. Well, Sir Mulberry has a great eye for swine, it seems, and is uncommon fond of 'em. And that brings me to the fact that he's a close friend of Colonel Pike's here—by which I mean to say that when this queer thing happened he told the colonel about it at once." Mutlow's face was extremely wooden. "For this particular boar, you see, he thought a world of—and if you're to believe his men about the place he'd be across and visit it most every morning. Then one day when the brute was full grown and Sir Mulberry had gone over as usual to have a word with it he found that it had been spirited away in the night. Only something else had been left in its place: a great boar in marble or some such stuff that must have weighed pretty well a ton. Did you ever hear of such a crazy thing? Just no sense in it. And soon the story was going round among the servants that it was the hand of God laid heavy on Sir Mulberry for his wicked pride in his pig. There had been a judgment in the night and the brute been ossified."

Colonel Pike pushed two empty port glasses into the rear file and brought forward a full one." Means petrified," he said.

"Ossified," said Mutlow with dignity, "I understand to have been what was popularly said; but petrified, of course, is right. The pig was petrified, so to speak; and so was Lady Farmer's dog.

"Lady Farmer's dog!" Appleby was again reduced to the dictaphone habit.

"Certainly." Colonel Pike deferred broaching the last of his ports in order to interrupt. "Everything round poor old Mulberry turning to stone. Lot of nonsense—but worries him, it seems. Keeping it as quiet as possible, but asked to have you sent down. Met you here to talk about it in an unobtrusive way. Glad to know how you explain it." And Colonel Pike looked up at Appleby in a sharply interrogative fashion.

"I'm quite unable to explain it, I'm afraid. It sounds nonsense to me too."

"Pity. Disappointin'." Colonel Pike frowned with disfavour at Appleby. "Should have asked for an older man. Feller with more experience no doubt put us wise at once."

"Very probably," said Appleby.

"However, presentable at least. So come along." Colonel Pike drained his last port and stood up. "Possibly that when you have a dekko at Mulberry the truth will dawn. Car outside. Mutlow, go away."

Mutlow went away. Appleby followed Colonel Pike to the innyard, in which a Daimler sleekly reposed. They climbed in. "Good feller, Mutlow," said Colonel Pike thoughtfully. "Thoroughly reliable man. Think a world of him. Where's Blight? Blight, you fool, wake up and drive us to Tiffin Place. Don't lose the way. Remember Kerrisk's cows on Nottle common. And don't go honking through Little Boss again and scaring Major Molsher's colts."

A few snowflakes were falling. Billy Bidewell, Spot and the cart had disappeared—and presently Snarl too was fading into distance. "Had Blight for years," said Colonel Pike. "Trustworthy. Great joy."

With infinite discretion the Daimler was skirting the paddocks beyond Little Boss. "Stopping with the Ravens?" said Colonel Pike. He shifted some inches further from Appleby, as if to gain a vantage ground for fresh social appraisal. "Know them? Of course I do. Important family down here. But went to pot rather—about a generation back. Writer-feller came into the estate. As a family a bit given to all that sort of thing. Bishops—no harm in that. But painters and professors and what-not too. No real harm, I dare say. Don't mean to be disrespectful to friends of yours."

"The writer was very popular in his time," Appleby said. "One of his brothers was a sculptor."

"That so," said Colonel Pike civilly.

"The whole place is full of vast marbles: bears, stags, lord knows what."

"So it is. Dine there about once in the twelvemonth. Nice girl."

"Very," said Appleby.

"Distracts the eye. But remember all that sculpture perfectly. Some very decent sportin' prints in the old gun-room." Colonel Pike appeared to consider that what was going forward was a little cultivated talk. "Used to think myself rather knowing in that sort of thing. Acquainted with Havell, by any chance? Got one or two rather nice efforts of his myself. Pheasant shootin'. Autumn tints. Very decent dogs." Colonel Pike sheered abruptly off this æsthetic debauch. "Turnips ought to do well," he said.

"Very." Appleby looked out intelligently over unintermitted expanses of snow. "About this turning-to-stone business at Tiffin Place: do you think it might be a joke with a sort of symbolical twist to it? What about Sir Mulberry—might he be described as a bit petrified himself?

Colonel Pike shook his head decidedly. "Mulberry," he said unexpectedly, "is less like a stone than a cloud. Plenty of him one minute, and then he's sort of drifted away the next. Must have been rocky enough in his time, I don't doubt. Contemporary of my own. But a provincial governor and all that when I was just foolin' about between up-stations and

Poona. Might apply to Mary, though—that's Lady Farmer. Once heard that young Mark Raven call her a stone-in-the-rain. What would you make of that?"

"A joke of the boldly borrowed kind. It means a mackintosh and a shooting-stick and the gaze fixed upon beagles or harriers in the distance."

"That's Mary all right." Colonel Pike seemed much impressed by the power of this image as now explained. "Still, it hardly seems a reason for all those rum goings-on. You haven't heard all of it yet. After the dog-business—But here we are. And—good lord—look at that."

The car, which had been sweeping up a long curved avenue, had now rounded a final arc and was approaching a broad balustraded terrace behind which stood a solid seventeenth-century mansion, admirably reposeful in its ordered infinity of square mullioned and transomed windows. At intervals the long line of the balustrade was strengthened by massive vacant pedestals. And upon one of these an elderly man, orthodoxly attired after the manner of the country gentry, stood posed in the dramatic attitude of the Marsyas of Myron.

"Yes," said Colonel Pike in answer to Appleby's enquiring glance. "That's Mulberry. As you see, the business is rather weighing on his mind."

Chapter 10

SIR MULBERRY FARMER's greetings were entirely without embarrassment. "Queer thing," he said when he had ascertained that his guests would stop to luncheon. "To start with I was filled with apprehension. There's no accounting for that."

"I can imagine that it is a very disconcerting experience." In talking to a country gentleman who stood under threat of petrifaction Appleby supposed that it was desirable to be soothing. "There's nothing out of the way in your coming to feel some sinister design in it, and being worried."

"Is that so?" Sir Mulberry looked at Appleby with discernible irony. "Perhaps the quiet sort of life we bumpkins lead counts. Unprepared for anything which might be fancied to have a hazardous side. Now come and look at the pig."

Colonel Pike snorted. "In Sir Mulberry's last eight years in India," he said, "he was shot at twenty-seven times. Other means of assassination were also tried. When he says it's queer that he's been rattled, he means what he says."

They had turned a corner of the terrace and were heading for the back of the house. Appleby refused to be disconcerted. "It doesn't necessarily follow," he said. "Presumably those people in India didn't start turning things to stone. And something utterly fantastic may disturb a man who takes shooting as all part of the day's work."

"Quite right." Sir Mulberry nodded emphatically. "Do you know, anything having to do with stone or statues fascinates me now? What you might call an *idée fixe.*" He chuckled. "Decidedly *fixe*, Mr. Appleby. Did you ever read of the Stone Men of Malekula? Identify themselves with their own statuary. Something of the sort was in my head when you arrived."

"So we noticed," Appleby said.

Colonel Pike frowned, as if disapproving of this manner of speech to a Lord Lieutenant. But Sir Mulberry nodded amiably. "It doesn't at all surprise me that I should respond eccentrically to the affair. As a family we are a bit like that, particularly in our later years. And, of course, I'm getting on. But what does surprise me is that I was scared. You understand?"

"Yes," Appleby said.

"Well, that's a start. And seeing the pig will be another. There's just time. Don't attend to the stable clock—hasn't gone for years. These are my wife's guineafowl. I was scared, and there was a reason, and I couldn't put a finger on it. You understand *that?*"

"Yes."

"Then you're ahead of the chief constable." Sir Mulberry vigorously laughed. "And here we are. This first freak was, of course, months ago. But I haven't let it be touched."

They were surveying a handsome brick building which it seemed invidious to think of as a sty. It had plainly been designed by a previous owner of Tiffin Place when much under the influence of the late Mr. Ruskin, and in detail it was not unreminiscent of a villa in the northern suburbs of Oxford. The only living occupant at present was a vast and lethargic sow; three Gothic courts were hers; and this spacious solitude she shared only with a large, lugubrious and indefinably inept white marble boar. Appleby took one glance and had no doubts left. The monumental creature had Theodore written all over it.

"Anybody could drive a cart in during the night and simply slide the tiresome thing down a plank." Colonel Pike was apparently explaining the hopelessness of arriving at any substantial clue to the mystery. "I wonder if it might have been stolen from a museum? It has the letters *T.R.* carved on the back."

"Has it, indeed?" said Appleby. "You know, it might be taken simply for a sculptural embellishment planned by Sir Mulberry—particularly in view of the somewhat ornate character of the surroundings."

Sir Mulberry Farmer had provided himself with a stick and was scratching the recumbent sow in a routine manner. "Just what we hoped," he said. "There was a fuss among the men when the creature was discovered—and no doubt some talk since. We just kept quiet. And, as a matter of fact, we've managed to be pretty mum about the whole affair. Of course, the old lady who went demented proved rather a difficulty, and the disappearance of the half-witted boy has been more awkward still. However, we've contrived to avoid any damned publicity." Sir Mulberry's eye, which had been fixed on his sow with an expression of affectionate regard, turned to the stone intruder and hardened in distaste. "Ghastly," he said. "Thoroughly coarse in the bone. Hind quarters high and narrow. To think of wasting all that marble on perpetuating a lard-hog." He shook his head gloomily. "Spot of luncheon won't be amiss. Then we can look at the dog, and that great staring waxwork, and the cow."

"The cow!" exclaimed Appleby, dismayed. This nonsense was altogether inordinately piling up.

Sir Mulberry looked at him in mild surprise. "It was the cow that turned that wretched old woman from Drool demented, wasn't it?" he asked. "Has Pike not told you—"

Appleby sighed—and remembered about the lady who no

longer let a room in that hamlet. "Ah," he said. "Old Mrs. Ulstrup. Of course."

They walked away. Colonel Pike covertly nudged his host. "Deuced queer his knowing about the woman at Drool. Other things, too. Young, of course. But great confidence. Think a world of him."

Lady Farmer was a lean woman with features so extremely like a hare's that to the urban mind she would have appeared natural only if hung upside down with her nose in a little silver can. And, as if to lend piquancy to this resemblance, she entered her diningroom surrounded by a small pack of beagles—creatures, Appleby supposed, not commonly admitted to such domesticities by the gross—and for a time seemed disposed to pay more attention to these than to her guests. Sir Mulberry did the talking, though with increasing absence of mind. And the cause of his distraction—Appleby suspected —was the salt. As Sherlock Holmes, noting Dr. Watson's eye travel to the portrait of the American general, and seeing his hands clench in a martial ardour, was able brilliantly to deduce that his medical friend was meditating upon the battles of the Civil War, so Appleby observing Sir Mulberry toy absorbedly with the contents of a silver salt-cellar, inferred that here was a man vividly envisaging the fate of Lot's wife. The truth no doubt was this: that deep in his unconscious mind Sir Mulberry longed for the stony change. It was a notion holding all those charms of security and convenience that psychologists associate with a return to the womb, while at the same time having the advantage of being altogether more dignified.

Appleby became aware that Lady Farmer had fixed him with a steely stare, much as if she had an insight into the fatuous nature of his present reflections. Being aware of a steely stare in a hare, as well as being suggestive of nonsense verses, was disconcerting in itself. Appleby was trying to think of an intelligent remark when Lady Farmer spoke.

"This is an extremely disagreeable business," she said. "It brings such extremely disagreeable people about the place."

"Ah," said Appleby.

"There was a journalist. The very morning after the pig.

A most impertinent man. Fortunately I discovered he was from the *Banner*—"

"The *Banner*?" said Appleby curiously.

"He had come straight down from town. The *Banner* happens to be owned by my brother." Lady Farmer paused grimly. "So the fellow went away."

"Extremely fortunate," said Appleby.

"Extremely disagreeable altogether," said Lady Farmer. "It brings a rag, tag and bobtail about the place. Mulberry, I don't remember that we have ever had to receive the police before."

"Come, come, Mary." Colonel Pike glanced in cautious apology at Appleby. "Policeman myself, after all."

"After the Hoobin boy, too"—Lady Farmer ignored the interjection—"after the waxwork affair a reporter came down. From the *Blare*. But as it happened the *Blare* had been bought the week before by Lord Sparshott, one of my dear father's closest friends."

"So the *Blare* fellow went away too?" Appleby asked this question absently. He was frowning as if at some problem laid out on the table before him. "But tell me about the boy Hoobin, Lady Farmer. He was employed here?"

"Quite recently my husband agreed to his being engaged to help the stable boys. They objected to his odd ways and he was quartered by himself. Then one morning this"—Lady Farmer paused, as if in search of a perfectly accurate expression—"this extremely disagreeable joke repeated itself. The boy was gone and there was a waxwork there instead."

"I suppose," asked Appleby mildly, "that it would be rather an exotic looking waxwork? Swarthy with suggestions of yellow, altogether ferocious in expression, and recalling the orient or the inner reaches of Asia?"

Lady Farmer looked uncommonly startled—which was the last touch in the hare-like effect. Sir Mulberry, who had been puffing out his cheeks as if meditating the possibilities of a Della Robbia *bambino* in nicely glazed terracotta, deflated them rapidly and looked at Appleby open-mouthed. Colonel Pike laid down a knife and fork with a clatter. "Precisely so!" he said. "But how—"

"It is what we commonly find," said Appleby solemnly, "in cases of this sort. The oriental or eurasian waxwork."

"By Jove!" said Colonel Pike. "Is that so?" He turned to Sir Mulberry. "Man has great experience," he murmured. "Took to him at once. Have everything explained in a jiffy. You'll see."

Perhaps it was so; perhaps everything could be explained in a jiffy. Appleby found himself looking more distastedly than was civil at Lady Farmer's beagles. They lay about, mildly salivating, and got in the way of the servants. As household pets even Bishop Adolphus's Tartars and Kurds would be preferable. . . . And there, of course, was the point. It was undoubtedly one of Adolphus Raven's waxworks that had taken the place of the Hoobin boy. The transmogrification of Sir Mulberry's prized Gloucester Old Spot into the ill-conceived marble lard-hog of Theodore Raven was equally beyond question. In fact, it had not been in vain that the road to Tiffin Place had lain through Dream Manor. The mystery of the one was the mystery of the other. And never surely had a detective arrived upon a case to find himself in unexpected possession of so much relevant information. Had he not been apprised even of the dementia of Mrs. Ulstrup, the pyromania of young Hoobin and the breed of pig purveyed to the squirearchy by Brettingham Scurl? The untoward end of Gregory Grope's grandmother, it seemed to Appleby, was his sole piece of local lore that had not yet entered the picture. The affair had all the promise of that extreme tidiness which marks a well-made play. The dénouement, therefore, must be as rapid and decisive as Colonel Pike could desire. He turned again to Lady Farmer. "I suppose," he asked casually, "you knew Heyhoe?"

Lady Farmer stared. "Everard Raven's man? Yes, I know Heyhoe. An extremely disagreeable old person."

"He's dead. They found him last night, buried in the snow."

Sir Mulberry emerged momentarily from the abstraction into which he had sunk. "All frozen and stiff?" he asked.

"Decidedly so. As stiff as a statue, as they say."

"No doubt he drank," said Lady Farmer.

"I suppose he did." Appleby paused. "Did you ever hear an odd story about him?"

Rather as one turns the knob on a refrigerator, Lady Farmer increased the chilliness of her stare. "I don't often hear odd stories about other people's servants."

Colonel Pike coughed deprecatingly. "Come to think of it, there *was* something about the old fellow. But I'm dashed if I can remember what. Except that he was the only man who could handle a great horse they kept over there."

"That's so." Appleby nodded gravely. "Billy Bidewell seems to do not too badly, but I'm told that, with Billy, Spot may revolt at any moment. Which is awkward, as Spot seems to be the only means of locomotion about the place."

"Ah," said Colonel Pike respectfully. "Bit hard up at Dream, one can't help seeing."

"I believe Ranulph Raven got through a lot of money. I wonder if any of you remember him?"

"Just remember seeing him about when I was a boy. Distinguished looking old chap in an artistic way." Colonel Pike shook his head. "Been told he was wild enough, early on. A bit of a byword about the county even. And that took some managing in those days. For instance, there was the old marquis at Linger Court. I remember my father telling me—" Colonel Pike caught the eye of Lady Farmer. "Or rather I don't."

"Ranulph Raven was celebrated in his time," Appleby said. "But I don't ever remember seeing a biography of him, or even a brief memoir. And I've rather come to feel that the family is glad to keep him quiet. Except as a legend, that is to say. Only a few of them seem really to know his books."

"Books?" said Sir Mulberry vaguely. "Do you know, that was why I was rattled. Something about a book. But I can't at all remember what. Odd."

Appleby looked quickly across the table. "You mean one of Ranulph Raven's books?"

"I'm sure I couldn't say." Sir Mulberry was drifting rapidly away again. He had clasped his hands lightly on the two arms of his chair and was making some calculations as to the right inclination of his head. This time, Appleby obscurely surmised, it was Houdon's celebrated figure of Voltaire.

"If you have finished your coffee," said Lady Farmer, "we may as well look at the dog."

They looked at the dog. "Extremely disagreeable," Lady

Farmer said. "Entirely misses the broad splay feet. And look at the tail—no bushy fringe hanging from the dorsal border."

Appleby, though unable to regard this latest petrifaction with the expert eye thus invoked, felt inclined to agree that no enthusiasm was possible before it. Theodore had lavished much anatomical care upon its production, but unfortunately no gleam of the canine—or even the doggy—had visited his work. Having the bodily form of some species of terrier, it remarkably managed to convey the suggestion of a snake. Lady Farmer was the last person to welcome such a changeling. It appeared moreover that the creature it had mysteriously replaced possessed as many virtues as this had vices—having been a dachshund with a body extremely long and cylindrical, legs notably thick and twisted, and quite uncommonly everted paws. Appleby listened to these particulars with forbearance and then proceeded to enquire into the facts of the case. But very little emerged. Lady Farmer's favourite dachshund had been secluded for a time in the stables, and one night the substitution of this stony monstrosity had taken place. A general acquaintance with the lie of the buildings, and the sort of casual information on kennel matters that might be picked up from a groom in a pub, were all that the perpetrator of this particular absurdity would have required. There seemed nothing for it but to pass on to the next exhibit.

And this the party did, in deepening gloom. No doubt it was the gloom that prompted Appleby to offer some remark indicating mild professional confidence. "I think," he said—they were viewing the cow—"I think it's possible to begin to see a little light in all this."

"See light?" said Sir Mulberry. "Nothing but grope in the dark, if you ask me."

Colonel Pike slapped his thigh—with the vehemence of one in whom appropriate intellectual reactions seldom occur. "Jove!" he said. "That's it—just come into my head. Told you I knew some yarn about the old fellow Heyhoe. No particular reason to be called Heyhoe at all. Father unknown—though there's a tale he was Ranulph Raven himself. But mother was old Mrs. Grope. Woman they found in the well."

Chapter 11

COLONEL PIKE had suddenly remembered that he was invited to tea at Linger Court. This had occasioned his departure in a great hurry, with demands upon Blight for a turn of speed which seemed altogether to ignore the convenience of Kerrisk's cows and Major Molsher's colts. And presently Inspector Mutlow arrived in a modest Morris and retrieved Appleby from the Farmers. He was in a state of considerable excitement. "Very curious things taken to happening in these parts, Mr. Appleby," he said as they drove off. "Very curious indeed."

"Well—yes, I suppose so." Appleby was not sure that he quite liked the tone of Mutlow's voice. "I must say that when it came to the cow and poor old Mrs. Ulstrup I did feel that things were becoming a bit out of the way."

"Cow? Ah—to be sure. But I'm speaking of last night Mr. Appleby. To begin with, a very peculiar thing happened at Tew. The lock-keeper's wife rang up about it less than a couple of hours ago. Didn't at all know what to do. Was she to let the carriage go on, or hold it? Such a thing hadn't happened before."

"Carriage?"

"Carriage." Mutlow reiterated the word with severe emphasis. "Turbill, the lock-keeper's name is—and he drinks. Late last night he was out taking a breath of air, no doubt so as to sober up a bit before going to bed. And down the river he sees coming what looks like a small barge with a deck cargo. There was never a light nor a sound from it, and down it came all the same straight for the lock gates, so that this Turbill thinks he'd better swing them open. And open them he does and in floats the craft. There was scarcely a blink of moon now, and he shouts at the thing and still there isn't a sound, so he goes and opens the sluices, and down the thing sinks into the lock until of course he can't see a thing. Well, Turbill hollers again that there's a bob to pay, and when still the folk on board make no reply he damns their eyes and goes off to bed. Thinking—you see, Mr. Appleby—that he's served them a nasty turn,

97

since the bottom of a lock isn't the easiest place to get away from in darkness."

"Dear me," said Appleby." And what did these people say in the morning?'

Inspector Mutlow, who was engaged in steering his way with all proper caution through Little Boss, glanced sideways at Appleby with the frankest suspicion. "There wasn't anybody. Turbill came out in the morning—with a nasty hangover, I don't doubt—and what he saw floating in his lock was an empty carriage. What you might call a gentleman's travelling-carriage of the old fashioned sort."

"Ah," said Appleby.

Inspector Mutlow heavily respired. "The result was that this fellow Turbill thought he'd got the horrors, and down he fell in a sort of fit and has been carried off to hospital."

"It appears to me," said Appleby, "that there is much nervous excitability in your district, my dear inspector. Old Mrs. Ulstrup goes off her head when required to milk a marble cow, and now this Turbill—"

"No doubt, Mr. Appleby, you will have your little joke. We understand that you have a bit of a fondness for that sort of thing." Mutlow paused on this dark saying. "But that's not all the queer doings," he presently proceeded, "that I've heard of last night. This carriage was seen earlier, mark you, floating down the Dream in clear moonlight. There happens to be a road-mender—"

"Who lives at the end of Noblet's Lane."

Mutlow frowned. "A road-mender called Scrase. And I must say that for a stranger you've come by a queer knowledge of these parts, Mr. Appleby. Well, this Scrase was making his way home late at night, and he saw the carriage floating down the river. Two people were sitting on the roof of it—a man and a woman."

"Dear me," said Appleby mildly.

"They were pretty well undressed—"

"*What?*"

"—and Scrase saw quite clearly that they were waving a couple of bottles—"

"Well, of all the infernal—"

"—and presently he heard them a-hollering and singing at the top of their voices—"

Words had failed Appleby; he was looking at the abominable Mutlow aghast.

"—all manner of filthy songs. This Scrase is an extremely godly man, it appears, and he was very much shocked."

"Was he, indeed? I shouldn't be surprised if another severe shock came his way quite soon."

Mutlow appeared uncomfortable. "It must be admitted, Mr. Appleby, that stories tend to get a bit exaggerated when they begin to circulate in these parts. For instance, there's that lad, Billy Bidewell. It seems he's been saying that last night you and Miss—"

"I want to find Gregory Grope." Appleby's interruption was decided. "Where is he likely to be?"

"The engine-driver?" Mutlow, evidently surprised, looked at his watch. "If he's on time, he'll be just about drawing into Sneak. But he may be well on the way to Linger. Unless, of course, he's running really *late*—in which case he'll still be at Snarl."

"Find him."

"Find him, Mr. Appleby?"

"There's a road within sight of the railway-line, I suppose? Cruise along it, inspector, until you spot Gregory Grope. He may take us a little way in our investigation." Appleby looked wrathfully at Mutlow. "Which is probably more than the vulgar gossip to which you have been listening will do."

Mutlow swung the car obediently down a by-lane. "No offence, Mr. Appleby, I hope. It's simply that something very queer has happened over at your friends' place at Dream. As I don't doubt you know. And now all sorts of strange stories are being built round it of what happened in the night. A regular sensation, the thing is like to cause. There's half a dozen reporters about the place already. And as soon as the colonel gets wind of it we'll have him over, drinking Mr. Raven's port and barking about dictaphones."

Ahead of them now could be discerned the line of a railway-embankment. Appleby searched it for the puff of smoke by which the late Mrs. Grope's grandson might be located. "You think there's the makings of a sensation in the Heyhoe affair? No doubt you're right, and it will put the little matter of the Tiffin Place petrifactions in the shade. Particularly as the Ravens probably haven't the advantage of being related to the

Banner and the *Blare*. . . . Has Heyhoe's body been competently examined?"

"Well, there was our local police surgeon this morning—"

"Humph."

"—but Mr. Raven, it seems, made a bit of a fuss, and they're having some big wig over later."

"Very wise." Appleby was leaning down under Inspector Mutlow's windscreen to light a pipe. "Your friend Billy Bidewell is of the opinion that this old man Heyhoe was simply put away by the Raven family acting in concert—the sufficient reason being that they felt he was a nuisance, and that Billy was now capable of managing Spot."

"Well, I'm blessed!"

"Quite so; it has your lock-keeper beaten hollow. But you can't see any better reason, can you, why the Ravens should do away with their coachman?" Appleby had sat up again and was looking sharply at Mutlow.

"Dear me, no, Mr. Appleby. Of course, I've barely heard the details since I saw you last. But it seems altogether mysterious. Not that one possibility hasn't occurred to me."

"What's that?"

"That this matter of the old man Heyhoe's death might be connected in some way with these queer doings at Tiffin Place."

Appleby puffed at his pipe and looked thoughtfully at Mutlow—rather as one might view a chimpanzee manœuvring a banana towards himself with a stick. "A very ingenious fancy," he said. "Does great credit, if I may say so, to your agility of mind. But a bit far fetched, all the same."

Inspector Mutlow—as no chimpanzee would do—began to whistle with a faintly ironical intonation. He was quite a songster, Appleby noted, and possessed of four or five notes to Billy Bidewell's one.

But a well-made play would have altogether more economy of incident. The old blind man who had so oddly questioned Mark and Judith Raven years ago; the illegitimacy of Heyhoe; the apprehensions of Sir Mulberry Farmer; Mrs. Ulstrup's marble milker; *Paxton's Destined Hour;* the Ranulph legend; the family preference for Adolphus, Theodore, and that Latinate Roger who had received the commendations of Dr. Jowett: to what neatly dropped curtain could all these lead? A play, the philosopher had sagely discerned, must not concern many actions of many men, or even many actions of one man, but one action of one man—one action, whole and completed. Well, who was the man here? Was he Ranulph Raven, who had followed his own numerous writings into oblivion round about the turn of the century? Ranulph had been stirring in his grave for some time, chiefly for the purpose of playing tricks upon his children. To his son Luke he had delivered a tombstone, and to that Caliban-like Heyhoe whom he had begotten—it was to be presumed—upon the late Mrs. Grope, he had offered the whimsical little gesture of a minor practical joke on Spot. What sense was there in all this, and in Heyhoe's macabre burial; where was there discernible a single action, whole and completed?

And now more Ravens were stirring. Theodore's ghost had marched on the stage and begun an exhibition of supernatural legerdemain on a characteristically massive scale. There are seances in which fans and handkerchiefs flutter across the room, in which buttons and coins and matchboxes, hot from the ether, materialize themselves and drop dramatically from the ceiling. But Theodore was playing this sort of game in monumental terms; large chunks of marble, with the faint displeasingness that marked them as authentic from the master's hand, were the counters in this gigantic spiritualist demonstration. And what of Bishop Adolphus—was he not prowling too? The waxwork which had taken the place of Hannah Hoobin's boy: had the ghostly Theodore borrowed it because he had no suitable marble to hand? Or was the wraith of Adolphus, having abandoned for the time its contemplation of the religious system of the Zend-Avesta, beginning to take his part in this tiresome family diversion? And plainly there were still plenty of Ravens in reserve: grandfather Herbert of the Foreign Office and the madrigals, for example, was no doubt capable of an outré posthumous behaviour of his own.

With his eye still on the railway line in quest of Gregory Grope, Appleby sighed—so that Inspector Mutlow glanced at him suspiciously across his wheel. It was, of course, all very confusing. And yet, æsthetically viewed, the whole random composition had its charm. The fact or notion of the Tiffin Place petrifactions was pleasing in itself, and it was almost a pity that hard sense, satisfying to Mutlow, must be screwed from it; that the cellar must be resolutely descended to and the port-drinking footman unmasked. Would it not be pleasant to retire from the elucidating of crime and give oneself to the creating of unashamed fantasies—in which champion milkers might turn to marble at one's whim, and no explanation need be required? From these dangerous thoughts Appleby was roused by the whistle of a locomotive engine somewhere ahead.

"That's Grope," said Mutlow. "He's whistling at old Amos Sturrock's goats." The car rounded a bend and a long curve of railway line lay before them. "But he's not going from Sneak to Linger. He's going from Linger to Sneak. He's forgotten Murcott's milk, if you ask me, and now he's coming back for it."

"We'll stop him. Draw up."

The train was now approaching. Its engine, it occurred to Appleby, might be of considerable interest to the compiler of the *New Millennium* Encyclopædia, since it had every appearance of being closely related to that Stourbridge Lion which delighted the hearts of the Delaware and Hudson Canal Company on the 9th of August 1829. Behind the engine were two closed trucks, and behind these was a carriage of the stubby or truncated proportions commonly found in nurseries. And this completed Gregory Grope's charge. Appleby stood up and waved vigorously. "Stop!" he shouted. *"Stop!"* And Inspector Mutlow, after what was evidently a moment's indecision and even disapproval, got up and did the same. *"Stop!"* they both shouted, and their gesturing arms collided in air. It was a vigorous demonstration that took on positive drama from the silent, snow-covered fields about them.

And now Gregory Grope himself was visible. He leant out of his cab and waved. Appleby and Mutlow continued to gesture wildly. Gregory Grope, much pleased, took off his cap and waved that. The train puffed slowly past. Mutlow, urged by Appleby, started the car, turned it, and followed. Appleby continued to wave. So did Gregory Grope—as also a youthful assistant, who now appeared beside him, brandishing a shovel. In the little carriage at the back a window was lowered and an old man with a white beard joined the orgy of salutations. The engine whistled with unexpected power. Mutlow, in a spasm of excitement, gave a long blast on his horn. In the closed trucks sheep bleated and cattle lowed. And then a look of pleased comprehension came over Gregory's features; there was a hiss of steam and clanking of buffers; and quite suddenly the little train was at a dead stop.

Mutlow and Appleby crossed to the line, and were received with the cordial hospitality that characterizes the English railway system at its best. "Jump in, sir," said Gregory; "jump in, whichever gent is coming." He turned to his assistant and gestured towards the furnace. "Another passenger, William. Better have a bit more steam. And now, sir, which way would you be wanting to go?"

This implied so accommodating a spirit that Appleby found it difficult not to beg to be wafted to Sneak forthwith. But professional austerity triumphed. "As a matter of fact," he answered, "neither. What I want is a word with you about your grandmother—if you can spare the time, that is to say."

The assistant put down his shovel, produced a catapult, and climbed from the cab. Gregory looked disappointed for a moment, but then leant out and squinted up at the red, wintry sun. "Running nicely to time," he said. "And it's wonderful the head of steam William can get up if we're a bit late. So go right ahead." He gave a wave to the old gentleman with the beard, who was taking the air still at his window while meditatively filling a pipe. "Signals up on grandmother, sir, right down the line."

"Do you remember your grandfather?" Appleby asked.

Gregory nodded vigorously. "It was grandfather," he said, "that started me off."

"Started you off?"

"Gave me the *Wonder Book of Trains*. After that I never looked back."

"Ah." Appleby was philosophic. "Many a man's ambition has been fired by the gift of a book, Mr. Grope."

"That's it, sir." Gregory Grope patted some worn but shiny brass contrivance in his cab. "Fired and stoked it, as you might say—and here I am. And we're not standing still either."

"Is that so?" . . . The old man with the beard had now got his pipe going and was puffing placidly at the landscape. The bleating and lowing of the freight had subsided. William—whether proposing a brace of rabbits or merely a little quiet tormenting of old Amos Sturrock's goats—had altogether disappeared. "Not standing still," said Appleby. "That's capital."

"There's talk of a branch line to Slumber." Gregory paused dramatically. "There's even talk of electrification, from time to time." His eye swept the half-dozen fields and the little valley which separated Sneak from Linger. "Like on the Chicago, Milwaukee and St. Paul run."

"Capital," repeated Appleby. "And no doubt even heavier traffic will be the result. Wake some people up, too. Brettingham Scurl will have to clear those pigs out of the waitingroom at Linger."

This was a great success. For Gregory, it was clear, took railways seriously—even if he was a little weak on the timetable side. Conversation became both amiable and intimate. The early sex-life of a grandmother is not a theme upon which any man can speak at first hand, but Gregory was able to provide a certain amount of family tradition upon the subject—which was one on which Appleby, despite the silent disapproval of Inspector Mutlow, displayed a positively prurient interest. When old Mrs. Grope married Gregory's grandfather her reputation for virtue had not been outstanding. Indeed, she had several times disappeared for considerable periods on end, so that it was supposed that she was on somewhat easy terms with members of the local gentry. On this Gregory had several stories, altogether unedifying in character, to which Appleby listened with the closest attention. His interest, indeed, only slackened when Gregory came to the middle phases of his grandmother's career; and it quickened again as the narrative approached the old lady's last years. Long after age had brought her to a merely contemplative habit Mrs. Grope, it seemed, had maintained a keen interest in sexual psychology and erotic science in general. And just as the great Sir Francis Bacon, climbing out of his carriage to stuff a dead hen with snow, died a martyr to Knowledge, so had Mrs. Grope in her humbler sphere ended her life in the disinterested pursuit of her studies. For having gone out one night to make certain observations in a nearby dingle much frequented by local lovers, she had allowed an unexpected wealth of material to blind her to the fact of an approaching storm—and when the storm in fact descended it was supposed that she had recourse to the fortifying effects of a bottle of gin which she commonly carried upon her person. This—together with somebody's regrettable carelessness with the cover of a well—was judged to have been the end of her. When brought up with the bucket she had been very decidedly beyond the reach of interrogation.

Questioning elicited a few further facts. Old Mrs. Grope had not been given to book-learning. Like another natural philosopher, Charles Darwin, she was markedly without literary interests or linguistic abilities. Her husband however—the same who gave grandson Gregory his *Wonder Book of Trains* —had been a reader. He had taken a particular interest in the works of the eminent local author, Ranulph Raven.

This was coming near the heart of the matter. "Did you ever," Appleby asked, "have any dealings with an old fellow from Dream by the name of Heyhoe?"

"I know 'un," said Gregory. "Surly old bastard."

"Bastard?' said Appleby hopefully.

"Bastard?" echoed Gregory—evidently puzzled. "Oh, *bastard*. Well, I don't know as to that."

"He's dead, as a matter of fact. Somebody buried him in a snowdrift last night." Appleby paused. "Set 'un, so to speak."

"Set 'un?" Gregory was mildly interested—but suddenly went off at a tangent. "More snow coming," he said with satisfaction. "William and me are like to have the snowplough out, come Wednesday. Come and see us, if you're anywhere near the line."

"I'll make a point of it." Appleby was extremely cordial. "But this Heyhoe—"

"But it's in America they have the champion snow-ploughs." Gregory's eye had kindled. "There's a picture in the *Wonder Book*—"

"So there is. I remember it very well. And so does Inspector Mutlow here. Somebody told me this Heyhoe had once worked on American railroads."

Gregory opened his eyes very wide. "I never heard tell of that, now! He'd worked all his days for the Ravens, to my thinking. Except when he went off—the shameless old brute —and lived on that wench over Tew-way. Before the hussy married t'other fellow. Heyhoe and his Hannah was a regular scandal about these parts, I've been told."

"Hannah?" It was now Appleby who was wide-eyed. "Do you mean the woman who's now Hannah Hoobin?"

"That's right. And didn't you say something about bastards? Well, there you are. Hannah Hoobin's boy—the half-wit, that is—is this dirty old Heyhoe's son."

Chapter 12

WILLIAM was now returning through the snow; in one hand he dangled his catapult and in the other—mysteriously—the carcase of a domestic fowl. The old man with the beard, having knocked out his pipe and deposited it unexpectedly in the band of his hat, was placidly consulting a large silver watch. Gregory Grope himself seemed perfectly agreeable to conversation both indefinitely prolonged and enigmatical in intention—but Appleby felt that the time had come to set the local railway system in operation once more. Reiterating, therefore, his lively expectation of pleasure from the snow-plough come Wednesday, he climbed down from the cab, with Mutlow following. William, having deposited his fowl in a box labelled *First Aid,* fell to raking cinders and shovelling coal, and Gregory, by dint of much tugging at a lanyard above his head, produced a very creditable whistle as the engine got slowly under way. Gregory waved and William waved; the old man with the beard raised his hand in a gesture at once economical of effort and expressive of the most patriarchal benignity; the sheep bleated and the cattle lowed. And so Gregory Grope's care and pride steamed away —incidentally, in the direction whence it had come, so that it had to be presumed that the matter of Murcott's milk was in abeyance once more. It steamed away most purposefully, nevertheless. Were the paint only a little brighter, Appleby thought, and the impression of speed more convincing, the whole would have been virtually indistinguishable from the more moderately priced sort of Hornby Train. Almost one expected a vast but juvenile Hand to descend from the heavens and transfer the complete outfit to a neatly compartmented cardboard box.

Appleby turned round and tramped towards Mutlow's car. "Well," he said, "what do you make of it all?"

"Very much what I was beginning to make of it before." Mutlow's response was prompt and decided. "This business of the old man Heyhoe at Dream links up with the queer doings at Tiffin Place. At Sir Mulberry's the boy Hoobin disappears and there's a waxwork left instead. That's strange enough. At Mr. Raven's Heyhoe gets buried alive in snow. That's strange enough too—and uncommon nasty as well. And now it seems the boy we've called Hoobin may be the old fellow Heyhoe's son. Mark my word, Mr. Appleby, there's a tie-up between them somewhere."

They climbed into the car. "If I may say so," said Appleby, "your district seems to be a hotbed of sexual immorality. The people are as promiscuous as old Amos Sturrock's goats."

"Amos Sturrock's goats are not promiscuous." Mutlow was suddenly indignant. "They're uncommonly carefully bred."

"No doubt. And so, perhaps, are Kerrisk's cows and Major Molsher's colts." Appleby was feeling cold, slightly hungry, and definitely depressed. "So let's say rabbits. Round about here you behave like rabbits, and the fact that one man is reputed another man's illegitimate son is scarcely a tie-up at all."

"Old Mrs. Grope fell down a well—which is what you might call a fatality, Mr. Appleby. And Heyhoe was *her* son. Heyhoe has been buried in a snowdrift—which is another fatality, I'm sure you'll agree. Now, Hannah Hoobin's boy was *his* son. Hannah Hoobin's boy has been turned into a waxwork—"

"Which is undoubtedly a fatality too." Impatiently Appleby slammed the door of Inspector Mutlow's car. "So drive to Mrs. Hoobin's now. And, if possible, take old Mrs. Ulstrup on the way."

"Mrs. Ulstrup?"

"The maid who milked the marble cow, my dear man."

Mutlow let in his clutch. "So many folk come into this that one fair loses count of them." He was silent for several minutes. "You don't seriously suggest that these affairs aren't connected up together?"

"Of course not." Winter light was dying from the afternoon sky, and the snow-covered landscape had gone bleak and ugly. Appleby stared sombrely out at it. "Of course not. Indeed, I've got further evidence that it is so. The waxwork and all that marble rubbish which has been turning up at Tiffin Place: it comes from Dream Manor."

Mutlow sat up abruptly over his wheel. "From Dream! But surely, then, the Ravens must have known?"

"I don't think necessarily so. Their place is as full of junk as a badly overcrowded museum. A lot could vanish without being missed. Any one could have stolen it. Heyhoe, for instance."

"Well, I'm dashed!" Mutlow looked at Appleby with a mixture of distrust and respect. "And I'm not surprised that you were a bit reluctant to see the whole thing as hitching up. A thoroughly unpleasant business for your friends."

"My friends?" Appleby frowned, absent and perplexed. "Oh, that! At midday yesterday I didn't as much as know that any of these Ravens existed."

"But Billy Bidewell says—"

"Bother Billy Bidewell for a great gossiping booby. The Ravens are interesting and rather pleasing folk, and I would be sorry to see them involved in a vulgar sensation."

"It looks like being that, all right." Mutlow spoke with unconcealed satisfaction.

"No doubt, inspector, no doubt. You will have your photograph in the national press, wearing your best bowler hat and pointing to the spot where you eventually found the body. I know the feeling. I had it years ago in the case of an old person called Gaffer Odgers."

"Find the body!" Mutlow was startled. "*You* found the body, I gather. You and this young Miss Raven between you."

"I mean the body of Hannah Hoobin's boy. Do you realize that this boy—a helpless, idiot boy—disappeared quite a while ago and that you've done virtually nothing about it? That you've moved in the matter only because a local big-wig has taken to feeling creepy, and to fancying himself the Discobolus or the Medici Venus? It's very bad, inspector, very bad. Colonel Pike may protect you to some extent, but I fear that the Home Secretary will take a serious view of it. Let us hope that Hannah Hoobin's boy is alive, after all. Let us hope that the whole affair is of a sort that can be—um— composed."

"Composed?" said Mutlow—somewhat weakly.

"Composed. And, now that we are beginning to see our way through it, we shall soon know."

"See our way through it?" Mutlow sounded his horn petulantly at an irresolute hen crossing the road. "The whole thing is plainly sinister, but just doesn't make sense."

"Possibly so. Or possibly contrariwise."

"Contrariwise?"

"Might be useful as a damned dictaphone."

"Really, Mr. Appleby—"

"I know, I know. And you must forgive me. My nerves are very bad." Appleby shook his head solemnly. "A presentment, inspector. Shall I be turned into a ferocious waxen Kurd? Or, puzzling over the case, shall I be made marble with too much conceiving—as happened, you will recall, to Milton when he started reading Shakespeare?"

Mutlow accelerated. "I don't know," he said, "that I see the joke. If it *is* a joke, that is."

"Ah—that's the question. The whole thing looks like a series of jokes—and so may Appleby's End."

"Appleby's—" Mutlow checked himself. "We have a station called that down here."

"Precisely. I got off a train there last night—and immediately stepped into a freakish universe in which such a coincidence will most assuredly not pass unexploited. There will be another Appleby's End as certain as *Paxton's Destined Hour.*"

Mutlow opened his mouth—and once more checked himself. "I never," he said carefully, "heard of *Paxton's Destined Hour.* Would it be of any use asking about it?"

"Very little. *Paxton's Destined Hour* is merely one fragment of the nonsense by which we are surrounded in this affair. But I suppose you've heard of the alphabet murders?"

"I don't know that I have."

"Dear me. Well, they began with the murder of Mr. Archer of Abernethy—a horrid business. And then it was the turn of Miss Bell of Bolsover. Poor old Sir Christopher Catt of Coldstream followed, and then a certain Mrs. Dawes, who lived at Dover—"

"I don't believe a word of it."

"Quite so; I'm making it up. But what is the point of the story? Obviously that only poor old Sir Christopher was really aimed at, and that the murder began with Mr. Archer, and ended with Mr. Ziesing—"

"Really?"

"—just to make things confusing. What do you think of that?"

"Very little." Mutlow spoke with conviction. "Very little indeed. Unless you were a scribbler looking for a short way to a long yarn, that is to say." Mutlow paused on this, apparently disconcerted by its approximation to the epigrammatic. "And I don't see what you're getting at, anyway."

"Then consider this. Suppose that it is to your prosaic, practical interest to do something uncommonly odd—and not be found out. The difficulty is clear: oddity almost automatically betrays itself. The needle gleams in the haystack, and can't possibly be missed."

Something seemed to strike Mutlow. "Talking of haystacks—" he began.

"So what you do is to stuff the haystack full of needles. You see? Oddity wherever the perplexed investigator turns. Now this affair—the Tiffin Place-Dream Manor affair—may very well be like that. A great many odd things have been happening; a good many more than you've heard of yet, inspector. They're strung together, very roughly, on a string which is itself pretty odd too—a string that leads back to Ranulph Raven, the father of the present elder Ravens, who wrote mystery-stories and the like half-a-century ago. But there may be nothing in that but a desire to lead us up the garden path. And just one of these queer happenings—it may be—makes sense. The others are like the deaths of Miss Bell of Bolsover and Mrs. Dawes of Dover—just extra needles in the haystack for the sake of muddling things up."

"I suppose there may be something in that." Mutlow visibly brightened. "The only sense in the whole affair might be this Appleby's End business you've been speaking of. Yes, I think it's a very likely idea. And simplifies matters a lot. Ninety per cent of what has happened is strictly meaningless and can be ignored."

"Just that. Only, you have to fix just *which* ninety per cent. And that makes it not so simple after all. In fact, that's the idea."

"I suppose so." Mutlow, thus briefly taken a turn round

Robin Hood's barn, was dashed again. "You don't think it *might* be Appleby's End? Figure it that somebody wanted to get you down to this district, Mr. Appleby. It's in this person's prosaic, practical interest—wasn't that your expression? —to get you down here and do something uncommonly odd —I think uncommonly odd was what you said. And sinister, of course." Inspector Mutlow's voice was faintly wistful. "Well now, if this person can create a whole bunch of queer doings and bring you down on the strength of them—which is where the usefulness of your belonging to the Yard comes in—and if then something equally queer happens to *you*— why, it's very unlikely that we shall be able to solve the matter."

"I agree with you there, inspector."

"Because we shall be beginning at the wrong end, and nothing will make sense. Suppose, Mr. Appleby—no offence, you understand—that there happens to you something like what has happened to Sir Mulberry's pig. Or to this Heyhoe, if you prefer it."

"Take it that I have no preference."

"We should naturally suppose that—that your sad misfortune, Mr. Appleby, was the *consequence* of your having come down and got mixed up with whatever the mystery was. Whereas it would really be the *cause* of the whole affair— and Heyhoe and old Mrs. Ulstrup's cow and the rest would simply be the additional needles stuffed in the haystack. Billy Bidewell"—this association of ideas seemed inevitable with Mutlow—"says there are some of those Ravens that are uncommonly interested in you. You're sure you have had no connection with any of them before? Suppose that some previous case of yours had resulted in bringing a friend or relation of theirs to the gallows, and vengeance had been sworn—"

"Good heavens!"—Appleby looked in frank astonishment at a Mutlow who was proving thus unexpectedly prolific of ideas—"you speak with the voice of old Ranulph Raven himself. This is just, I imagine, how his yarn-spinning mind worked. 'Vengeance had been sworn.' Who can doubt that the phrase is endemic in his works."

"That's just it!" Mutlow tapped his steering-wheel incisively. "Something in the blood, as you might say. Their minds work just as this tale-spinning old man's did. In fact, I think we've got a line on this whole case. Only, of course, we'll have to wait."

"To wait, inspector?"

"Certainly. You see, it hasn't happened yet. The real needle is still missing from the haystack. Only the red herrings have been displayed so far. They're still planting the trees that are going to prevent my seeing the wood." Mutlow, his imagination evidently afire, swung hazardously towards the ditch. "But presently the hour will strike. Presently, Mr. Appleby—mark my words—the real blow will fall. And I must say"—Mutlow was suddenly handsome—"that I shall be uncommonly sorry not to have the benefit of your collaboration in clearing the thing up."

"I see." Appleby looked at this rural colleague, genuinely impressed. "Well, well. And do you know, one of those Ravens has already offered to do me a memorial? As a joke, of course. But the sinister underlying irony is now revealed."

"A *memorial*? You mean something *carved*—and out of *marble*, or something like that?" Mutlow was now deep sunk in a sort of detective ecstasy. "Well—there now! Once one just gets a hold on cases of this sort it's astonishing how quickly everything links up. Which one is the sculptor?"

"The girl. And she's going to do the John Appleby Memorial for Scotland Yard. Only it may, perhaps, just be called Object."

"Object?"

"Miss Raven's work is modernist in manner."

"Is *that* so?" with Mutlow this seemed to clinch the matter. "I'm inclined to think we may set about getting a warrant."

"Possibly so." The late afternoon air was chill, and Appleby buried his nose in Mark Raven's shapeless tweeds. "Of course, I haven't had the opportunity for much conversation with Miss Raven. But I do not think it would misrepresent the situation to say that she and I are engaged."

"Engaged! But you say it was only yesterday—"

"That's how I see the matter."

It would have been difficult to say whether Appleby's voice indicated resolution or resignation—which was one more enigma for Mutlow to meditate. And for some time he meditated. "You know," he said eventually, "it *is* a confusing

affair. And at times I almost think you're concerned to keep
it so."

"My dear fellow, one gets these fancies after a long day."

"I suppose that's it." Mutlow's voice was apologetic. . . .
And now the car drew up before the ivy-clad cottage of old
Mrs. Ulstrup of Drool.

Chapter 13

A FLAT clerical hat, battered and of a type no longer much
favoured by ecclesiastical outfitters, had been thrown care-
lessly down in the porch; it was to be conjectured, therefore,
that Mrs. Ulstrup was in process of receiving spiritual advice.
And a voice, resonant, cheerful and eminently of the pulpit,
spoke from within. "Just on the boil," said the voice. "Ready
in a jiffy."

Appleby knocked and the door was opened—or rather
manipulated, for it seemed to be possessed of only one hinge
—by a red-faced, white-haired clergyman standing some six-
feet-four in badly cracked shoes. "Come in," said the clergyman; "come in, by all means. I don't know you from Adam
—though I've always had a shrewd idea, mark you, that
Adam would be eminently recognizable if one passed him in
the street. Bother this door! I must tell the village carpenter
that here is something very like a work of corporal mercy.
A part of the country this, gentlemen, in which opportunity
for Works fairly abounds. A wise dispensation, no doubt,
since we come rather noticeabley short at present in the matter
of Faith. Come in. Smith is my name and this is Hodge, my
cat." He pointed to a large brindled creature sedately posed
in the crook of his arm. "I was just going to butter the buns."

They entered what proved to be a stone-flagged kitchen,
oddly poised between cosiness and dilapidation. The Reverend Mr. Smith appeared to be labouring with some success
on behalf of the former quality; his professional outfit consisted of half a pound of butter, a packet of tea and several
paper bags. And his voice boomed out again amid much

chinking of crockery. "At least you look respectable—but are you gay? Our hostess—who will presently appear—is none too generously dowered either way, I am sorry to say. At a guess"—and Mr. Smith glanced up fleetingly from his operations—"I should say that you were a couple of policemen come to enquire into a theft of poultry. If so, I advise you to see that boy who stokes Grope's engine. I've had an eye on him for some time. Not a bad boy, mind you, but decidedly given to what you might call collective farming. Indeed, I don't know that I could point to a more collective boy in the whole district." And Mr. Smith, chuckling hugely, lifted the kettle from the hob.

"What," asked Appleby, "of Hannah Hoobin's boy?"

"Went to work at Tiffin Place," said Mr. Smith. "Didn't like the job, and therefore left the district. I don't know why your friend should look so uncomfortable about it."

Appleby glanced at Mutlow. There was no doubt that the Hoobin affair had been kept altogether quieter than was proper, and that Colonel Pike's assistant was now feeling uneasy on this score. There was also no doubt that Mr. Smith was a person of observation and intelligence—the first intelligent person, Appleby reflected, that he had met since saying good-bye to Judith that morning. And—since observation will go a mile while gossip travels a furlong—he was eminently a man to cultivate. "You are quite right about our calling," Appleby said. "This is Inspector Mutlow of the Yatter police; my name is Appleby, and I am a detective-inspector from Scotland Yard."

"Can you butter scones?" Mr. Smith appeared not at all impressed by this information. "Capital. Both halves, if you please; and don't stick them together again. Mrs. Ulstrup is naturally something of a connoisseur in butter. Mr. Mutlow, I will trouble you to put that plum cake on a plate. The plate with the cow. I have sometimes pleased myself with the fancy that our friend's kitchen is like a Hindu domestic interior—if Hindus have domestic interiors. The sacred animal is everywhere in evidence, as you will have observed."

This was unchallengeable. Cows and calves decorated such crockery as was in evidence; two large china cows, such as used to distinguish the windows of old-fashioned dairies, stood on each side of the fireplace; smaller china cows lined the mantelpiece; and on the walls hung two large oleographs, presumably after Cuyp, in which cows, milkmaids, pails, joint-stools and enormous narrow-necked jars were built up into opulent cylindrical compositions. Appleby surveyed the collection with interest. "Can you tell me," he asked, "if all this is a recent development with Mrs. Ulstrup?"

"Dear me, no! It is innate, Mr. Appleby—or virtually so. As the Roman twins were suckled by a she-wolf, I have sometimes supposed that Mrs. Ulstrup must have been suckled by a Friesian or a Jersey. And since girlhood she has been celebrated in this part of the countryside for her skill in vacimulgence." Here Mr. Smith paused and looked sharply at Appleby.

"I gathered she has been a milkmaid."

"Capital!" Much pleased with this little test of the literacy of the metropolitan police force, Mr. Smith lifted the lid from the teapot and stirred vigorously with a spoon. "I maintain," he said, "that it assists the infusion. Now, where were we. Ah, milking, to be sure. You will remember that Horace in the *Georgics*—But stay! I think I hear Mrs. Ulstrup coming from her room. As King Duncan said of an altogether more formidable lady: See, see our honoured hostess. Inspector Mutlow, be so kind as to open the door."

From some room beyond the kitchen there had come a very slow step, and now Mutlow opened the door to reveal an elderly woman of ample proportions who paused on the threshold. Mrs. Ulstrup, framed against a further vista of bovine portraiture on the wall of what appeared to be her bedroom, raised one foot from the ground and then slowly put it down again where it had stood; after this she turned her head very gradually from side to side—rather as if performing some exercise in a beauty manual; then she put out her tongue and contrived to lick her nose; and finally she simply stood where she was, rhythmically moving her jaws. Just as it was evident (once more) that Dr. Watson imagined himself upon a battlefield of the Civil War, so was it evident that Mrs. Ulstrup imagined herself in the middle of a nice daisyed and buttercupped field. The melancholy fact was patent. The lady believed herself to be a cow.

"Excellent!" said Mr. Smith, and looked as delighted as if the door had opened upon a dryad of the grove. "Come along, my good soul. Admirably buttered scones and not at all a bad plum cake." And then, since Mrs. Ulstrup showed no sign of stirring, "Coop!" said Mr. Smith vigorously; "coop, coop!" And slowly Mrs. Ulstrup responded. Heavily, on a slightly zigzag course, and dipping her head at each step, she crossed the room and sat down by the fire. Mr. Smith began pouring tea. "What might be termed a vacillating nature," he said. "Now, if the old lady had devoted her life to Sturrock's goats, no doubt she would have turned capricious."

Mutlow, upon whom learned little jokes were not likely to make any impression, picked up the scones and walked over to Mrs. Ulstrup. "Seasonable weather," he said encouragingly.

Mrs. Ulstrup, who had been exercising her lower jaw in a slow rotary motion, reared her head slightly in air and once more licked her nose.

Mutlow frowned. "And nice," he said more severely, "to see a little bit of sunshine."

Mrs. Ulstrup blankly stared.

Mutlow took a deep breath and his voice became frankly threatening. "Turnips ought to do grandly," he said.

Widely and dramatically, Mrs. Ulstrup opened her mouth. Then she inserted a scone, closed her jaws upon it, and fell to her rotary manner of chewing once more.

Mr. Smith took a slab of plum cake. "I fear," he said, "that Mrs. Ulstrup will not have a great deal to say to us. Indeed, I must admit that even the common courtesies of speech have of late begun to fail her. But it is often so with people of ruminative habit." Mr. Smith chuckled again at this, placed a large cup of tea before Mrs. Ulstrup, and patted her affectionately on the nose. Whereupon Mrs. Ulstrup made a contented noise and took another scone.

"I understood," said Appleby, "that the—the disorder we are witnessing had its origin quite recently, in a distressing experience to which Mrs. Ulstrup was subjected at Tiffin Place. But it appears from what you say, and from the decorations and embellishments of the house—"

"Quite so, quite so." Mr. Smith bit with zest into his plum cake, and nodded a vigorously affirmative head. "Mrs. Ulstrup's misfortune—for so, I suppose, we must regard it—has been much exacerbated since her return from Tiffin Place. But she has always been this way inclined. I have sometimes wondered whether there is not some anatomical abnormality. Looking down from the pulpit—for Mrs. Ulstrup is an excellent churchwoman, I am happy to say—and viewing her ceaseless masticatory activity, it has occurred to me to wonder whether perhaps there might not be two stomachs?" And Mr. Smith looked enquiringly at Appleby, as if out of a great scientific innocence.

"This bovine behaviour," said Appleby, "is more likely to be the reflection of some conflict in the unconscious mind."

"Is that so?" Mr. Smith was largely impressed.

"A traumatic incident in the early years of childhood—"

"Dear me! Like little Harpad."

"Little Harpad?" Appleby was puzzled.

"You will read about him in a fellow called Freud—a wonderful fellow, though as much an artist as a scientist, I should be inclined to say. This little Harpad, when more or less a baby, had an adventure in the fowl-yard, and for years afterwards he would do little save crow like a cock. Now, Mrs. Ulstrup appears to fall roughly within the same category of human behaviour, does she not? So what you say about the Unconscious interests me very much. What, Mr. Mutlow, is the Unconscious?" Mr. Smith reached for the kettle and watered the teapot. "What we think of as the Unconscious is very much what the Romantics thought of as the Child— but, of course, stood on its head. Now, a child, whether standing on its head or not, should be treated firmly and kindly—which is no more than the wisdom of one's grandmother or one's nurse. I would be a little more precise, however, and postulate a sort of wary indulgence. And there you have the rules, too, for coping with the Unconscious." Mr. Smith took up a knife and cut the whole remaining plum cake into large chunks. "Wary indulgence, Mr. Appleby —and plenty of plum cake. Be so kind as to pass Mrs. Ulstrup the plate."

Appleby did so and Mrs. Ulstrup, rather as if she were a creature of the circus, neatly helped herself with her fore hoof. "But surely," said Appleby, "her condition had changed suddenly for the worse when she came back from Tiffin Place?"

"Most decidedly so. And I see you know something of the affair. Sir Mulberry Farmer had a beautiful white cow—a

South Ham, I believe—which he had great hopes would prove a champion milker and win a cup at our local show. Sir Mulberry, I am glad to say, strongly supports that sort of thing. Well, Mrs. Ulstrup here, since highly expert in these mysteries, was engaged for the milking, and moved over to Tiffin Place. But within a week she was back, and in this— um—untoward condition. Moreover, before lapsing into silence she told, I am sorry to say, a regular tale of a cock and a bull."

"A bull?" said Mutlow hopefully.

Mr. Smith frowned. "My dear sir, it is a common phrase— and most notably occurs in Sterne's *Tristam Shandy*. Mrs. Ulstrup came back with a fantastic story. She went in to milk the cow one morning and there it was as usual, gleaming white in its stall. But when she endeavoured to carry out her purpose and applied herself to the creature's udder, she received the unconscionable shock of discovering that the brute had been turned to marble in the night. A sufficiently queer fantasy, gentlemen, and concomitant doubtless with the unfortunate posture of affairs which you now witness. Mr. Appleby, pass Mrs. Ulstrup's cup. Inspector Mutlow, be so good as to replenish Hodge's saucer with milk."

"It's true," Appleby said.

Mr. Smith reached for the sugar basin. "Dear me! I confess that it seems to me a singularly purposeless suspension of the operation of natural law. A marble cow! Could it be some prank of the stable-lads? But no—to me at least it suggests a somewhat sophisticated mind. Literature holds many myths about being stricken to stone, whereas I judge it a thing not current in folklore. And why has not more been heard of this? Our unfortunate friend here has been needlessly under the odium of prevarication. Give her another piece of cake." Abstractedly Mr. Smith took another chunk himself. "And what became of the changeling cow?"

"I suspect that Sir Mulberry simple locked the door on it." Did anything of this talk, Appleby wondered, penetrate to Mrs. Ulstrup's dreaming mind? "Over this and other matters he has been much upset, and disposed to have as little idle talk as possible. There have been other odd happenings. Hannah Hoobin's boy, whom you suppose to have left the district, was changed into a waxwork."

"A waxwork? It probably came from Dream Manor, where they have poor old Bishop Adolphus's collection. And—dear me, how a life of simple pastoral care dulls one's wits!—the marble cow is doubtless from Dream too, and will be one of Theodore Raven's amiable ineptitudes. The plot thickens, Mr. Appleby! Or shall we say solidifies? See if Mrs. Ulstrup would care to go back to the scones."

Mutlow, who had been making a gloomy study of one of his numerous notebooks, looked up sharply. "You seem pretty quick at the bearings of all this, sir." He regarded Mr. Smith with the uncompromising suspicion which he seemed to reserve for those capable of cerebration. "Quite on the spot, as one might say."

"Thank you, inspector, thank you! I chance to know the Ravens very well. This is a straggling parish, and my rectory is, as it happens, the nearest habitation to theirs. I must have been one of the first to hear the strange news of the man Heyhoe this morning. Miss Clarissa was good enough to send a message over by Peggy Pitches. And Peggy Pitches told me that Billy Bidewell had told her how Miss Judith and our young friend here"—and Mr. Smith bowed politely to Appleby—"had been benighted. In a haystack, I think she said."

"Quite so," said Appleby firmly. "A commodious haystack, Mr. Smith."

"I should have judged it to be more Mrs. Ulstrup's line. I remember how my dear father was accustomed to define any forward young woman as the haystack going after the cow." And Mr. Smith's features disposed themselves in lines of emphatic merriment around shrewdly observant eyes. "He meant to indicate that an impulsive girl is sometimes an embarrassment. It may be so. Certainly she is always a responsibility."

"No doubt," said Appleby.

"As for Heyhoe, his fate tacks on to other untoward matters at Dream. A strange place. I never knew the old squire, who died long before my present incumbency here. And the family—why, I know not—seldom speaks of him. He was a writer of romances, as you are doubtless aware, and he made something of a fortune and lost it again. Ranulph Raven—a good name for a railway bookstall. I wonder when the railways started bookstalls? Gregory Grope would know."

"Gregory Grope knows quite a lot." Appleby stretched out his hands to the excellent fire burning in Mrs. Ulstrup's grate. "For example, that his grandmother liked spying on lovers."

Mr. Smith raised his eyebrows. "It is a common disorder," he said placidly.

"And less harmful than incendiarism."

"Incendiarism?"

"Incendiarism—which was at one time the diversion of Hannah Hoobin's boy. Both are decidedly degenerate forms of sexual behaviour. So it is interesting, perhaps, that Gregory Grope's grandmother and Hannah Hoobin's boy are conceivably blood relations."

"Dear me!" Mr. Smith turned to poke the fire—but his expression, it struck Appleby, was that of a man rapidly thinking. "I must confess that you take me out of my depth. And even in your colleague I believe I perceive an inner floundering."

Mutlow nodded. "I don't understand it. I don't understand why we are here at all."

"My dear inspector, every day I meet people who are in precisely that predicament. I commonly recommend getting a start on clearing the back yard. But let us return to Hannah Hoobin's boy. And let us hope that *he* returns to *us*. For the plot thickens still." Mr. Smith looked grave. "And by no means so agreeably, this time."

Appleby nodded. "Quite so. And the relevant facts seem to be these: Gregory Grope's grandmother was by way of bestowing her favours on the local gentry, and on more than one occasion she disappeared for a time, as if she were being kept by somebody in another part of the country. Now the man Heyhoe is admitted to have been the illegitimate son of Ranulph Raven, and the chronology of the matter at least does not exclude the possibility of Gregory's grandmother's having been the mother. And next we have the fact—or rather statement by Gregory, for it is no more than that—that Heyhoe in his turn was the father of Hannah Hoobin's boy."

"I see." Mr. Smith pushed away his teacup and looked thoughtfully at Appleby. "And old Mrs. Grope fell down a well, Heyhoe has been buried in snow, and Hannah Hoobin's boy has been changed into one of Bishop Adolphus's waxworks. Finally, you, my dear sir, appear from Scotland Yard, drop in to tea with the good Mrs. Ulstrup and myself, and invite me to make sense of these matters." Mr. Smith paused. "I believe that your colleague here, if he think hard, will be able to make sense of them. But, for my own part, I emphatically declare myself unable to do so."

Mutlow beamed. "No doubt it takes the professional angle," he said. "And I must say I'm beginning to see some possibilities."

But Appleby was looking keenly, almost hopefully, at Mr. Smith. "You honestly find it doesn't make sense?"

"That is what I find. The sequence of events we have just reviewed is, of course, susceptible to a certain rational explanation—and Mr. Mutlow, it would appear, is on the track of it. But there has been a number of other circumstances—circumstances of which I suppose you to be pretty well informed—which simply do not cohere."

Inspector Mutlow, rather as one who would direct traffic at an intersection, held up a heavy hand. "The needles," he said oracularly. "What you're talking of now is all the other needles in the haystack."

Mr. Smith looked mildly surprised. "I fear I don't follow you. Perhaps you mean all the other bats in the belfry? For the whole affair has a bizarre quality which suggests madness at every turn. I am not confident that a great deal of harm has been done, so far. We must ask ourselves, however, if the matter has now reached some critical stage."

Appleby looked curiously at the acute and comfortable Mr. Smith. "I think it has," he said.

"Dear, dear!" Mr. Smith took out his watch. "I see that presently I must be off. My two lads are down from Oxford for the Christmas vacation, and at such seasons I like to be home at a reasonably early hour. However, a few minutes remain. Inspector, pray make way for our friend."

Mrs. Ulstrup had finished her tea, and appeared to feel that there was no further occasion for the discomforts of the circus. Abandoning, therefore, the chair on which she had been somewhat awkwardly perched, she now moved across to the fireplace and lay down comfortably on the hearth rug. Mr. Smith watched this proceeding with perhaps a shade of helplessness. "Really," he said, "I could wish that she had taken it into her head to be not a cow but a sheep. I should then have been sustained in my professional labours by a good deal of scriptural metaphor. For who ever heard of the parable of the lost cow?" Mr. Smith glanced at Mutlow, whose disapproval of this fancy was evident, and then back at Mrs. Ulstrup as she lay placidly disposed in opulent curves. "Like Cleopatra's ladies in the play, she may be said to make her bends adornings. But the inspector, I see, is impatient for conference more serious than this. I repeat, therefore: madness at every turn. Consider, for example, Mr. Luke Raven's tombstone. For you have doubtless heard of that."

Appleby nodded. "I have. Or consider Sir Mulberry Farmer. His behaviour has become first cousin to Mrs. Ulstrup's—only decidedly more protean. At one moment he toys with the idea of having become the Hermes of Praxiteles, and at another he feels strongly drawn to some barbaric and megalithic art in the South Seas. For other things have happened at Tiffin Place, you will understand, besides the translation of Mrs. Ulstrup's cow."

"You scarcely surprise me." Mr. Smith paused and looked thoughtfully at the fire. "Do you know, I am strongly reminded of something I have not read for a long time—one of Ranulph Raven's stories."

Appleby sat up with a jerk. "You mean some one specific story?"

"No, I cannot say that. Indeed, I have no very clear memory of one of his stories as distinct from another. Such things do not dwell in the mind. As you grow older, Mr. Appleby, you will find that you turn more and more to your Chaucer and your Horace."

Mutlow grunted impatiently. "Now, sir, tell us just what you mean, if you please. Not that it sounds at all likely to be important, if you ask me."

"In all probability you are right." Mr. Smith was quite unoffended. "It is no more than a stray thought that has floated into consciousness."

"Do you mean," asked Appleby, "that what you have called the bizarre elements in our case are reminiscent of Ranulph Raven's writing?"

"Very possibly they are. I have a notion that his short stories in particular are full of inexplicable circumstances strangely resolved. But I am thinking of the honest and com-

monplace melodramatic writing which is the basis of most of
his novels. It is stuff in an accepted Victorian taste, and runs
on through Dickens to the end of the century. Lost heirs and
missing wills and clandestine marriages, Mr. Appleby. That
sort of thing."

Chapter 14

IT WAS now dusk and Mrs. Ulstrup's kitchen, lit chiefly from
the flickering grate, was a place of dull reddish light and
dancing shadows—much like Cinderella's kitchen in the pan-
tomime before the dramatic entrance of the Good Fairy.
Perhaps this lady would presently appear and transform
Mrs. Ulstrup either back into an elderly woman or through
some yet further metensomatosis? It seemed scarcely a probability worth waiting for—and meanwhile there were other
tasks before the end of the day: and notable among them an
interview with Hannah Hoobin, mother of him who appeared
to be known only as Hannah Hoobin's boy. But one or two
matters remained on which Mr. Smith might have valuable
information, and Appleby now addressed himself to eliciting
these. "I am staying with the Ravens," he said, "simply because I made their acquaintance quite fortuitously last night.
I suppose you know them fairly well?"

"Everard Raven and Miss Clarissa—who, I believe, is only
a distant relation—are among the most regular of my congre-
gation, and with the former I frequently discuss matters of
common interest. Of late he has been giving increasing
thought to religious matters, I am glad to say." Mr. Smith
chuckled. "Or I *should* be glad to say, were I not cognizant
of the fact that what he likes to call the doggy letter is hard
upon him. He has also discussed Romanticism and Represen-
tative Government with me, just as he has discussed Railways
with Gregory Grope. I feel that Gregory and I have some
title to be considered among the many scholars and men of
science whom the *New Millennium* declares itself as drawing
upon."

"But it appears that—apart from picking other people's brains—Everard does all the work himself. He must be a most industrious person."

"Eminently. Have you seen what he calls his Scriptorium? It is in most marked contrast with the rest of the house, and suggests notable efficiency. And yet I don't know whether Everard Raven really possesses that. Is he, as Byron so admirably describes Gibbon, 'laborious, slow, and hiving wisdom with each studious year'? I really couldn't say. Only I see from Mr. Mutlow's kindling eye that *Childe Harold* is a favourite with the Yatter constabulary."

Mutlow scowled at this innocent bandinage. "Byron?" he said. "Didn't he get himself into trouble over—"

Mr. Smith held up a hand in which a last fragment of plum cake reposed. "Ah, my dear inspector, the professional angle again! Let us pass on to the other Ravens. The melancholy Luke is very fond of our church and churchyard—but not at service time, I am sorry to say. He is a friend of the Longers—the marquis, as you may know, is of somewhat saturnine temper himself—and visits frequently at Linger Court. As a consequence, he has been given a key to the Linger vault, and sits there amid the bones of long-dead Longers, composing poems. Poetry, of course, is in the Raven family. You will have heard of Herbert Raven, well-known for his revival of the madrigal and the aubade."

"A gifted family running to eccentricity," pronounced Mutlow heavily. "Just the place to look for trouble, if you ask me."

"But I notice," said Mr. Smith benignly, "that your London colleague does *not* ask you. Possibly he is conscious of your own marked disinclination to ask *him*? You must forgive my interest in the organization of the police force. It is something quite new to me."

"And Robert Raven?" asked Appleby. He was obscurely aware that Mr. Smith, still amiably discoursing, had concentrated his mind on some pressing business of his own. "What sort of a man is Robert?"

"A delicate watercolourist, Mr. Appleby, and one with a considerable reputation in embroidery."

"Embroidery?"

"Ah, I perceive that you have not penetrated much below the ferocious outer integument of Robert—though you must have marked too, I think, his gentle manners. I sometimes associate him in my mind with the Tchambuli."

Mutlow tapped his notebook with a pencil. "Come, come, sir," he said. "There are no gentry of that name in this part of the country, I very well know."

"My dear inspector, the Tchambuli live in New Guinea, south of the mountain-dwelling Arapesh and west of the cannibal Mundugumor. A most interesting culture. The men, although of virile appearance and demeanour, spend their time indoors in the pursuits of weaving and painting, while the women—"

"Who's been eating my cake?" In the shadowy kitchen a new voice broke in upon Mr. Smith's ethnological discourse. The three men looked around, startled. And then, with even more emphasis, the voice spoke again. *"Who done it?"* demanded the recumbent Mrs. Ulstrup. *"Who's been and pinched my cake?"*

"It's gone, all right," said Mutlow.

"You're sure she didn't eat it herself?" Appleby asked.

"Quite sure. She left a bit on that plate there, and I shoved it to the corner of the table nearest the door."

"Then you must have shoved it too far, so that it fell on the floor." Appleby peered under the table. "Better bring the lamp over and look for it. Mrs. Ulstrup seems quite upset."

Mutlow brought the lamp and grovelled. "Nothing here," he said. "Nothing at all. Must have been mice."

"Nonsense—mice can't make away with a sizeable chunk of plum cake. Look again."

"I tell you, it isn't here." Mutlow rose, red-faced and wrathful. "Must have been the cat."

"Hodge? He hasn't stirred."

"Well, then, Mr. Appleby, a rat. At any rate, it's gone. Good heavens! Where's Mr. Smith?"

They stared round the fire-lit kitchen. Mrs. Ulstrup, her weak indignation quickly expended after the manner of her kind, had returned to ruminative ease, and might never have heard either of plum cake or of the divine gift of articulate speech. The door was open. Mr. Smith had disappeared.

"Well, I'm blessed!" said Mutlow. "I thought he was a queer customer—coming like that to give the old girl tea!—but who would have thought he'd behave so?"

Appleby frowned. "What do you mean—behave so?"

"Bolt like that, of course. Make off with a piece of cake."

"My dear man, it was his own cake." The fatuity of this conversation was reducing Appleby to bewilderment. "And why shouldn't he give the old girl tea? It's what's called the visitation of the sick."

"I'd call it the visitation by the cracked. Rushing off with a hunk of his own cake! It makes it pottier still." Mutlow had opened one of his notebooks as if urgently compelled to commit this conviction to writing. Then he shut it again in despair. "It's just awful, all this," he said. "No sense in it at all. Just one perfectly idiotic thing after another. A clutter of ghastly, disconnected lunacies. It's impossible even to keep them all in one's head. The old man they buried in the snow, for instance. I've almost forgotten about him."

Appleby laughed. "Pins and needles," he said. "So many red herrings that the haystack has fairly got pins and needles. But here is Mr. Smith back again."

It was true that the large form of Mrs. Ulstrup's pastor was framed in the doorway; he was panting heavily and clasped a stout stick which he must have snatched up from beside his clerical hat in the porch. "Missed her," he said; "—and not for the first time. Got away with a capital selection of *exuviae* too."

Appleby, who had thrown himself down rather wearily in a chair by the fire, sat up again abruptly. "Selection of *what?*" he asked.

Mr. Smith laid his stick on the table. "We are in the presence of sorcery."

This time it was Mutlow who reacted violently. "Sorcery? Of all the damned nonsense—"

"Do not swear, sir!" Mr. Smith, suddenly drawn up to his full six-feet-four, was revealed as a formidable—and angry—specimen of the muscular Christian. Then he turned to Appleby. "Sorcery," he repeated. "It is not, of course, so common as witchcraft proper. But it does turn up from time to time."

"I saw her hand come in at the door," said Mr. Smith, "and then she snatched the cake. Of course she must have been watching and so knew who had been eating it. Something left by Mr. Mutlow would be useless for her purpose—unless her purpose is to sorcerize Mr. Mutlow, that is to say."

"Sorcerize *me!*" Mutlow peered rather nervously about him in the shadows of Mrs. Ulstrup's kitchen. "I never heard of such a thing."

"Possibly not. But I fear, my dear inspector, that your nescience is scarcely very strong evidence against the objective existence of a phenomenon. I doubt, for example, whether you have ever heard of the planet Pluto. But the planet Pluto exists."

"I should have thought"—Appleby was frowning into the fire—"that Mrs. Ulstrup was sufficiently sorcerized already. It is your opinion that we have just been visited by some woman concerned to gain an occult power over her?"

"There is no other explanation. As I pursued her I saw that she had not only the fragment of cake (which would be especially valuable as having come direct from Mrs. Ulstrup's lips) but a large bone evidently purloined from the larder. These *exuviae*—a scientific term which I see is familiar to you—would of course, according to the theory of sorcery, be transmitted to the sorcerer, who would then have Mrs. Ulstrup within the malign power of his, or her, art. Had I caught the woman I fancy that I should have extorted a confession from her. But, most unfortunately, she eluded me in the dusk."

Appleby shifted the lamp on the table and looked hard at Mr. Smith. "You speak of all this, sir, in a somewhat equivocal way. Do I understand you to mean that what you call the theory of sorcery vindicates itself in practice? In short, do you *believe* in sorcery?"

Mr. Smith smiled—a whimsical smile such as he had not before offered. But his words were carefully chosen. "I do not know that I can tell you offhand whether we are required to believe, or required to disbelieve, in sorcery. The subject is dark and intricate."

"But I'm not seeking theological information." Appleby shook his head impatiently. "I'm asking whether you yourself believe in such things."

"My dear Mr. Appleby—does the inspector here believe in Pluto? We don't know, and it would be pointless to enquire."

And Mr. Smith fell to packing up the tea things. "By the way, Mr. Appleby, are you fond of beagling?"

"Beagling? I've been out with beagles, from time to time."

"Ah. It occurred to me to wonder if you were familiar with the habits of hares."

Inspector Mutlow's car chugged competently through the dusk. "I agree with you," said Appleby. "I agree with you entirely. Sorcery is the last straw. For what may we predict as a consequence of its intervention? Far greater complexity and confusion; obscurities such as our case has not shown hitherto."

Mutlow groaned. "And what would you be thinking of that old parson, Mr. Appleby? A bit touched, if you ask—if I'm not mistaken."

"I should describe him as intelligent, learned and impulsive. And possibly as being wise as well. Consider his attitude to Mrs. Ulstrup. The poor woman has taken refuge from some nervous conflict in the notion that she is a cow. On that basis she is getting on very nicely. Now, I suspect that theology disapproves of people imagining themselves cows—"

"There was Nebuchadnezzar," interrupted Mutlow unexpectedly.

"Yes—and I've no doubt that he was badgered and told that it had all happened because of his sins. But Mr. Smith in this instance keeps his theology in his pocket, and acts as if dropping in on an old cow and taking tea with her were an everyday affair. He spoke very cautiously of sorcery. Nevertheless I think we may add unorthodoxy to his attributes." Appleby paused. "Intelligent, learned, impulsive, wise and unorthodox. What do you make of that?"

"It sounds like one of those old-fashioned tombstones. By the way, what was that he said about Mr. Luke Raven and a tombstone? I didn't follow that at all."

"Somebody sent Luke Raven a tombstone, complete with the date of his death in the then near future. It didn't come off."

"It would be chiselled on."

"What?"

"If it didn't come off."

Appleby groaned in his turn. "Our brains are turning to train-oil and will be useful only to Gregory Grope. I mean that Luke Raven didn't die."

"Of course he didn't die. He's alive." Mutlow took one of his swerves towards the ditch. "I always think one gets sleepy driving through the evening air."

"Then you had better recite poetry in order to keep awake. It's what the airmen do."

"I don't know any poetry." Mutlow made this statement simply. "I never liked it much."

"What do you read?" Appleby was somewhat inclined to give rein to the field-naturalist's instincts when adventuring among his rural colleagues. "For instance, did you ever read any of Ranulph Raven?"

"Yes. Mother had some books of his, and I remember reading a story or two sometimes on Sundays when it was wet."

"Of course. And did you ever read *Paxton's Destined Hour?*"

"No."

"Or *The Coach of Cacus?*"

"No."

"Or one about a fearful maid who came upon a gentleman buried up to the neck in a spinney?"

"No." Mutlow's voice was wholly unresponsive. "But I remember reading one called *The Medusa Head.*"

"Called *what?*" Appleby's question was almost a shout.

"*The Medusa Head.* I don't know why. It was about a family portrait that seemed to have the power of paralysing any living creature that looked at it. First it was the owner's canaries, which had been hung in a window in the picture gallery. One morning they were found stiff and dead, staring at this portrait. Then it was his dog. It was found staring at the portrait too, cold and as stiff as a statue. Then the owner's wife was found there, staring at the thing in the same way—and as you might say turned to stone. After that—"

"I see. And would you say that it was interesting?"

"Interesting?" Mutlow's voice was puzzled. "How could it be interesting—just a lot of rubbish in a book?"

Appleby sighed. They drove in silence through the gathering dusk.

"But about that sorcery, you know," said Mutlow; "I think there may be something in that. And it's serious when that sort of thing starts up in a countryside. Leads to trouble."

"Ah."

"Probably nothing to do with this Tiffin Place affair. But I would like to look into it, all the same."

"I judge that you will be invited to pursue it."

"What's that?" Mutlow was suspicious once more.

"Nothing at all."

Again they drove in silence. "Hoobin's," said Mutlow briefly.

And Hoobin opened the door. It had not occurred to Appleby that there might be a Hoobin; he had thought of the household in terms simply of Hannah Hoobin and the vanished Hannah Hoobin's boy. But not only was there a Mr. Hoobin; at the moment there was a visitor as well—and an irate visitor at that. The Hoobin home was small—and even in the darkness discernible as squalid—and it echoed to angry voices. Mutlow frowned as he listened, convinced that altercation among the labouring classes calls for immediate police intervention. "Now then, now then," he said, "what's all this?"

"It be thee, be't?" Hoobin, who was an elderly man contorted like a thorn tree, held up a candle and viewed Mutlow with sullen distrust. "Has't found t'half-wit?"

"No, we haven't."

Hoobin's brow cleared slightly. "Two on you, be there? Come in and turn un out." He jerked a thumb over his shoulder. "Summat for you to do for your money besides feedin' your fat bellies." he added more expansively. "Come in and turn t'pig man out."

"What big man? What are you talking about?"

"T'pig man. Scurl. Hark at un."

From within the cottage voices were growing louder—a high-pitched man's voice and a higher-pitched woman's. "Look at it again," said the man's voice. "Look at it as long as you like. It's the law, I tell you, and it'll take more than your ugly mug to change it."

"Get out on here," said the woman. "Get out on here afore I take the broom to you."

"Broom?" The man's voice was elaborately scornful. "Your

dirty hovel hasn't seen a broom this twelvemonth." There was the sound of somebody displeasingly spitting on the floor. "Why don't you keep the brute in here and let him feel home-like?"

"Get out on it, I say." The woman's voice rose to a crazy scream. "Come back come Easter and I'll let you have the chitterlings to choke on." She paused. "But they'll have taken you up by then, Brettingham Scurl. They'll have taken you up for the Abbot's Yatter alms-box."

Hoobin had turned round and now Appleby and Mutlow followed him into an untidy kitchen which compared most unfavourably with Mrs. Ulstrup's. "Aye, said Hoobin. "And for Dr. Whitehead's chickens."

"And for what happened to little Sarah Pounce," said Mrs. Hoobin.

"And for what George Potticray told his mother."

"For what you did in the Shrubsoles' byre."

"For the way they found—"

Brettingham Scurl, who was a diminutive creature in a suit of cheap townee clothes, interrupted this increasingly mysterious invective with a yell of rage. "Give him up!" he screamed. "I've got the law on you and you know it. Give it up or pay the money now. I'll have you before the Sessions. I'll have you gaoled. You never had the money. It's fraud. It's conspiracy between the two of you." He brandished a document in air and advanced threateningly upon Mrs. Hoobin. "You!" he howled. "You and your fire-bug bastard! You rakes, you jakes, you lousy callet—"

Mr. Hoobin took a step forward and seized Brettingham Scurl by the ear. "Out on thee!" he roared.

With surprising power Brettingham Scurl twisted himself free and hit Mr. Hoobin hard on the jaw. Then he snatched up a lantern which was burning smokily on the table and made for a farther door. "I'll out with it," he cried. "And you'll be in for assault if you try to stop me. For I've the law on you. Assault and battery is what it'll be, you slut, you trollop, you great cuckoldy booby of a Caleb Hoobin." And Brettingham Scurl disappeared in darkness. Whereupon both the Hoobins pursued him, roaring and screaming the while with inexpressible rage and dismay.

The emotions of Inspector Mutlow were scarcely less ex-

treme. That such a scene should transact itself within the very
ambit of the law outraged him profoundly. Bellowing angrily,
and rather—Appleby thought—like the elephant Babar when
disposed to smash everything to bits, Mutlow pursued the ill-
conducted peasantry into a muddy and malodorous yard. It
scarcely seemed a trail likely to lead to the heart of the
Ranulph Raven Mystery; nevertheless Appleby followed in
time to see his colleague, by some titanic exertion of police-
manship, momentarily dominating the situation. "Explain
yourselves," Mutlow was saying; "explain yourselves, or it's
the lock-up for the lot of you."

"You can't have the law on me." Brettingham Scurl was
standing sulkily by the parapet of what appeared to be a
sizeable pig-sty. "You can't have the law on any of us for
transacting lawful business on private premises. Indeed, you're
trespassing, that's what you're doing. Policeman, are you?
Let's see your warrant-card. And let's see your warrant for
stepping in here unasked too."

"He be asked, all right." Mr. Hoobin was breathing heavily.
"He be asked in to cast thee out, Brettingham Scurl. And I'll
have the law on thee for what that foul mouth of yourn did
say afore witness."

Brettingham Scurl began waving his document again, whereupon Mutlow snatched it from his hand and read it by lantern
light. "Well," he demanded, "where's the pig?"

Triumphantly Brettingham Scurl pointed into the recesses
of the sty. "There he is," he said. "Hark at him."

There was a moment's silence in which a deep porcine
grunting could be heard through the darkness. Mrs. Hoobin
began to flap her arms wildly. Mr. Hoobin, now gloomy and
uncertain, glowered at everybody in turn. "He's been before
the magistrate," said Mutlow to the Hoobins. "And he's got
his order—though he has no business to be serving it himself."

Brettingham Scurl's triumph was redoubled—and so was the
grunting from the sty. Mrs. Hoobin had gone pale in the
lantern light; Mr. Hoobin's glance was circling the yard
warily, much as if in search of a weapon. "What's it all
about?" asked Appleby mildly. "Have they taken his pig?"

"It's the time-payments." Brettingham Scurl was suddenly
and politicly civil. "They've failed on their time-payments on
one of my pigs."

Appleby stared at him. "You mean to say you sell Gloucester Old Spots on the instalment plan?"

"Certainly, sir. And Middle Whites. There's a lot of folk round about here has my Middle Whites that way. The Gloucester Old Spots are mostly for selling outright to the gentry. They would suit you very nicely, sir, if I may say so. These Hoobins bit off more than they could chew when they paid a deposit on one of them. And now I'm going to take my pig." And Brettingham Scurl swung one leg over the wall behind him.

Mrs. Hoobin, a woman of displeasing articulation, let out a squawk which represented a new low in sheer vocal hideousness; Mr. Hoobin was tapping urgently on the roof of the sty; and from the darkness the grunting was now like the ticking of a clock. Appleby stepped forward. "One moment," he said. "Mr. Scurl, I'm interested in what you say, and I believe a Gloucester Old Spot would suit me very well. What's the sum owing to complete the deal? I'll pay, and the Hoobins and I can come to some arrangement later."

This was too much for Inspector Mutlow, who thrust his hands in his pockets and contrived to give what is so much rarer in life than in literature—a hollow laugh. The Hoobins conferred together in whispers. But Brettingham Scurl had no hesitation in pronouncing the suggestion excellent. And presently, stuffing a considerable sum of money into a greasy pocket-book and giving his late creditors a wide berth, he faded into darkness and was presently heard heading for Linger on a motor-bicycle.

Mrs. Hoobin was now weeping noisily; Mr. Hoobin swore under his breath; and as the clatter of the engine died away the grunting from the interior of the sty was somewhat uncertainly resumed. Appleby took up the lantern. "We're well rid of that Scurl," he said cheerfully. "I didn't at all care for the man. And now let's look at the creature we've rescued from him." And Appleby made as if to step over the wall in his turn.

With a yell of despair Mrs. Hoobin threw herself forward and had to be collared by Mutlow. Mr. Hoobin turned to her sullenly. "Peace, woman!" he said. "There's nobbut to get un out." He banged on the roof of the sty. "Come out, thou," he bawled. "Come out on it and show thyseen."

From the sty came a last dejected grunt and then a stirring as of a lithe and active body in straw. Appleby held the lantern at arm's length over the wall—and was hardly able to suppress a cry. In the low doorway there had appeared a chaos of wavy yellow locks, unkempt and dirty; beneath these, and on either side of a long nose, were eyes which were at once amused and crazy; and beneath these showed a shapeless mouth and a twisted grin. Far from looking half-witted, Hannah Hoobin's boy looked wholly mad—which is a very different thing. He also—Appleby realized with a sudden tingling of the spine—looked exactly like a juvenile and uncouth version of Mark Raven.

Hannah Hoobin's boy stood up and shook himself like a dog come out of water; then he swung on to the wall and perched astride it, evidently both scared upon discovery and delighted at being the centre of attention. Unlike either his blubbering mother or his sullen putative father, Hannah Hoobin's boy was a not unattractive specimen of his species. When brought before a bench of magistrates given to the conscientious reading of scientific little books on juvenile delinquency he would stand every chance of getting away with a good deal.

Before this crazy and feral charm, however, Inspector Mutlow showed no present sign of going down; instead he started forward with something like a howl of rage. "I'll learn you, you beastly little brat," he bellowed; "I'll learn you, you young scoundrel!"

Hannah Hoobin's boy looked momentarily downright frightened; then (with what, in one possessed of his wits at least, would have been considerable moral courage) he gave a low, deep grunt, eminently evocative of the very spirit of Gloucester Old Spots.

Mutlow helplessly spluttered. "Where's the pig?" he demanded inconsequently. "Where's Scurl's pig?"

Hannah Hoobin's boy took his hands from tattered pockets, picked several straws from his hair, and then luxuriously and expressively stroked his belly. "Ate un," he said. "Breakfast, dinner, supper. Breakfast, dinner." He looked at his mother. "Supper?" he asked hopefully.

Mrs. Hoobin, convinced that her son was about to be hauled off to jail, fell to blubbering again upon this pathetic question. The elder Hoobins, it seemed to Appleby, were both of markedly low intelligence. This might explain a good deal. For it seemed clear that some fantastic deception must have been imposed upon them. "Well, well," he said amiably, "I'm sure the boy is much more interesting than a Gloucester Old Spot. I'm quite glad I have a share in him. And now we'll all go inside and have a little talk about it."

They returned to the Hoobin kitchen, Hannah Hoobin's boy shedding straws as he went and Mutlow bringing up the rear, muttering. The displeasure of Mutlow was easy to explain; he had experienced another encounter with the unexpected, and there was nothing of which he more strongly disapproved. Old Mrs. Grope had fallen down a well and Heyhoe had been found buried in snow; heredity therefore required that the disappearance of Hannah Hoobin's boy should have an issue at once more sinister and conclusive than this of his discovery alive, well, and lavishly dieted on pork in a pig-sty. Had the boy been found quartered, cured, smoked and hanging in joints from the maternal rafters Mutlow would have been altogether more pleased.

Appleby on the other hand, who had been tired and dispirited at the end of his day's tour among the curiosities of the Linger country, was now discernibly in good spirits. He watched with a benevolent eye while the boy, tattered as the prodigal in the painted cloth and equally fresh from the swine, applied himself to such victuals as Mrs. Hoobin could provide. And he studied the family. Mr. and Mrs. Hoobin, he concluded again, were extremely stupid—and what is called sane. The boy was as undoubtedly crazed—but his mind was as quick as it was aberrant. And that he traced his descent from a Raven it required only half an eye to see.

"Well," said Appleby, "how did all this happen?"

"Yes," said Mutlow, "how did it happen? Out with it, before you're off to the county jail."

Mr. Hoobin cursed; Mrs. Hoobin wept; the boy quickened the pace of his eating, as if distrustful of the adequacy of prison fare.

"Oh, come," said Appleby. "They didn't constrain the boy to live in a sty, you know. And they've fed him well. I don't believe a charge of neglect would stand for a moment."

"Neglect!" Mutlow spluttered indignantly. "These people

have compounded a felony; that's what they'e done."

"What felony?"

"Well, a misdemeanour. Turning cows and things to marble. They've obstructed me in the execution of my duty."

"My dear inspector, when you came here previously to en-quire for the boy did you explain that it was in pursuance of a criminal investigation? Did you tell them of these various odd happenings that Sir Mulberry didn't want advertised?"

"Of course I didn't. I simply demanded to know the where-abouts of this brat."

"And the Hoobins refused to give you any information. They were legally entitled to do so." Appleby chuckled. "Take them before a magistrate and they may very well say that they regarded you as an unsuitable associate for their boy."

Mr. Hoobin nodded. "That's right," he interjected with large, stupid cunning. "That's it, mister. We didn't like un. There's always plenty about a countryside that'll take advantage on a half-wit. And we didn't like the look on un."

"And now, I think we'll have the truth." Appleby turned to Mrs. Hoobin. "What frightened you?"

Mrs. Hoobin hesitated. Then, slowly and without speaking, she turned to an untidy dresser behind her and rummaged in a drawer. From this she presently produced a much-thumbed scrap of paper which she handed to Appleby. Printed on it in bold letters and a staring red ink was this injunction: SOME-THING HAS HAPPENED AT TIFFIN PLACE THEY WILL TAKE THE BOY AGAIN HIDE HIM A FRIEND.

"And what does the boy say?" Appleby tried a direct ap-proach to the bright-eyed, gobbling youth at the table. "What did you make of it, Mr. Hoobin?"

The eyes of Hannah Hoobin's boy rounded at this mode of address. "Mischief," he said decidedly.

"I'm sure you weren't far wrong. And who do you think this message came from?"

"Fairies," said Hannah Hoobin's boy. His voice was as decided as before.

"Ah." Appleby looked abstractedly at Mutlow, who—de-spite his weakness for witchcraft and sorcery—was displaying at this suggestion all the indignation of an aggressive rational-ist. Then his glance turned to Mrs. Hoobin, but he continued to address the boy. "Do you know the folk over at Dream? Do you know an old man called Heyhoe?"

"I know un. He be purple."

"Purple?" Appleby was puzzled.

Hannah Hoobin's boy, who appeared to have formed a high opinion of this stranger's abilities, looked surprised. "The air about him be purple when he moves," he explained. "I be purple too. But most folks hereabouts be yellow." The boy paused and then jerked his head at Mutlow. "He be mucky green—which is what I've never seen before."

"Is that so?" Appleby was perfectly serious. "A mucky green aura is something quite out of the way?"

The boy nodded, equally serious. "Only pigs be mucky green," he explained.

Mutlow breathed heavily. Appleby picked up the scrap of paper again—with exaggerated caution, as if it were a dangerous charm. "You've none of you had anything stolen from you recently?" he asked. "Anything that could be taken to a witch or a sorcerer?"

Blank silence greeted this question. Then the elder Mr. Hoobin spoke. "Old Gammer Umbles that lives Tew-way be a witch," he said informatively. "But us never had nothing to do with hern."

"That's very wise of you." Appleby rose, patted Hannah Hoobin's boy amiably on the shoulder, and moved towards the door. "Let him sleep in his bed again," he said. "Whatever happened at Tiffin Place had nothing to do with him, so nobody's going to take him." He paused. "To-morrow, by the way, it's possible you'll have quite a number of visitors."

"Visitors?" Mrs. Hoobin looked obscurely alarmed, and her glance travelled about the untidy kitchen—conceivably in search of the broom of which Brettingham Scurl had declared himself to see no evidences. "Us be to have visitors?"

"Several of them. Very pleasantly spoken gentlemen who will want to have quite a lot of talk. Well, talk away—and particularly the boy." Appleby chuckled. "But not free."

Mr. Hoobin was staring open-mouthed. "There be money in it?"

"Decidedly. Don't you, my dear sir, make the mistake of talking just for beer. Make it a fiver before you open your mouth to anyone. And another fiver if they want to take photographs."

In the Hoobin pantomine it was Appleby himself who was the Good Fairy after all. His aura must have been golden—and now, with Mutlow following him, he withdrew while still surrounded by it. Mr. Hoobin accompanied him through the untidy little garden. And at the gate Appleby asked a final question. "That boy," he said. "Are you his father?"

Mutlow was starting his car. Mr. Hoobin stood silent for a moment, and there was no sound except the spluttering of the engine. Then he spoke. "Be I the one that got t'half-wit?" he said.

"That's what I'm asking."

Mr. Hoobin considered. "Mister," he said heavily, "did 'ee ever see a saw?"

"Dear me, yes."

"And would 'ee ask which tooth cut board?"

Chapter 15

DARKNESS HAD fallen and it was snowing again; snowflakes danced in Mutlow's head-lights; far away a melancholy hoot told of Gregory Grope chugging between Snarl and Linger, dreaming of the Flying Scotsman, the Golden Arrow, the Berlin-Constantinople Express. Linger Court, Tiffin Place, Dream Manor, the rectory of the reverend Mr. Smith, Mrs. Ulstrup's cottage, the hovel of the Hoobins: England in all its venerable and grotesque stratifications had crept under a single blanket. The scattered lights that appeared and disappeared as the car ran through the hedgerows told of labourers' wives stirring porridge, of butlers coaxing up the temperature of claret, of parlour-maids disposing respectable silver on carefully patched damask, of anomalous proceedings in the kitchens and diningrooms of the dissipated, the simple lifers, the artistically inclined. . . . Gregory Grope's engine hooted again—this time from farther away. "It *ought* to come together," said Mutlow irritably.

"Of course it ought. Only there's rather a lot to fit in." Appleby, huddled still within Mark Raven's baggy tweeds, tapped the modest row of gauges on Mutlow's dashboard. "Look at these. You could wire them up in a number of ways and get some very odd results. This affair's like that. Any number of little wires, and if we just get a terminal or two wrong the final report will be grotesque. Or—what's worse—it may be both incorrect and specious. Have you any kids?"

"Four boys." Mutlow spoke with all the casualness of the proud father.

"Well now, suppose you got out the Meccano and made a pretty elaborate crane. Then suppose you took it to pieces again and handed just those bits to your boys and told *them* to make a crane. Each boy would produce something different, and each would have a few bits over, which they'd have to use up just anyhow. We've been given just such an assortment of bits—but we don't even know whether they should make up into a crane or a windmill or a bridge. For instance, why am I here? Why did your precious chief constable get me down? What am I supposed to be investigating?"

Mutlow slowed down and carefully negotiated a bend. For a moment he seemed nonplussed by this batch of questions. "Certain events at Tiffin Place—" he began heavily.

"Events? What do you mean by events? Practical jokes? Would you say it was my business to go chasing about the countryside after a practical joker?"

"The cow was valuable." Mutlow paused on this, as if acknowledging that it was a somewhat lame rejoinder. "And that boy had disappeared. It looked as if there might be something sinister about that." Mutlow was confident again. "I tell you frankly, I never expected to see the lad alive."

"Don't you mean that late this afternoon, and when you had heard of certain other matters, you *started* not expecting to see the Hoobin boy alive?"

"I wouldn't say you were wrong in that, Mr. Appleby."

"But you think it's improbable that we're any longer investigating anything in the nature of a series of practical jokes?"

"I do." Mutlow was wholly decided. "We're investigating murder—and perhaps attempted murder as well."

"But you won't murder somebody by persuading him to hide in a pig-sty."

"There's that Heyhoe."

"Um."

"And old Mrs. Grope. I suppose you'll agree"—Mutlow was massively sarcastic—"that you *do* murder somebody if you persuade him to fall down a well."

"But old Mrs. Grope's falling down the well never roused the faintest suspicion of foul play. It's merely that certain facts the authenticity of which is still extremely doubtful have suggested to us one possible interpretation of these facts. Can you imagine yourself asking your local coroner to reopen the inquest on Mrs. Grope—just on the strength of that interpretation?"

"No, Mr. Appleby, I can not." Mutlow, though not perhaps distinguished by any talent for seeing life whole, had a capacity for seeing minute sections of it with tolerable steadiness. "But the point is that Mrs. Grope was Heyhoe's mother. And you can't get away with Heyhoe."

"I shouldn't at all want to attempt anything so disagreeable. But if you're going hot-foot after homicide you may find Heyhoe a broken reed. What do you think the doctors will say he died of?"

Mutlow hesitated. "Exposure."

"Precisely. And how do you know he didn't die of exposure *before* he was buried in that grotesque way? He was old, drunken, and wandering about on a freezing night. Within an hour the fact of his being dead would be indubitable to anyone who came upon him. His burial after that would simply bring us back to the level of macabre joking."

In the faint light from the instruments Mutlow looked genuinely shocked. "It would still be a crime," he said briefly and after a pause.

"That's very true. A judge would take an uncommonly dark view of it. But how would Ranulph Raven regard it? For that's the question."

Mutlow swung round and stared at his companion. "Ranulph Raven! I don't understand this Raven business at all. It seems plumb crazy to me. How should he come in?"

"Because everything that's been happening—and more has

been happening than you've heard of yet—is related either closely or vaguely to something or other in this old fellow Ranulph Raven's books. It's a correspondence so odd that it's difficult to recognize. For instance, you yourself have told me the story of some yarn of Ranulph's you once read as a boy, while quite failing to see that it bears a point by point resemblance to all this turning-to-stone business at Tiffin Place."

"Good lord!"

"Why was Sir Mulberry—a notably courageous man—rattled or scared by those idiotic incidents? Because buried somewhere in his mind—and at a level where one can bring very little sense of proportion or common sense to bear—he had this yarn of Ranulph's. And if the analogy from that yarn—*The Medusa Head*—continued it would be his wife, Lady Farmer, who would be overtaken by some uncanny fate in the end. That's clear enough. And in this affair a little clarity is pretty well worth its weight in gold."

"It is that, Mr. Appleby. And I would like to be well rid of it, I don't mind telling you. But this sorcery—"

"And now, Heyhoe." As the little car hummed through the late evening Appleby was settling down to something like a review of the case. "Again there is a correspondence with a Ranulph Raven story—or something like. But first you must realize this: just as these recent events hitch on to Ranulph stories, so often do the stories themselves hitch on to events in the past. Ranulph, that's to say, wrote up actual incidents and sensations round about him. There's nothing odd in that. But sometimes he wrote up fantasies: the things actual people whom he met confessed to him they dreamed of. As a consequence of this we have something much more remarkable: *Ranulph Raven stories sometimes had the appearance of coming true*. Put it like this. He wandered about this countryside, and he had a certain power of reading people's *futures*. He would get at bents, plans, ambitions, some of which would be sinister or sensational. Some of these he would write up. And some of these again—very few, but enough to attach notions of the uncanny to him—would later actually fulfil themselves. Now Heyhoe—"

"Wait a minute!" There was a quite new sharpness in Mutlow's voice. "Was he proud of this? Did he make a business of it?"

"Yes—or at least I fancy so." Appleby glanced with unusual interest at his companion.

"He would like this notion of a yarn coming true. It would amuse him to think of such a thing happening long after he was dead. And what *is* happening? What that old fellow Smith said. Something just like a Ranulph Raven story. And it's happening in his own family. An honest Victorian story of doubtful heirs and—yes, by heaven!—secret marriages. Lord knows what sense can be in all the details, Mr. Appleby. But the core of the thing is clear. Ranulph was *married* to Mrs. Grope; and Heyhoe, therefore, was legitimate. Heyhoe was *married* to Mrs. Hoobin. That's it! A perfect Raven yarn. Hannah Hoobin's boy is the legitimate heir of Dream."

"Well, well!" Appleby's voice held considerable respect. "You mean that there is probably a Raven story that runs on these lines, and that it amused Ranulph to plan for its coming true bang in the next generation of his own family? Decidedly a sardonic humour he must have had. But it's not impossible. It's not impossible, at least, that his own valid marriage was with Heyhoe's mother, and that he had a mind perverted enough to take pleasure in the idea of complications resulting some day. But he certainly could not have had any hand in planning the legitimacy of Hannah Hoobin's boy—who was begotten by Heyhoe some twenty or thirty years after Ranulph's death. There's a snag there."

"Maybe so. But scrap the notion of malice or design on Ranulph Raven's part and simply put it like this, Mr. Appleby. As a young man he was foolish enough to marry the woman who later became Mrs. Grope. Somehow he kept it quiet, and the man we call Heyhoe, who was really his heir, lived at Dream as a servant. Eventually Heyhoe married—also for some reason clandestinely. He married this woman who is now Mrs. Hoobin and there was born to them the half-witted boy. You see what that means. A place like Dream is entailed to legitimate issue, no doubt. So the present squire, Mr. Everard, and all the crowd of Ravens who live with him, have no real right to the place at all. Very well. Suppose now, they find out that old Mrs. Grope knows the truth—"

"In that case, wouldn't she have proclaimed it long ago? If she knew herself to have been Ranulph Raven's wife, and her son Heyhoe entitled to rank as a gentleman, surely she would sooner or later have come forward with it."

Mutlow shook his head. "We don't know the early circumstances. Ranulph may have been Mrs. Grope's first lover. Conceivably she may have believed herself to have been seduced by means of a mock marriage, and only later have discovered that it was valid—by which time she may have been scared of the Gropes. But as an old woman she would become independent again, and perhaps try blackmailing the folk at Dream. Whereupon she fell down a well."

"And then?"

"The Ravens got busy and ferreted out the fact that the half-wit too was legitimate. So both he and Heyhoe had to go."

Appleby laughed. "They had to go. But the boy didn't go. He stopped in a pig-sty. As for Heyhoe, he went all right—but not at all after the fashion of his mama. Mrs. Grope had an accident on a dark night. Heyhoe too was out on a dark night. But instead of having an accident which might get two or three lines in a local rag, he dies in conditions so fantastic that to-morrow every national paper will very likely be splashing them. Moreover he is found under circumstances that directly parallel a Ranulph Raven story." Appleby frowned. "No, that's not right. He is found under circumstances which recall some actual happening in the neighbourhood long ago. Billy Bidewell's grandmother told him of it—the story of a fearful maid who came upon what appeared to be a severed head grimacing upon the ground. Ranulph may have known the story, but seemingly he never wrote it up—for the Heyhoe affair doesn't suggest any part of his writings to Miss Raven, and she knows them well. So where are we—if your theory is sound? The Ravens have decided on eliminating their legitimate relation Heyhoe—and they do it after a sensational fashion, reminiscent of a story Ranulph didn't write, and of a kind certain to attain the widest notoriety. Moreover, they have already set an authentic Ranulph story—The Medusa Head—in operation at Tiffin Place, seemingly as part of a plot against Heyhoe's half-wit son. This too will be sure of publicity now, and it is linked in turn with tricks they must simply have perpetrated upon themselves: notably

the *Paxton's Destined Hour* trick, seemingly directed at Luke
Raven. They make all this pother—and to absolutely no purpose. Or rather what is achieved is exactly the reverse of what
they could conceivably be expected to desire. For the boy is
unharmed—he has had to survive nothing worse than roast
pork three times a day in a pig-sty—and a veritable spot-light
of publicity is thrown upon the Raven family history over
three generations. Now the Ravens, my dear Mutlow, are able
people. That they should make such an absurd hash of pre-
serving their property is incredible. Intellectually incredible.
But your theory is psychologically incredible too. The Ravens
are not the sort of people who bother about property—which
is why it fades out on them. They're the artistic sort, who
mildly and intermittently feel that it's nice to have money
about, and who are prepared to use their wits occasionally
to get it. But none of them would push an old woman down
a well, or refrigerate a half-brother to death. Yours is as
ingenious a theory as a colleague has ever presented me with.
I congratulate you on it sincerely. But it won't do. Not only
are there parts not built in—"

"Needles, Mr. Appleby. The needles put into the haystack
to serve as red herrings."

Appleby shook his head. "I don't think so—for the simple
reason that they're *not* red herrings. They're not drawn *across*
the trail; they're *on* it. They lead back to Ranulph Raven and
his stories. They've made us keep our eye on Ranulph and his
kind of yarn, and so set us on this notion of legitimate marriages and so forth within twenty-four hours of our really
getting to grips with the case—within twenty-four hours of
Heyhoe's death. The blind man—have I told you about that?
—and *The Coach of Cacus* and *Paxton's Destined Hour* and
The Medusa Head and the gentleman who took an earth bath
in his spinney: all these are not red herrings; they're spotlights. We'll get at the truth if we just stick to that."

Mutlow laughed—with unexpected heartiness and satisfaction. It seemed as if Colonel Pike's harassed henchman was
taking hold of the notion that there could be simple joy in
the chase. "Mrs. Ulstrup's cake," he said; "I don't know that
there's much spot-light about that. On the other hand it's certainly a part not yet built in. And I dare say you're right,
Mr. Appleby—or I don't say you're not. And there'll be a

spot-light on us, sure enough; let's hope we cut a decent figure in it. Which means finding the villain of the piece and laying him by the heels."

Appleby considered. "We may find him," he said carefully. "But I doubt whether we shall lay him by the heels."

Mutlow drove for some seconds in silence. "It would be hard to tell just what you mean by that."

"What if the villain of the piece died last night?"

"Heyhoe! How in the world could he be responsible for all this? But, if so, he's escaped justice all right."

"Undoubtedly. Except perhaps the poetic kind."

"Now, Mr. Appleby, that's another queer saying. You really think Heyhoe was responsible for all those freaks?"

Appleby turned up his coat-collar against the chill evening air. "I wouldn't mind betting," he said, "that you'll be convinced of it before the night's over."

Chapter 16

"HALF-PAST seven," said Mutlow. "You'll be glad to get back to a bit of dinner and the young lady, I don't doubt."

"Decidedly," said Appleby.

"And, however it may be about Heyhoe"—Mutlow was encouraging—"I shouldn't be surprised if you get the whole business finally sorted out in the morning. For you must be called a fast worker, Mr. Appleby, if we may judge by the speed with which you've hitched yourself up."

"Miss Raven has had her part."

"Of course she has." Mutlow, whose feelings were now evidently of the friendliest, switched from jocoseness to tactful understanding. "I quite well remember how it is. Would you have any idea when you would be getting married?"

"I haven't discussed the point. But if required to guess I should say Thursday or Friday."

"Is that so, now?" Mutlow seemed somewhat awed. "It shows that as often as you step on a train or a bus you just don't know. In the midst of life—"

"I hope it won't be as bad as that. By the way, it looks rather as if Dream is on fire."

"Good heavens!" Mutlow stared ahead and pressed his foot on the accelerator. "I believe you're right, Mr. Appleby. And here's the avenue."

The car swung off the road and now straight ahead of them a bright glow lit the sky. From somewhere ahead, too, came the roar of a powerful engine and the raucous hoot of a siren. Appleby leant forward, frowning. "Odd," he said.

"Odd? It's that blasted Hoobin boy again, take my word for it. You ought to have let me clap him in jail, Mr. Appleby, indeed you ought. But that engine's coming this way. . . . *Look out!*"

A powerful car, with blazing headlights and screaming siren, had hurtled round a curve of the drive and shaved past them, making for the highroad. Mutlow swore and pressed the accelerator again. But Appleby sat back. "It's not a fire," he said. "Whatever it is, it's not a fire. The light's too steady and too yellow. Here comes a motor-bike. And a second one following. Is he coming through our windscreen? No, he's just got past. . . . Good lord!"

They had swung round a final bend and now the ancient manorhouse of the Ravens lay sprawled in front of them. And on a broad, snow-covered lawn before the house a circle of cars was parked, each with its headlights blazing. In the pool of light thus created something like a random camp had been pitched. Folding chairs and tables lay about singly and in groups; at these men sat scribbling in notebooks or tapping at typewriters; at a larger table near the center there was something like a buffet or bar. Hard by this, too, a species of scaffolding was being erected, while two men from amid a huddle of movie cameras shouted directions to the workmen. Engines roared, typewriters clattered, men shouted—and now there was a rush of the particularly quick-witted towards Mutlow's car. The doors were flung open; flashlights spluttered and flared; camera shutters clicked.

"It's not Dream that's being set on fire," Appleby said. "It's the Thames."

Robert Raven stood in the hall, outglowering the Tartars and the Kurds. Scattered about the floor lay a litter of evening papers, and these the manservant Rainbird was endeavouring to clear up. Whereupon Robert Raven would repossess himself of each in turn, briefly scan its front page, toss the paper in air, dust his fingers lightly against each other, and wait for the next. "Billy Bidewell is drunk," he said. "Peggy Pitches has been given eighteen pairs of silk stockings and had her head turned into the bargain. Mark knocked down a man who had got into Judith's studio with a camera—with rather too vigorous a punch, apparently, so that he's lucky not to be in jail. Judith has announced that she's going to be married to you on Wednesday. Everard approves, but Clarissa says that we must insist on the Archbishop of Canterbury's imposing a decent delay." Robert advanced upon Appleby as if meditating some sudden privy injury to his person. "I congratulate you most heartily and hope you will be very happy. To-morrow morning I'll start working you a firescreen. Unless you'd prefer a couple of water-colours of the west wing? I'm rather pleased with the way I get the ivy sometimes. It's stuff with a texture much easier to handle in oil." Inconsequently Robert snatched another paper from Rainbird. "FOLK-LORIST TELLS," he read.

"I beg your pardon?"

"It means Billy Bidewell. BODY IN SNOW. FOLKLORIST TELLS. Some rubbishing story of its once have been quite the thing to bury people in that way. Listen to this. *'The victim once chosen,' said Mr. Bidewell, 'it was only a question of waiting for a heavy fall of snow. Then they would set 'un.' Mr. Bidewell added that his late grandmother, also a well-known folklorist, had frequently told him of an incident which has come to be traditionally known as 'The Tale of the Fearful Maid.' Unfortunately before being able to recount this anecdote Mr. Bidewell, who is a thoughtful young man with something of a scholar's stoop and evidently of a delicate physique, was taken ill and had to retire to his room."* Robert Raven broke off. "Means dead drunk. *It is hoped however that Mr. Bidewell, whose antiquarian knowledge should be of considerable assistance to the police in their investigations, will be well enough to be further interviewed to-morrow."*

Appleby divested himself of Luke Raven's inky cloak. "Stinkweed was rife in the ditches," he said, "and ruddocks were like little leaping flames in every hedge. Once Billy gets going on Gammer Bidewell's story he will leave our rural novelists standing. Did you ever hear of the howling and hollering head?"

"Never." Robert had snatched another paper. "Listen to this, Appleby. DREAM VOYAGE'S GRISLY END. YOUNG SCULPTRESS' ORDEAL."

"Sculptress? A capital word, sure to be specially pleasing to Judith." Appleby picked up a paper on his own account. "STRANGE DEATH IN SNOW," he read. "Rather tame, that one. Good Lord! HAYSTACK REFUGEES FIND HEYHOE RIGID. There's talent there."

"There's atrocious vulgarity, you mean." Robert Raven soke with mild heat. "I'm afraid all this will upset Everard very much. Ever since he started in on this popular work —cheap encyclopædias and so forth—he's been a bit touchy. . . . Who was Gaffer Odgers?"

"Gaffer Odgers?" Appleby was dismayed.

"Listen. *An old friend of the Raven family, Detective-Inspector John Appleby of Scotland Yard, a brilliant young officer frequently in the public eye since his association a number of years ago with the ghastly case of Gaffer Odgers's oven.* . . . It sounds unpleasant."

"And it was unpleasant. By the way, when I marry Judith I shall retire."

"Is that so?" In his ferocious fashion Robert looked more cheerful. "D'you do anything yourself?"

"Do anything? Oh, I see. Well, not watercolours, or anything like that. But I was going to be a farmer before I took to police work, and I expect I'll go back to that."

"Capital. See you keep Judith a big barn. I should divide it up, if I were you." Robert was unexpectedly practical. "Two-thirds studio and one-third nursery, so that she can potter to and fro. As the family increases the proportions will be reversed. Of course, one day she'll have Dream."

"Surely Mark will have that."

"Not a marrying sort—and certainly won't want to live as the bachelor country squire. I'd advise you, by the way, to see to the drains. And talking of drains"—Robert picked up another paper—"can anything be done about all this?"

"I'm afraid not. You see, this is a mere mild beginning; just what rather conservative local journalists were able to get off this morning. The people camped outside now are the experts, and in the morning papers you'll see them really begin to exploit the business." Appleby glanced rapidly down another column. "So far, the really sensational element hasn't been tapped. The local people haven't got on to it. When the odd connections with your father's stories begin to emerge the Dream affair will inevitably be raised to the rank of a first-class sensation. I've had some experience in these matters, and I'm afraid there's no avoiding it. Not even if, like the Farmers over at Tiffin Place, you were pals with half the newspaper proprietors in England. And I suppose you're not?"

"Newspaper people?" Robert was horrified. "Dear me, no. Everard's publishing people are bad enough. Except for their cigars."

"Cigars?" It was Everard Raven's voice, and a moment later the harassed owner of Dream stepped from amid a congeries of Kurds at the foot of the Regency staircase. "Cigars?" Everard threaded his way forward, rather like somebody with a minor speaking part advancing through a crowd of supers. "My dear fellow—my dear John—I'm extremely glad to see you back. This is a very sudden decision of Judith's, but I assure you we are all very pleased—though Clarissa may take a little humouring, I think I ought to say." And Everard shook hands with evident warmth. "In addition to which it has its providential aspect. I mean that you are just the person to advise us in this very embarrassing situation in which we find ourselves. Now, what was I saying?"

"You were saying cigars," said Robert helpfully.

"That's it! D'you know, one of these reporter fellows offered me a cigar? In my own house—and a person I'd never seen in my life before! It is very difficult to know what to do in such untoward situations."

"And what, in fact, did you do?" Robert asked.

"I bowed formally, and rang for Rainbird. Unfortunately Rainbird didn't come. And the fellow didn't in the least understand that I was displeased by his lack of breeding. So I took the cigar. It seemed the simplest thing to do." Everard looked from Robert to Appleby, vaguely troubled. "An entirely trivial incident, of course. But this sort of thing takes one sadly out of one's depth. And—do you know?—one of Adolphus's waxworks is missing. Apparently it has been gone for quite a while. Rainbird says he thought it had gone to be repaired. Who ever heard of repairing a waxwork? Particularly one of Adolphus's." Everard checked himself in this rambling and looked about him in a pathetically bemused way. "But I am altogether forgetting more important things. A suitcase has arrived for you, my dear fellow, and dinner is at half-past eight. And, most important of all"—and Everard beamed with sudden and complete cheerfulness—"here is Mark, who will no doubt find Judith for you. Mark, my dear chap, here is your brother-in-law waiting for you say the right thing."

Mark Raven had appeared from somewhere beneath the staircase; his yellow locks were filmed with cobweb and he was clutching several dusty bottles. "I've found some of Herbert's Mouton Rothschild," he said, "and a stray case of Bristol Cream. So we can look on the bright side, after all." He came forward, shook hands, and stood contemplating Appleby with a sort of malicious remorse. "At the best of times I should say there was only one tolerable way of looking at a projected marriage, and that's through the virtual opacity of a glass of decent claret." Mark glanced from Appleby to his cousins, tossed his head violently, and suddenly ferociously scowled. "Confound it all," he said, "it's a bit thick."

Everard was distressed. "Really, Mark, I'm sure we ought to be extremely pleased. The acquaintance may be short, but if Judith—"

"Don't be silly." Obscurely furious, Mark banged down the Mouton Rothschild in a spine-chilling way on a table. "I knew this was going to happen, the way she looked at him in that railway carriage."

Appleby smiled. "But I felt," he interrupted, "that I was being looked at rather like an unhewn block of soapstone."

"Precisely. That was exactly it." Mark's malicious grin momentarily returned; then he scowled again. "Let them marry, by all means. He seems quite a decent chap—"

Robert Raven, who had been peering at the claret, turned round again with the air of one who has a decisive card to play. "And he's going to farm," he announced.

"—quite a decent chap; and I should say that in Judith he gets a bargain as women go. So far, so good. But what I'm saying is—"

"And here is Luke." Everard turned to where his melancholic brother, in a dinner-jacket and a frayed boiled shirt obscured behind an enormous tie, was descending the staircase with a gloomy deliberation suggestive of a skeleton about to keep a date with a feast. "Luke, my dear fellow, you will be delighted to welcome John, I am sure. And, Mark, if there is to be claret—and I wholly approve—it ought to have been brought up hours ago. How upsetting a state of siege is! Do you know, those people were climbing in by the servants' hall, so that I had to order that the shutters be put up? Now, what was I saying?"

"The claret," said Robert.

"To be sure—the claret. Mark, take it to Rainbird and see what he can do." He turned to Appleby. "And Robert will take you along to the studio. Judith has been working quite steadily all day."

"Except"—Luke Raven spoke for the first time, and in sepulchral tones—"when being subjected to the indignity of interview by the police."

"But it might have been very much worse." Everard, harassed as he was, seemed determined to see the bright side of things. "This fantastic publicity"—he waved a hand as if to indicate the present strange assemblage on the lawns outside—"is very distressing, of course. But think how much more upsetting it would be for Clarissa and Judith if the first dreadful suspicions had proved true!" Everard turned to Appleby. "Perhaps you haven't yet heard? The affair of Heyhoe has grown even more unaccountable, but at the same time rather less grim. We were much shocked by the tenor of the police enquiries this morning. There was minute questioning as to what had happened to each of us after the accident at the ford. As it chanced, we had all separated in quest of assistance, and finally made our journeys home independently. We could not, therefore, render any account of one another's movements. Judge of our horror, then, when it began plainly to appear that some of us were being held suspect of a most atrocious crime!" Everard Raven paused, glanced about him, and shook his head in sudden vexation. "Mark has taken the claret," he said, "but quite forgotten the sherry. And I do like to see sherry in a decanter. But—dear me!—I fear I have quite lost the thread of what I was saying."

"Suspect of a most atrocious crime," said Robert.

"Precisely! It was plainly in these people's mind that some of us had wantonly seized upon this faithful old fellow and buried him in the snow, there to await—"

"But the doctors turned it down." Robert Raven, hitherto extremely patient, seemed to feel that Heyhoe's death was occasion for more matter and less words. "We got a couple of competent ones over later in the morning. And they're quite sure for reasons of their own that the old man died first and was forced into the snow drift afterwards. He had a bottle of gin, it seems; and he went wandering about in the snow, and the gin was too much for him. Then somebody found him, dead as a door nail, and played this queer trick. As Everard says, it makes the whole affair more unaccountable than ever."

"I think not." Appleby shook his head decidedly. "There are one or two rather puzzling elements in the whole matter, it can't be denied. For instance, there is a little affair of a piece of cake which is at present worrying me a good deal. But if there was reason to suppose that Heyhoe had been murdered I should be very puzzled and worried indeed."

Everard Raven looked bewildered. "I'm afraid I don't at all follow you. Can you tell us why?"

"Because Murder and the Fine Arts are never bedfellows—whatever De Quincey may say."

But for once even a literary allusion appeared to give no pleasure to the editor of the *New Millennium*. He passed his hand over his brow. "How much I wish," he exclaimed, "that this was all over! Coming upon the usual quiet tenor of our life at Dream, it is really very disturbing—very disturbing indeed."

Luke Raven, who had been communing quietly with a Kurd in a corner, raised first his eyes and then his long and beautiful hands. Broodingly he gazed at these, as if taking satisfaction in penetrating to their enduring skeleton. "Disturbing?" he echoed. "Know that what disturbs our blood is but its longing for the tomb." He took out his watch and gazed at it as one who knows that every second spans out man's mortality. "I wonder," he said, "if they managed to get any potatoes? There are few things so good as a roast potato for allaying the fever of the bone."

Chapter 17

JUDITH RAVEN put down her mallet. "Well?" she said presently.

"Appleby's End." Appleby looked at his affianced bride with a good deal of natural curiosity. "I think we might begin with that. Is there a story of Ranulph's called Appleby's End?"

"Yes. The place had that name long before there was a railway station. And I suppose it caught his eye."

"I see. And is it about a man who is invited to stay at a strange house with sinister consequences?"

"He doesn't get married." On Judith's face there was a faint replica of Mark's malicious smile. "But sinister is the word. Spooky doings in long, gusty corridors, with the carpets rising on the floors and the rain driving and the ivy tapping on the window panes. And madness ending all."

"You're not mildly apprehensive? You won't mind being tied for life to a madman?"

"I'm not apprehensive."

"Or annoyed?"

Judith frowned. "That's very hard to answer. If Ranulph's ghost brought you here for sinister purposes—ineffective, mind you, so I'm *not* apprehensive—he at least *did* bring you here. I'm not quarrelling with him. Come and look at the Appleby Memorial."

They turned round and faced the long studio, which occupied the ground floor of an entire wing of the house. Now somewhat ineffectively lit by lamps slung near the ceiling, it showed as vast and cavernous; and its chilliness on this winter evening was accentuated by the familiar marmoreal glitter of Theodore Raven's massive statuary. Colossal torsos, involved figure compositions, prowling or crouching animals lay about without care of disposition as in some Cyclopean fantasy; near at hand they writhed and contorted themselves in an ecstasy of eternally thwarted muscular effort; farther off, shadows compassionately enfolded them until in the recesses of the studio they lost distinguishable form and showed like

153

icebergs looming in a mist, their cold breath going out before them. But what lent strangeness to the scene was the fact that these inferior productions of Theodore's genius had become a quarry for the exploring chisel of his descendant. Some had radically changed their very mode of being. Of Thusnelda in Chains only a pair of manacled limbs remained; the rest of her had been worked over with a cunningly obliterating hand until she showed like a vast pebble long polished by an infinite sea—a pebble deep within which slumbered some rudimentary vital form. Others had undergone a metamorphosis startlingly partial. General Wolfe reading Gray's Elegy before Quebec displayed the musing soldier unconscious that his legs were turned to gnarled roots and his arms to branches—while behind him stood an untouched aide-de-camp, stolidly regardless of this martial Daphne's leafy change. Stout Cortez stared at the Pacific as intently as was possible to one whose head had turned to a flaming torch, and Xerxes as he wrote his Cartel of Defiance to Mount Athos was ignorant that his broad back had taken on the form of a chest of drawers. But these surrealist flights were in a minority; on stands and trestles all about the room were Judith's Objects: spheres and cubes and ovals in groups of two and three and four—conversation pieces from some private universe in which the abstractions of solid geometry owned a mysterious life of their own.

For a time Appleby moved silently and attentively from composition to composition. It was an austere world and markedly superior to Gaffer Odgers's; even its nightmares—and he glanced back at Xerxes—had their lurking meaning —which Gaffer Odgers assuredly never had. . . . He stopped before an effort of Theodore's which appeared to represent a charging buffalo. "Have you," he asked, "missed a cow, and a boar, and a dog?"

Judith puffed dust from the buffalo's threatening horns. "There's a cow and a boar and a dog missing," she said carefully.

Appleby moved on, and paused again before one of Theodore's vainly soliciting goddesses. "Mark said it was a bit thick," he said.

"A bit thick? One has to thicken the neck and the ankles and so on, so as not to break the line." And Judith stared at Theodore's goddess with a grave innocence.

"But then you said just the same last night. That it was a bit thick, and a false position. And do you remember how you told me that you have a compact with Mark not to tell each other fibs? Is that going to apply to me?"

"Yes."

"Then isn't it going to be—"

"I'm marrying you for your wits—partly." Judith, who had appeared troubled, was now looking at him again in simple mischief. "I expect to see you work it out for yourself. And I don't need to tell you either fibs or otherwise. I can just keep mum."

"But can you keep mum—for instance, about last night? That Heyhoe business gave you a bit of a shock?"

They were now standing before one of Theodore's works in a sentimental mode: a mother with a child in her arms. But the child had been chiselled down to represent a skeleton, and the mother's head had become a skull. "The Heyhoe business?" said Judith gravely. "Well, I did find it rather macabre."

"And disconcerting in that it didn't hitch on to any Ranulph story?"

"Quite so."

"I've discovered it hitches on to what might well be a Ranulph story—only he doesn't seem to have written it. Billy Bidewell—"

"Ranulph did write it." For a moment Judith seemed tired and impatient. "Only it was never published. Everard told me this morning." She looked at the statue before them in evident distaste and ran a finger cautiously along one of the child's ribs. "My salad days," she said, "when I was green in judgment. But what ever shall I do when Theodore is all used up?" She paused. "John, what first struck you about this whole business?"

"That it was the work of an artist—and therefore quite probably of somebody with Raven blood. Perhaps of somebody interested in dreams because brought up at a place called Dream. For dreams, you know, use whatever is lying about. A dream takes up a hundred hints from the common business of the day and weaves them into whatever structure it has on hand. A man called Appleby and a place called Appleby's End: there's pure dream material in that—and it's not been missed." He paused and looked seriously at Judith. "Only, of course, this is a thoroughly practical and business-like dream—or was meant to be."

"And you seem to be a thoroughly businesslike analyst." Judith looked at her watch. "Only ten minutes to get into other clothes." She moved towards the door, and then halted. "If I *were* marrying you for your wits it looks as if I should be getting a bargain. For I take it you have the whole affair taped?"

"I don't understand it all, by any means. And—what's more —I doubt if anybody does."

Judith looked at him, open eyed. "Is that just being oracular? Is it the professional manner?"

"It is not. I'm not bringing anything professional into all this. You see, there's enough trouble been brought in already. Heyhoe's death, chiefly—which is what has brought down all that mob of journalists and reporters. It's exciting, no doubt. Quite wakes the place up, doesn't it? Heyhoe died, and there was his body lying in some lane, and the dream-artificer promptly exploited the fact and made the correct move. It was a bit macabre, as you were pleased to say. It was also a mistake. This ingenious dreamer overreached himself. In England one can't do that with a body—however dead—and get away with it. The explanation will be demanded—and will continue to be demanded, even if half-a-dozen of my colleagues are sent down from the Yard in turn and fail. Not that they would fail, for there are lots of them a good deal smarter than I am."

Appleby was now pacing up and down the chill studio with a vigour that sent little clouds of marble dust eddying round his feet. Judith had sat down on the stomach of a Dying Gaul and was eyeing him warily—and at the same time with rather more satisfaction than wariness.

"That's the first spot of trouble, Judith Raven. It's either awkwardness at the next assizes or compounding a felony—if it can be done."

"But in Sherlock Holmes there's a man who conceals the body of his wife after she dies in a vault or something until he can meet his creditors by winning a horse race. He even gets somebody to impersonate her—and nobody has impersonated Heyhoe, have they? And he doesn't get into any trouble at all. The coroner is most sympathetic."

"Bother Sherlock Holmes. And you may take it from me that the judge won't be sympathetic—quite contrariwise. And that's only trouble number one. Trouble number two concerns the habits of hares."

"Of *hares?*"

"Of hares. That's the unknown element at the moment. And trouble number three is that it looks as if the engineer is going to be hoist with his own petard." Appleby halted. "I suggested to the local police inspector that perhaps in the burying of Heyhoe there was a sort of poetic justice. That's as may be—and Mutlow will go away and chew on it. But possibly poetic justice isn't going to stop there." Appleby paused. "Judith, how would you describe the whole business from *The Coach of Cacus* incident down through Luke's tombstone to the present moment?"

"Describe it, John? I think I should describe it as blocking out. But that's a sculptor's word. Call it spade work."

"Precisely. But what if it's labouring another man's ground?"

"I don't understand you a bit."

"Or if the spade went right into a nest of hornets?" Appleby opened the door. "You know what's been happening at Tiffin Place?"

Judith hesitated for a moment. "You're asking too many questions. But, yes—I do."

"Our reporter friends will be on to that in no time. And to much else—for the thing ramifies like anything, as you very well know. A great big rambling mystery—if not too complex—is just meat and drink to them. But—mark you—it needs a focus. And that's where Heyhoe was to come in. A sound instinct there, no doubt. Still, I don't know that Heyhoe *will* quite do—or not now. You see, for newspaper purposes the core of the thing ought to be murder." Appleby was pacing up and down again. "A blood-soaked hatchet. Brains scattered about the carpet. Something going bad inside a trunk. Dismembered—"

"Shut up, for goodness' sake."

"Very well. But what's *not* wanted is something finical, and merely finical. A series of odd happenings, linked together in rather a complicated way by an obscure and rather literary thread, a booksy thread—" Appleby paused and stared thoughtfully into the gathering darkness of the studio, where Judith was now extinguishing the lamps. "It's not really satisfactory—or not without a centre in some brute and readily intelligible fact. And Heyhoe isn't quite that—or not now. But the whole thing has possibilities still, they'll feel. And so they'll cast about. . . . Judith, do you remember old Mrs. Grope?"

"You mean Gregory Grope's grandmother?" Judith looked puzzled. "I remember her very well. She had some sort of accident."

"She came to a mysterious end on a dirty night."

"Like Heyhoe, you mean? Is that what you're driving at?"

"Exactly so. And she was Heyhoe's mother."

Judith looked completely startled. *"Heyhoe's mother?* I had absolutely no idea—"

"I know you hadn't. There's quite a lot in this business that you had no idea of. In fact, that none of you had any idea of. And that's the trouble. Moreover, there are still mysterious things happening that I don't understand myself—though I'm beginning to have a glimmering. So we have two jobs in front of us."

"Two? I should have thought one was enough."

"Two. Getting to the heart of the mystery." Appleby chuckled. "And getting away again."

They returned down a long corridor hung with vast canvases dimly discerned. Broken wheels, the bellies of horses, gleaming steel, patches of scarlet and gold, cannon mouths flowed endlessly past them; once they came to a corner and were abruptly confronted with a line of bayonets; a little farther on, the rays of a solitary lamp fell dramatically on a soldier who brandished a sword in one hand while with the other, and with two rows of admirably regular teeth, he contrived to tie a bandage round an extensively shattered knee.

"Great-aunt Elizabeth," Judith said. "She admired Lady Butler and tried the same line herself. She was a friend of Tennyson's, and particularly good at breaking down in the right place when he read his poetry aloud. We don't know whether he broke down when she showed him her battle-pieces. . . . Hullo, Rainbird seems to be holding the fort. And against the police, too. Does that mean we are all going to be rounded up?"

A flurry of cold air blew down the cavernous hall where the Kurds and Tartars, in ranks as stiff and unwavering as one of great-aunt Elizabeth's British regiments under fire, opposed a hostile immobility to a constable who was talking urgently to Rainbird through an open glass door.

"The household," Rainbird was saying firmly, "is about to dine. Come back, young man, in a couple of hours. And if you want something to do in the meantime go and clear those folk off the lawn. Pitched themselves there without Mr. Raven's invitation, they have; and it's plain trespass." Rainbird peered out into the night. "A good many of them gone, I'm glad to see. But there's three or four cars there still."

"The cars be no business of mine."

"Then they ought to be. What's the good of a gentleman paying his taxes if the likes of you can't see that he's permitted to live undisturbed on his own estate?" As he uttered this manorial sentiment Rainbird endeavoured to edge the door to.

But the constable was obstinate. "Them as wants to live undisturbed," he said, "ought to avoid carryings-on. And, by all accounts, there's been a power of carryings-on at Dream."

"There has been untoward circumstances." Rainbird was dignified. "There has been untoward circumstances, without a doubt. But your sphere, my lad, is protecting cottagers' poultry. Now, be off with you."

"I mun see 'un." Under stress of an offended dignity the constable was becoming as massively rural as Billy Bidewell. "Here be message for Inspector Appleby."

"Mr. John"—Rainbird pronounced these words presumably for the first time, and with great formality—"Mr. John is dressing for dinner and not to be disturbed for the convenience of his professional subordinates. If you care to wait we shall be pleased to accommodate you with a chair in the servants' hall. In which case you'll kindly step round to the back and enter by the offices."

Appleby came forward. "All right, Rainbird; I haven't gone to change yet." He turned to the constable. "Now then, what is it—a message from Inspector Mutlow?"

"Yes, sir. He sent me across as soon as he got in. It's about Woolworth, sir."

"Woolworth—the threepence and sixpence-a-time fellow?"

"No, sir." The constable looked mystified. "Ten shillings a time, he be."

"Who be?"

"Woolworth, sir. Woolworth be the Sturrocks' bull, over Tew-way."

"I see. Well, what's happened to Woolworth?"

The constable lowered his voice. "Sturrock do say some-one put the pins to 'un."

"Put the pins to him! Do you mean that somebody has been using this old, unhappy creature as a pin-cushion?"

"Witchcraft!" Judith had come forward and addressed the constable. "They found a model of Woolworth?"

"Yes, miss. Very nicely done in clay, it was, and hid right in Woolworth's straw. And pins, miss, so that Sturrock be afeard that poor Woolworth—"

"When was this discovered?" Appleby was glancing through the outer door and up the long dark drive to where the head-lights of a car were sweeping towards Dream.

"Not an hour since, sir. And Inspector Mutlow thought it was important-like—"

"He was perfectly correct. Moreover, it is most vital that the affair should be widely known at once. Did you ever have your picture in the papers? No? Well, here's your chance. Over there on the lawn there are several gentlemen in cars. Tell them you've got something new. Tell them you oughtn't really to mention it—"

The constable scratched his head, much bewildered. "But you just said, sir, as how the affair—"

"My dear man, it's nice to have your picture in the papers —but why not have five pounds as well? Tell them you rather think it's confidential still—and then give them Woolworth hot and strong. Ram home the pins good and hearty. Good night." And Appleby gave the constable a friendly but decisive shove and shut the door.

Judith was looking at Appleby in complete bewilderment. "Witchcraft," she repeated. "But it just doesn't fit in or make sense. It's got nothing to do with us. And why should you be so keen—"

"You know my methods, Judith." Appleby's eye had brightened; he was contemplating Rainbird as if inspiration glinted from every crease of that melancholic serving-man's frayed shirt. "Weren't you citing Sherlock Holmes? Well, he had nothing on this. And—listen!—the next batch of mysterious strangers is arriving. We must seclude ourselves." And Appleby grabbed Judith by the wrist and hauled her within one of those curious contrivances, midway between a sentry-box and a family sarcophagus, which the eighteenth century considerately provided for the porters in its draughty halls. Rainbird, faintly raising an eyebrow at the skittishness of young engaged persons, opened the door once more. For a car had drawn up outside, and now two men were advancing side by side up the steps. Appleby peered out at them. "Observe," he said in a hoarse whisper, "that the taller of the two has recently changed his occupation. How do I know, Judith? Elementary, my dear. He has the weaver's tooth and the compositor's thumb; no other deduction is possible! And the shorter—what shall we say of him? Is he a musician, or does he work a typewriter? Mark a certain refinement about the features—"

"Do shut up. It's—"

"—but mark too the worn line two inches above the cuff—"

"You silly ass!" With a strength born of much kneading of clay, Judith vigorously pinched her fiancé on the thigh. "It's Mr. Scott, the publisher."

"Of course it is. Ranulph Raven's publisher. And the other fellow is no one less than Liddell, the news editor of the *Blare*. What would he be doing round these parts, I wonder? But Rainbird is receiving them coldly. You can tell from the back of his neck that there is a frosty gleam in his eye. Publisher Scott is claiming old acquaintance. Editor Liddell is producing his card. Rainbird sees nothing for it but to show them into the library. Editor Liddell is plainly a stranger; he edges apprehensively past the first rank of Tartars—"

Judith scrambled out of the sarcophagus. "If you do retire from the police why not get a job as a radio commentator? The Mayor has finished his speech. There is breathless expectation in the crowd. And now Lady Augusta has risen. I think —yes, I think—that the Mayor is about to hand her the trowel. We'll be certain of that in a minute. It's a lovely afternoon, a perfect afternoon; there must be at least four hundred people here; five hundred, perhaps I should say. Lady Augusta has taken the trowel; there's a man standing by with some mortar all ready—"

"And here comes Everard. He looks worried. Can it be that he is wondering whether the cabbage soup will go round?" Appleby followed Judith across the hall. Everard Raven, once more in his faded pink wine-jacket, stopped on seeing them.

"Judith, here is Scott come unexpectedly down. I wonder what can bring him to Dream? We must welcome him, of course, though I fear his visit must be described as a shade untimely. However, it will be a pleasure to have him meet John."

"Perhaps that's why he has come," said Judith gravely. "And isn't there somebody else?"

Everard glanced at a slip of pasteboard in his hand and looked more worried still. "A fellow who seems to have given him a lift. Another of these intolerable journalists, I fear."

"News editor of the *Blare*," Appleby said.

"Dear me! Well, Rainbird must simply turn him out. He must invite him out of the library and tell him pointedly that I am not at home." Everard glanced at the card again. "A. H. Liddell. It wouldn't be Archie Hamilton Liddell, by any chance?"

"That's the man." Appleby was decided. "Used to sign articles as A. Hamilton Liddell."

"Oh dear, oh dear!" Everard's voice rose to something like a wail of despair. "We were up at Corpus together. And Corpus men always continue to acknowledge each other, I suppose you know. An excellent custom, I am sure. Have you ever remarked the cold glare that marks the meeting of Balliol men wherever they be? Judith, I am afraid he must be asked to dine. Pray see Clarissa and let her speak to Rainbird and have him approach cook. It may be that there are some tins of sardines—" And, agitatedly dodging Kurds and Tartars, Everard toddled off across the hall.

"Well, well!" said Appleby. He looked speculatively at Judith. "And all for Hannah Hoobin's boy."

Chapter 18

THE DINING-ROOM had been illuminated with unwonted splendour; one could see the cobwebs in the corners, and the places where the wallpaper was peeling off, and a large patch of green and brown and yellow where the damp was coming through. But one could also see more of the artistic treasures of the Ravens, for hung round the room in pairs were the masterpieces of Gawain Raven R.A. (1827–1884) and Mordred Raven A.R.A. (1840–1900). Gawain, like Jan Davidsz de Heem and Adriaen van Utrecht, appeared to have painted straight from his stomach; his canvases were a riot of boars newly slaughtered, hams long since cured and now part demolished, half-empty glasses of wine, meat, game and vegetables piled in cornucopian profusion, and in the corners oranges and lemons carefully studied while in process of peeling. Mordred had painted from elsewhere; Susannah and the Elders was the subject by which his imagination had been most compelled, and covering the greater part of all his canvases were ladies so uniformly rosy that one was compelled to suppose him as having worked exclusively from models who had come straight from an uncomfortably hot bath. Occasionally Gawain appeared to have painted in a good square feed for Mordred's nymphs and goddesses—commonly in the form of an inordinate picnic displayed upon a grassy sward. And once or twice Mordred had provided Gawain with a background in which female forms, browned to a duskier hue, disported themselves on the surface of a canvas within the canvas. But this scarcely mitigated the somewhat overpowering regularity with which the pictures delivered their alternate summons to bed and board; and there was positive relief to the appetites as well as to the eye in certain large blank spaces arbitrarily disposed about the walls. It was to be suspected that the Ravens had been compelled at times to eat their way not only through copies of Dodsley's Miscellany, Dryden's Fables, and the voluminous works of Voltaire in full calf, but also through the fantasmal boars, hares, cucumbers and pineapples of Gawain's inspiration—and even to submit to the further indignity of being supported by whatever Mordred's rose-red Paphians could bring in. A critic of the family unamiably disposed might have maintained that their behaviour-pattern approximate to that of a cannibal culture of the baser and more utilitarian kind. They devoured their kinsmen not for the sake of any mysterious power thereby gained, but simply of necessity when having a thin time. And this state of affairs—Appleby reflected as he sipped his claret —had its place in the deplorable mystery which it was now so desirable to elucidate or dispel.

And meanwhile the mystery held the board. Everard Raven had made some attempt to treat it as a subject unsuitable for present airing, but any resolution he brought to this course had been defeated by the general inclination of the company. Mr. Liddell was openly curious; Mr. Scott was discreetly so; and of the family only Miss Clarissa appeared to be entirely un-oppressed by a sense of awkward issues pending. For the soup had been not cabbage but artichoke; a mushroom omelet had followed; and now at a side table Rainbird was operating upon a noble loin of pork. These dishes, although possibly not of the first elegance, were amply sufficient to vindicate the dignity of the establishment—and moreover Peggy Pitches, albeit in a pair of new silk stockings of a shade scarcely congruous with a parlourmaid's attire, was manipulating the vegetable dishes competently enough. Miss Clarissa, therefore, had reason to be soothed. She had even made some entirely amiable remarks to Appleby. And now she was talking to Mr. Scott on her left hand.

"The unfortunate man who died last night," she explained, "was far from reliable. I could not conscientiously describe him as a valued servant."

"His new situation," said Mark, "is scarcely likely to be such that he will require a testimonial."

"Although he had been with us for a number of years. Everard, for how many years had the man Heyhoe been in your employment?"

"Really, Clarissa, I can scarcely tell. Certainly, for a long time."

"Quite so. And he was excellent with Spot, Mr. Scott. And with the two horses we had before Scott—I mean Spot. And with the four horses we had before the two horses we had before—" Miss Clarissa paused, as one to whom a point of interest has just occurred. "Everard," she continued, "I think it might be a good idea to keep four horses again. One would then have no hesitation in calling out the carriage."

"None whatever," said Everard.

"And Bidewell might be put in livery."

"Bidewell?" said Mr. Liddell. "Is that the thoughtful young man with the scholar's stoop?"

"And who has some knowledge," asked Mr. Scott, "of a piece of folklore about a head, which recalls the circumstances of Heyhoe's death?"

"I can scarcely subscribe to the scholar's stoop." Everard Raven fidgeted with the stem of his wine glass. "But, as for the piece of folklore, it does appear—"

"And you have a Ranulph Raven story, turning on the same circumstance, preserved in manuscript?"

"That is so." Everard looked round the table, frowning in perplexity. "But just how—"

"There may be something in this." Mr. Scott tapped the table for emphasis, and turned to Mr. Liddell. "Liddell, don't you agree with me?"

"I am certainly inclined to agree. But, you know, it's uncommonly bewildering."

"Very bewildering indeed," Appleby interjected decidedly. "I don't know that I've ever come across anything more so. A literary sort of affair, too."

"Ah," said Mr. Liddell with distaste. "Booksy."

"Booksy?" said Everard with dismay. "What a dreadful word."

"Exactly so. All this odd echoing of Ranulph Raven's stories—"

"Is most absorbingly interesting," said Mr. Scott.

"Interesting?" Mr. Liddell shook his head. "To you and me—yes. I don't mind saying that I shall be uncommonly intrigued to hear the explanation of it. But whether we could put it across—well, that's another matter."

Everard Raven set down his glass. "Put it across? Really, my dear Liddell, I quite fail to understand you. Here is a series of unaccountable events, most distressing to us all—and our only concern must be to avoid a vulgar scandal. I realize your professional interest in the affair, but I am sure that as an old friend you will agree to view that matter in a different way from these newspaper people who have been crowding about all afternoon. Indeed, I am hoping that you may have sufficient influence with them to—well, to tone the affair down. Nothing would dismay us more than some horrible form of publicity."

"It would be most repugnant to us," said Robert Raven—mildly and with a ferocious grimace.

"Entirely contrary to our family traditions," said Luke.

Mark tilted his chin and emptied a glass of claret. "We should never hold up our heads again," he said.

"Oh, come, come." Mr. Scott looked alarmed. "You must all please take a rational view of the affair. Just what the explanation of all these odd happenings can be I don't profess to know. But you must realize that the public is bound to be interested—"

"I'm not so sure about that." Mr. Liddell spoke with the gloom of a man who has rather rapidly reached the bottom of his first bottle. "I'm not at all sure about that. It's complicated. And there's what can only be called a strong intellectual element." And Mr. Liddell's features assumed an expression of distaste which was only modified as Rainbird approached with a decanter.

"The public can be *made* interested." Mr. Scott paused. "And we should be quite willing to acknowledge that as being in the nature of a service, my dear Liddell. In fact, there would have to be recognition—tangible recognition—of your part."

Everard Raven poised a spoon absently before Peggy Pitches' bust. "I am entirely at sea," he murmured.

"We are all wholly bewildered." Mark Raven grinned wickedly. "Judith, what can our unexpected guests be after? And can it be possible that your young man knows?"

Mr. Liddell was shaking his head thoughtfully. "I see the force of your argument," he said to Mr. Scott. "But can the thing be handled? That's the question. And I say at once that something very much simpler would have altogether more appeal. That's the opinion of the fellows out there." He gestured towards the garden. "It's got them guessing, I don't mind telling you. So much so, that they've agreed to hold everything till to-morrow. They felt that if they rushed things the whole story would be in a muddle still when to-night's papers were going to bed."

Mr. Scott nodded with satisfaction. "So much the better. We have upwards of twelve hours to get the whole thing planned."

"Simpler?" Appleby interrupted once more. "Have you heard of the sorcery, Mr. Liddell? It seems to have nothing to do with our affairs here at Dream, but you might be interested in it, all the same."

Everard Raven had produced a handkerchief and was mopping his brow. "I think," he said, "that as we are squarely faced with our own untoward affairs we should stick to them and avoid distractions."

"I quite agree, Raven." Mr. Scott was emphatic. "If Mr. Appleby would defer—"

But Mr. Liddell brushed his fellow guest aside. "Sorcery?" he asked curiously.

Appleby nodded. "Only this afternoon I was visiting an old woman of the name of Mrs. Ulstrup in a neighboring village. And—would you believe it?—somebody crept in and stole a piece of cake from her for the purpose of some sort of sinister magic. The local vicar knows quite a lot about it, by the way. It would probably be worth your while to have a chat with him. And then, only a few hours ago, there has been the queer affair of Sturrock's bull."

Mr. Scott set down his knife and fork and glared at Appleby. "To get back to Ranulph Raven—" he began.

But Appleby was explaining about the pins. And Mr. Liddel listened with close attention. "Well, I'm blessed," he said. "Bewitching the poor brute. And a bull, too—not a cow. There's always a bit of appeal in a bull. Yes, that's an uncommonly interesting thing."

Mr. Scott shook his head vigorously. "Interesting? It's quite stupid, if you ask me—and leads nowhere. Now Heyhoe—"

"Very definitely leads somewhere," Appleby broke in. "But how many people know in just what direction? I'm not sure that it wouldn't be as well to leave him alone until we find out."

Everard Raven, harrassed but still mildly cheerful, glanced down the table. "John," he said, "pray let Rainbird give you a little more pork."

It was a piece of hospitable care that was commonplace enough. But its effect was unexpected. Rainbird laid down his carving knife and advanced upon the diners. "Beg pardon, sir," he said. "Beg pardon, marm."

Chapter 19

THE SMALL decorums are those the violation of which is most startling. The company stared at Rainbird as if suddenly whisked into the presence of Balaam's ass. And in the momentary silence there could be heard from outside the curtained windows the roar of motor-car engines starting into life and the crunch of wheels gathering impetus on the snow.

"It was the pork, sir." Rainbird was apologetic. "It was your naming the pork, sir, that made me feel I'd better mention of it."

Everard Raven looked at his butler in astonishment. "Mention it, Rainbird? What in the world are you talking about?"

"Well, sir, nothing exactly in the world at all, if I may so express myself. Or half in the world, like."

Mark Raven turned round to scan the bottles and decanters, apparently suspecting that the explanation of this dark speech might lie in several surreptitiously consumed bumpers.

"The witches, sir." Rainbird's voice sang dramatically. "They've been seen not an hour ago."

"The witches?" Miss Clarissa Raven raised a pair of lorgnettes as if to convince herself that this was still her valued domestic who stood before her. "What witches, Rainbird, in heaven's name?"

"Why, marm, them as was a-trying to sorcerize old Mrs. Ulstrup and put the pins to Woolworth."

Everard Raven shook his head with an expression of unusual irritation. "Nonsense, my good fellow. These are simply old wives' tales that have been going round the district."

"Beg pardon, sir, but Inspector Mutlow says——"

"Inspector Mutlow!" exclaimed Appleby. "Is he here again?"

"Yes, sir. Waiting in the Scriptorium, sir. And Inspector Mutlow says, sir, that the marquis was most emphatic."

Luke Raven, who had been continuing to eat roast pork with the degustatory concentration common in the melancholic, set down his knife and fork. "The marquis!" he cried.

"Just so, sir—and who could ask for a better witness than his lordship—unless it were the duke himself from Scamnum?" Rainbird put this nice point in the law of evidence to the company at large. "The marquis had arranged for a car to meet him at the junction, it appears—at Linger, that is— and seemingly it broke down in the snow. Whereupon, sir"— Rainbird paused with satisfaction on this expression—"whereupon, sir, his lordship was pleased to step into the waiting room. And there the witches was. A whole sabbath of them."

"A sabbath!" Appleby was incredulous.

"Well, sir, at least three. There they was, sir, in Brettingham Scurl's waiting-room."

Judith Raven was looking at Appleby with a mingling of bewilderment and suspicion. "And what, Rainbird," she asked, "were the witches doing in so disagreeable a retreat?"

"If you please, Miss Judith, they was killing swine."

Mr. Scott had sunk back gloomily in his chair. But Mr. Liddell had jumped to his feet. "Do I actually understand—" he began.

Appleby interrupted him. "I suppose, Rainbird, that the witches were provided with a cauldron?"

"I understand they had something of the sort, sir."

"And they would be singing? Something like *"Double, double, toil and trouble, fire burn and cauldron bubble?"*"

Rainbird looked much impressed. "These are the very words, sir. Inspector Mutlow says his lordship noted them very particular. He had a kind of feeling, it seems that he had once heard them in his childhood. But no sooner had his lordship entered the waiting-room than the witches ran out screeching and disappeared, and there was nothing left but the carcass of one of Scurl's Gloucester Old Spots."

Mr. Liddell was still on his feet, and looking round him wildly. "Do you mean to say," he demanded, "that a nobleman of the county is actually prepared to swear that he has had an interview with *witches?*" He paused. "What was all that noise of cars?"

"That would be the gentlemen of the press, sir—those that have been hanging about the grounds. A good many of them, it seems, have driven off to Linger Court."

"Where's my hat? Find my coat!" Mr. Liddell had thrown down his table napkin and pushed back his chair. "There hasn't been a story like this—"

"My dear fellow, pray compose yourself." Everard Raven had risen too and was endeavouring to pat Mr. Liddell back into his seat.

"Have another glass of claret," said Robert.

"Wait for the port," said Luke.

"And the brandy too," said Mark. "We should like you to compare it with what the Longers offer you later in the evening."

"Rainbird," said Miss Clarissa, "I do not recollect one of our guest's having called for his hat and coat before. Possibly it is customary in hotels. Pray gratify Mr. Liddell's wish.

"Really, Clarissa, I must beg you to be calm." Everard was himself extremely agitated. "Liddell is naturally interested in what Rainbird has had to say, but I am sure he will not think of depriving us of his company in the middle of dinner. I am looking forward to offering him one of the Millennium people's excellent cigars."

Mr. Liddell, clearly much torn between professional instinct and social duty, finally sat down again. And Mr. Scott, who during this commotion had been fortifying himself with a couple of glasses of claret, leant earnestly across the table and addressed him. "You must consider, my dear chap, that the Heyhoe affair has already made the late editions to-night. And some rattling good men have been working on it all evening. And I believe the news-reel people have been on to it. The thing's as good as launched."

Mr. Liddell shook his head sulkily. "It's out of to-morrow's dailies, I tell you. And if it's not carried to-morrow evening it's as good as dead. By the next morning nobody will remember anything about it."

"But consider." And Mr. Scott spread out his hands beseechingly. "Consider the whole extraordinary affair. A popular novelist who has been dead for something like half a century—and suddenly his yarns start coming true! Mr. Luke Raven here received a tombstone straight out of a story called

Paxton's Destined Hour. Just think of that. Then, again, a story called *The Medusa Head*—"

"Bad title." Mr. Liddell scowled gloomily at his empty glass. "Not point one per cent of the newspaper public could tell you who Medusa was."

"Never mind, man, never mind! At Tiffin Place the most extraordinary things have been happening, and are a good deal bruited about the district already. A valuable cow—"

"We should have to be dam' careful about Tiffin Place." Mr. Liddell, who had sent an enquiring glance in the direction of Rainbird and the decanters, turned to Mr. Scott again and shook his head solemnly. "Fact is, the folk there are friends of our owner, Sparshott. Name of Farmer, isn't it? And *they* aren't after publicity." Mr. Liddell watched his glass being replenished. "Mind you," he continued in a mollified tone, "I don't criticize you people for wanting to look after yourselves. An affair like this doesn't happen very often, after all." His eye grew abstracted again. "But then, neither does witchcraft these days."

"Look after ourselves?" asked Everard Raven. "How confusing all this is! To a quiet-living scholar like myself, happily engaged on humdrum tasks—"

"Quite so, Raven. Quite so." Mr. Scott waved a hand impatiently. "Now, my dear Liddell, it seems to me that perhaps a little private talk—"

The end of Mr. Scott's sentence was drowned in a sudden uproar from the direction of the kitchens. There were shouts, a scream, the crash of much falling crockery. Then a door flew open and an arm appeared grabbing vainly after a hurtling object apparently compounded of mud, snow and rags. "Keep her out!" the object yelled. "I seen her, I tell you. Followed me right through the spinney, she did. Keep her—" The terrified jabber died away as the object discerned the august company into which his precipitate flight had taken him, and as a face at once awe-struck and tearful was turned towards them it was possible to recognize Gregory Grope's assistant.

"William," said Appleby, "whatever is the meaning of this? And what has been following you?"

Apprehensively William glanced round the room and at the closed doors. His eyes widened as they fell on the resplendent compositions of Gawain and Mordred, and his nostrils perceptibly dilated at the aroma of roast pork. "Please, sir, it was the——" He gulped desperately and fell to snivelling.

"William," Appleby said, "has been out after rabbits and is undoubtedly hungry. We must give him a good square meal. But first perhaps he will tell us——"

"It was the witch, sir." With a great effort William contrived articulate speech. "Followed me right up to the kitchen door, she did, a-waving and a-screeching like anything. I thought I was a sure goner."

"I see. And I suppose she had her broomstick?"

"Yes, sir." William nodded, dark-eyed and breathing quickly. "Her hat and broomstick, sir. And she carried her great big brindled cat. That be how I knew she were the witch."

"Of course it was. And now——"

Once more from outside there came the cough and purr of starting cars. And once more Mr. Liddell leapt to his feet. But this time he made resolutely for the door. "Witches!" he cried. "Your whole countryside teeming with them. Stealing cake. Bewitching bulls. Killing pigs. Pursuing beautiful country boys. By heaven, it's the greatest thing in a decade!" And Mr. Liddell rushed from the room.

There was a moment's bewilderment, and then the rest of the company followed.

"My tombstone!" shouted Luke.

"Sir Mulberry Farmer's marble milker!" called Robert.

"Judith's blind man!" cried Everard.

"Heyhoe and the howling and hollering head!" roared Mark.

"*The Coach of Cacus!*" screamed Mr. Scott. He grabbed Appleby by the buttonhole and endeavoured to hurry him on. "And we didn't tell you about this one," he bellowed. "*Appleby's End*, Liddell. *APPLEBY'S END!*"

Precipitately the Raven household rushed down the long hall, dodging as in some nightmarish obstacle race the impassive Tartars and Kurds. It was in vain. The front door stood open upon an empty lawn. Far down the drive several tail lights faintly glimmered—and even as they looked a large car shot out from the shelter of the east wing and with a wave and a whoop Mr. Liddell was gone. There was a fitful moon. And from the remoter darkness about them came sounds of dispersed and uncertain tumult as the denizens of Sneak and Snarl, of Sleep's Hill and Boxer's Bottom, of Drool and Linger and the nearer Yatters bestirred themselves about the greatest witch-hunt of the age.

Everard Raven gazed out blankly upon the churned-up snow, the vacant lawn, the sprawling eaves and gables of Dream—mysterious, silent, and hung with little icicles that glittered in the moonshine. "A frost," he said. "Scott, my dear fellow—an absolute frost."

Appleby mildly disengaged Mr. Scott's finger and thumb from his button-hole and gave one gentle sigh of relief. He walked over to Judith and took her hand. "A frost, Everard? As a lexicographer you ought to speak more accurately. What you mean is a close shave. But I think there's a visitor coming. I wonder, will he make up for Liddell's departure?"

They looked down the drive once more. From some side path there had emerged a tall figure carrying a bulky gladstone bag. He gave a friendly hail, and presently it was possible to recognize the reverend Mr. Smith. In the crook of his free arm nestled the dignified Hodge.

"Good evening," Mr. Smith called out cheerfully. "Is the hour too unseasonable for a visit?"

Everard Raven looked at him dazedly as he strode up the steps. "Not at all, my dear Smith; not at all. We are delighted to see you at any time. You are on your way home from your pastoral cares?"

"Precisely so." Mr. Smith set Hodge down on the mat. "My evening's activities—which have been not inconsiderable—could scarcely be better put. Rainbird, be so good as to take care of this bag. It contains—um—jam. Bless my soul! What ails the boy?"

William, whose equanimity had been somewhat restored by the prospect of roast pork and who had ventured cautiously into the hall, was once more hollering. And the reason was plain. His eye was fixed on Hodge.

Appleby patted him on the shoulder. "William," he explained, "has just seen a witch. And, as it happens, she appears to have had a cat much like Hodge."

"Dear me!" Mr. Smith picked up his cat and held it out before him. "William," he asked gravely, "do you think this was the witch's cat?"

William once more controlled his snivelling. "Oh, no, Mr. Smith."

"Ah," said Mr. Smith. "Well, well! And I wonder if I might ask Peggy Pitches to give Hodge a saucer of milk?"

Chapter 20

THE DEPARTURE of Mr. Scott was civil but prompt; he shook hands with Clarissa and Everard and walked off austerely into the night. For some moments the owner of Dream rather ruefully watched the dim figure receding down the drive. Then he turned round with resolute cheerfulness. "Well, well, it would have been pleasant to have our friends for a little longer. But perhaps it is even nicer to be just ourselves again. Smith, my dear fellow, you know that I count you as one of the family whenever you care to drop in. And now let us see whether Rainbird can give us coffee in the Scriptorium. And when Peggy Pitches has found Hodge his milk she will give William his roast pork. Yes, we shall make quite a snug evening of it."

"In conversation," said Luke sepulchrally, "with this Inspector Mutlow."

"Dear me—I had quite forgotten him." Everard was dashed. Then he brightened again. "But John, I am sure, will be able to manage all that. And, Mark—you had better go to the library and fetch the Millennium people's cigars. They may help. And brandy. Tell Rainbird to bring the brandy with the coffee. And I wonder if this Inspector Mutlow would care for a pie? Gratifying the physical man is important on these occasions." And Everard Raven as he made this tactful disposition of things beamed with an innocent cunning.

"I am inclined," Appleby said, "to advise against the pie. But the brandy and cigars can do no harm. What can do harm is indiscreet speech. So take your cues from me—and from Mr. Smith."

"From Smith!" Everard was startled. "I hardly see—"

"We must all regard ourselves as hares." Appleby had stopped in the hall and now looked round the group of his future relations. "That's what we are—little hunted hares. And Mutlow is a whole pack of beagles in full cry. And Mr. Smith, here—and his two sons if I am not mistaken—are fellow-hares who have been obliging enough to cross the scent. But the situation is critical still. Now, come along."

The Scriptorium was a room almost as large as Judith's studio, and consisted for the most part of long tables covered with galley-proofs, of innumerable filing cabinets, and of shelves of reference-books prominent among which were encyclopædias in half a dozen European languages. The general effect was efficient but markedly drear—and much as of some unholy cross between a scholar's study and a prison workshop. Had not a spark of rebellion, Appleby reflected as he glanced round, been among the first things he had marked in Everard's eye? Here was the explanation. But the farther end of the room had a less bleak appearance; here there was a circle of sofas and chairs before a large fireplace; and in front of these Inspector Mutlow restlessly paced.

Appleby walked straight forward, and the Ravens somewhat uncertainly followed him. "Mutlow," he said, "it was good of you to come over again. But I really don't know that you ought to have spared the time. This is a bad business that has started up around you."

"It certainly is." Mutlow looked peculiarly solemn. "When once countryfolk get imagining things about witches—"

"Quite so. And the trouble is that you can never be quite sure that there isn't something in it. Mr. Smith, you agree with me? Anyhow, with the inspector as preoccupied as he is going to be it is a good thing that the Tiffin Place and Heyhoe affairs have been cleared up."

"Cleared up?" The dictaphone habit came irresistibly upon Mutlow as he glanced with his familiar air of suspicion round the Raven circle. "I haven't heard of that, now, Mr. Appleby."

"Well, virtually cleared up. I hope you won't go away quite yet. For we really need your help in talking the whole matter out."

"And," said Everard Raven, "you must have a glass of brandy. Robert, bring a rummer."

"And a cigar," said Mark. "Don't hesitate to pick and choose."

"Sugar, Mr. Mutlow?" Clarissa dabbled with her Queen Anne silver. "So intelligent of Rainbird to secure a supply of coffee. A most reliable man."

Appleby sat down near the fire. "I have to explain to you all," he said, "that this afternoon Inspector Mutlow made a most penetrating analysis of the case. Perhaps I should say of the cases, for it was not until he had worked upon the matter that it became apparent that the whole affair was properly one. And now"—and Appleby looked gravely round—"I am sure none of you will want me to mince matters. It will be best that we have the whole truth at once."

"I really think," began Everard apprehensively, "that the presence of the family solicitor—"

"Not at all!" The astuter Robert interrupted sharply. "Let us have the whole truth at once by all means."

"The whole truth," corroborated Luke. "*Ruat coelum.*"

"The whole truth?" Mr. Smith sat back comfortably in his chair. "Here will be novelty, indeed. For I do not recall ever having encountered anything of the sort. Half the truth— yes. Even three-quarters is common enough. The whole truth, however— But I am encroaching upon Inspector Mutlow's time, which is now more valuable even than commonly. Mr. Appleby, pray proceed."

"The truth is this." Appleby's voice had become even graver. "Inspector Mutlow found very good reason for the darkest suspicions against this whole family. The death of old Mrs. Grope, followed by that of Heyhoe, as also by some obscure plot against the unfortunate youth known as Hannah Hoobin's boy—"

"Old Mrs. Grope?" Everard Raven was completely bewildered.

"The woman who is thought to have fallen down a well. Certain circumstances—family circumstances into which, at the moment, I need not enter—made it advantageous to you, Everard, and to the family in general, that first this old Mrs. Grope, and then Heyhoe, and then the boy, should be—well —liquidated."

"Good heavens!" Everard was staring aghast.

"Liquidated?" Luke was so astounded that he positively ceased to look melancholy.

Robert put the brandy decanter down on a table. "This is very serious," he said quietly.

"Quite so. It appeared, I say, that two crimes and one obscure attempt at a crime might be charged against you all. The subsidiary mystifications, such as the affair of Luke's tombstone and the proposed exploiting of a chance encounter with a person named Appleby: all these, it appeared, might be no more than so many false trails. What the inspector, in fact, brilliantly called the extra needles in the haystack."

"The haystack?" said Judith, startled.

Mutlow looked confused. "Yes, Miss Raven. I don't know what put such a figure in my head."

"But now another possibility struck the inspector." Appleby reached forward and replenished Mutlow's rummer. "It set a wholly new interpretation upon the affair, and accounted for the known facts a good deal more adequately. Mutlow saw that it was more probably—indeed, almost certainly—the old man Heyhoe himself who was at the bottom of the whole thing."

"Did I? Well, I suppose I did." Mutlow was looking at once mollified and harassed. "And that the burying of Heyhoe in the snow was—was poetic justice."

"Poetic justice?" said Clarissa unexpectedly. "Boiling oil would have been poetic justice for that old wretch."

"Really, Clarissa!" Everard was much distressed. "Have a cigar. I mean, pray take another cup of coffee."

"For when we reviewed the whole run of the case we found one wholly discrepant factor. The false trails were not really false trails. They were—again in Inspector Mutlow's phrase—spotlights. And they were spotlights playing upon Ranulph Raven and his books—particularly upon the odd way in which his writing had come to be regarded as having a prophetic slant to it. Now, if the family circumstances to which I have alluded were as we believed, it would be utterly against your interests as a family to have any attention drawn to Ranulph, and you would certainly not proceed to liquidate old Mrs. Grope and the rest amid a profusion of circumstances gratuitously tending to cast that spotlight upon Ranulph's life. On the contrary, it would be in your interest to keep Ranulph well buried. With Heyhoe, however, just the reverse held. These family circumstances were such—or he suspected them to be such—that it was to his advantage that the widest notoriety should be given to Ranulph and his biography. Heyhoe, in fact, wanted public interest in this forgotten writer thoroughly aroused and his whole history dug up. And with the cunning of an uneducated, half-senile but extremely formidable old man he took the extraordinary way to it that he did. Queer things began to happen which would be bound very soon to unearth the whole Ranulph Raven legend; the newspapers would be sure to take it up and, from right back in the last century, his whole early history would be laid bare. And this, I say, because of certain circumstances, Heyhoe had reason to believe would be to his advantage. Mutlow, I think I have more or less done justice to the series of deductions by which you have solved this case?"

Mutlow was staring open mouthed at Appleby. At length he spoke with difficulty. "Certainly," he said. "I think you put it very well." His confidence grew. "Very well indeed, Appleby."

But Everard Raven was gaping too—as indeed was the whole family. "Really," he said, "I can't make head or tail of it. Except that it seems too dreadful—too dreadful for words. Robert, Judith—whatever have we done? If only—"

"And so there is the truth of the whole matter." Appleby cut briskly in. "And, fortunately, there is now really no criminal case to pursue. I say fortunately because this extraordinary and very serious affair of witchcraft and sorcery is likely to occupy all the inspector's energies for some time. I am sure you will all agree that his handling of it is likely to be such that he will gain the greatest credit."

"Certainly." The Reverend Mr. Smith was emphatic. "When Inspector Mutlow runs the weird sisters to earth his career will most assuredly be made."

Mutlow looked about the company with a mixture of bewilderment and caution. "I'm not sure," he began, "that in *this* case—"

"Ah, very true." Appleby again replenished the rummer. "Your exposure of Heyhoe's tricks might well make your reputation. Only the matter of Hannah Hoobin's boy was a little unfortunate. There is no doubt that you were led into an error of judgment in not insisting upon a vigorous enquiry earlier. As I said before, the Home Secretary—"

"I suppose you're right again, Mr. Appleby." Mutlow's voice was reluctant. He rose to his feet and drained his liqueur brandy in a fashion that made Mark Raven visibly shudder. "And I certainly do want to get on to this witchcraft and sorcery business. Crowds of newspaper men are scouring the country over it already, it seems. And if I can just get the hang of it—" He moved towards the door, while the Raven family watched him breathless. He stopped. "I'm sure I have got it right about Heyhoe," he said. "But it seems to me the law ought to take an interest in what Mr. Appleby called these family circumstances. After all, a good deal of property may depend—"

"The whole matter will be thoroughly enquired into." Appleby was suddenly authoritative. "But at the moment it is not a matter for criminal investigation."

Mutlow nodded. "Then the whole Heyhoe business and all the freakish things he did had better lie quiet. I'm sure Sir Mulberry will be best content to have it that way. But wait a minute"—and Mutlow's brow suddenly darkened—"there *is* a criminal matter still, I think you'll agee. There's that poetic justice. For how I understand it is this: Heyhoe had been playing all these queer pranks out of the books by way of stirring up folk to go and enquire into the life of this Ranulph —you know why." Mutlow looked suspiciously round the Raven circle. "You know why—and the truth there will have to out sooner or later, I don't doubt. Half-wit or no half-wit. But what I'm saying now is this: Heyhoe was up to all that devilry, and you found him out. You found him out, some or all of you, and you hoist him with his own—"

"Petard," said Appleby.

"Just that. Poetic justice. You made one of this Ranulph's tales come true about *him,* so to speak. The tale of the fellow buried so as he looked just like a decapitated head. Now I don't question but that Heyhoe was dead already, for the doctors are sure of it. But then you took the body and did that to it. And I'll tell you I think it was a right nasty thing to do." Mutlow was suddenly indignant. "And it's criminal, what's more. So I'm afraid it will be either a summons or a warrant in the morning."

Everard Raven gave a groan of despair. "But my dear officer, if you would only consider—" He fell silent as Robert's hand fell warningly on his shoulder.

Appleby had risen and was imperturbably choosing a cigar. "Mutlow," he said, "that is the one particular in which you went wrong. And I don't doubt that it was my fault. It seemed as if one of the people here present must have been responsible for burying the old fellow—or it seemed so because the notion fitted in so well with this picturesque if rather unlikely idea of poetic justice. Heyhoe's monkeying with Ranulph's stories had been found out—and by way of revenge his body was, as it were, thrust into one of the stories. But it is really plausible? If one pauses only for a moment one sees that it is not. The thing would be utterly pointless. And one doesn't exercise poetic justice on corpses, after all. So where did we go wrong? Consider first just what has to be accounted for."

"An old man buried in a snowdrift after a fashion he couldn't have contrived himself." Mutlow was decided. "That's what we have to account for."

"Exactly. But if we go on from that to seek the man—or woman—who did the burying we skip a point. Or say that we neglect another figure in the drama. Spot."

"*Spot*, Mr. Appleby?"

"Yes, indeed. For consider the situation. Here is Heyhoe wandering round in the snow, with a bottle of gin in one hand and Spot's bridle in the other. He sits down still clutching the brute; he drinks, is bemused, falls half asleep or into a stupor. Very presently he is dead. But still he is clutching Spot's bridle—and I suppose you know what a dead man's clasp can be like? The horse is uneasy, tries to wander off—and presently bolts, terrified. He drags the dead man through the snow, makes for the bridlepath leading to his stable, skirts a snowdrift but drags the body right into it and is pulled up short. He rears and prances in a a panic, scattering snow everywhere, obliterating his own traces. Then something snaps or slips and he makes for home. And there is Heyhoe's body, tugged with the animal's full might into the snowdrift. Presently there is another considerable fall—Miss Raven and I walked through it—which is quite sufficient, together with the trampling of the searchers and those who dug out the body, to obscure any signs of what had actually happened. The whole thing amounts to no more than that: an unfortunate accident."

Everard Raven, who had been agitatedly moving his glasses from one part of his long nose to another during this recital, now laid them down and momentarily buried that organ in a rummer. Fortified thus, he managed to address Appleby. "And you really suppose that this was the manner of Heyhoe's end?"

Appleby turned to Mutlow. "What do you think?"

"There's not a doubt of it!" Mutlow, now conscientiously relieved from the unnatural necessity of hounding the local gentry, was suddenly expansive. "And it shows how careful one should be about—about testing one's hypotheses. And I'm not sure it wasn't you yourself, Mr. Appleby, who was a bit hasty there."

"Undoubtedly it was."

"Now, what I've always said—" Mutlow sat down again and his eye seemed to go in quest of the brandy bottle. "What I've always said is—"

From somewhere out in the darkness first a long, low howl and then a series of rising and bloodcurdling screams nipped Mutlow's discourse in the bud. Everybody sat up or leant forward, startled and listening. Again the same sounds were heard, and this time there was added to them a vast and hideous yowling as of some gigantic, demented and supernatural cat. Mr. Smith, who had a few moments before strolled over to a window, came back to the fireside and placidly stroked Hodge. "Dear me," he said, "what an extraordinary din."

"It's the witches!" Mutlow had sprung up in great agitation. "And they're not a quarter of a mile off. I—"

"The witches?" Everard Raven looked even more bewildered than usual. "It sounds to me the sort of noise young men make at night in the streets of Oxford when they're celebrating having been out with the drag."

"There it is again!" Mutlow was looking round hurriedly for his hat. "And—good heavens!—listen to that."

The uncanny sounds had been repeated, though now a little farther away. And this time they were followed by other sounds unmistakably human—the angry shouts, cries and halloos of a pursuing mob. And Mark Raven was following Mutlow to the door. "Won't you stop for another brandy? How sorry we are! Put a few cigars in your pocket instead. . . . Dear me, the man's gone!"

Appleby had crossed over to Mr. Smith. "You don't think," he said in a low voice, "that there's any danger if they catch up with them? It sounds a pretty angry crowd."

Mr. Smith chuckled comfortably and gave Hodge's whiskers a friendly pull. "My dear sir, the witches are no more than two lads in flannel trousers and tweed jackets, perfectly well known in the district, who are taking an evening stroll in the snow. They can change from hunted to hunters instantly at need. In addition to which Charles is a Rugger Blue and Arthur is likely to be amateur middleweight champion of England." Mr. Smith rose to his feet again, with the air of surveying his own gigantic person from his white hair to his cracked and ancient shoes. "We are an old-fashioned family, Mr. Appleby, and muscular Christianity is our *métier*." Mr. Smith tickled Hodge on the ear and his expression grew serious. "I fear that you have unpleasant news for our friends, and that I myself bring the confirmation of it. But at least we have avoided the catastrophe which their levity has nearly brought upon them."

Chapter 21

"OF COURSE," said Appleby, "Heyhoe never conceived or carried out such a series of bizarre incidents as have occured, nor was Spot in any way responsible for burying him in the snow. It is only the motive with which Mutlow has departed— satisfied, as it seems—that bears some approximation to the truth. For—as Liddell discerned—publicity for Ranulph Raven and his works was what you were after. It was simply the cannibal instinct of the Ravens that was at work once more. But you had no idea of the noose into which you were doing your best to run your necks."

Rather nervously Luke Raven inserted a finger under his collar. "O what a tangled web we weave—" he began.

"Quite so. And which of you began the weaving I have no idea. Clearly the inspiration came from the odd encounter with the blind man that befell Mark and Judith years ago. Apparently you didn't interpret it aright, but it did suggest to you the unusual way that Ranulph went to work and recalled the old legend of some sort of prophetic element in his writing and its curious relationship to reality. That was a sort of seed that lay in one of your minds—I suspect Judith's, I may say— and germinated not very long ago when the family realized that it was more than usually hard-up. Could you turn Theodore into bathroom tiles or sell a little more Gawain or Mordred? And, if not, was it conceivable that the long-since defunct reputation of Ranulph could be profitably revived? He would be copyright still for a few years and there was even a certain amount of unpublished material. Surely there was some promise in that?

"But on their own merits Ranulph's books would never rise again; they were as defunct as grandfather Herbert's madrigals. It was a sensation that was wanted—something that would be written up lavishly in popular papers and create an interest in this forgotten writer that clever editors and publishers could exploit. There would be money in that; big money, even. When I first met Everard we were sitting amid a litter of newsprint that showed what big business a current sensation can be. Set going and keep up only for a few weeks the notion that the forgotten writings of a Victorian novelist were beginning to come true and your fortune would be made. What with cheap editions, serials and cinema rights the the bag could be reckoned in tens of thousands of pounds. And eventually, you supposed, when the mystery proved insoluble, interest would subside and the whole thing be let die. I don't doubt that you made a miscalculation there, and that so oddly profitable a piece of mystification would eventually have been exposed."

Mark Raven, standing before the fireplace, took a swig of brandy almost as undiscriminatingly as Mutlow had recently done. "It must be admitted," he said, "that you know all about us. May we ask just how you tumbled to it?"

"I had two immense advantages—and the first was distinctly unfair. Judith, who began by pitching up the Ranulph legend hot and strong, presently ceased to be altogether un-interested in me—and as a result ceased to be sufficiently whole-hearted in her fibs. Having marked me down, it seems, with breath-taking speed, she came to feel that piling on the Ranulph deception was a bit thick—as later you were good enough to do yourself. But the second advantage came before that. As soon as I saw that board at the station telling me that I had been neatly derailed at a place called Appleby's End I knew that something was up—and that Everard was at the bottom of it. He knew my name—and perhaps my profes-sion, since an old photograph of myself was lying about the compartment thoroughout our journey. The coincidence was much too striking to be true—and in fact, of course, Everard was brilliantly improvising—as he was to do again, all too brilliantly, a few hours later. Appleby's End was a local name that had caught Ranulph's eye, and he had given it to a story. And here was an Appleby looking for a night's lodg-ing! Surely something could be made of this in the grand plot that was going forward. Anyway, Everard picked me up on spec. And it made me suspicious of him from the first.

"And now go back to the way your plans developed. First there was the little affair of *The Coach of Cacus*—a mere trial run, which came to nothing, and was merely by way of seeing what you could do. Then you started on *Paxton's Destined Hour* and were all set for real publicity. That a dead novel-ist's son should be served with a tombstone just as a character in one of his books had been would be sensation enough. But you had bad luck. Your family solicitor—whom Everard was so anxious to call in this evening to protect him from Mut-low—happened to be down here at the time. And with the wise discretion of his kind he insisted that so odd a matter be kept quiet. So presently you turned to *The Medusa Head*. Here was all this marble of Theodore's lying about, and no-body so much as willing to make a tile out of it. And here on the shelf was a yarn of Ranulph's in which all sorts of crea-tures were mysteriously turned to stone. The combination of circumstances was irresistible! And so the campaign against the Farmers was launched—with Spot and a farm-cart, no doubt, to do the carrying. It was well-organized this time, and was going to be the big thing. You even had matters so arranged that reporters were on the scene in no time. But again you had ill luck—on this occasion the most wretched luck. The Farmers were strongly opposed to publicity, and as it happened they had a pull both with the *Banner* and the *Blare*. Whereupon you went so far as to persuade the Hoobins, who are both a shade simple, to get their boy away from Tiffin Place and hide him. And you replaced him with one of Adolphus's waxworks. But again nothing much happened, for the local police didn't make quite the stir they ought, and so the Medusa mystery hung fire. And this was the state of affairs when I had the good fortune to meet Everard on the train. He was feeling rather blue—was not *Patagonia to Potato* almost out, and *Religion* barely on the stocks, and the *Revised and Enlarged Resurrection* looming ahead as soon as the *New Millennium* should be finished? And was not the whole great Ranulph plot horribly indecisive? So that when he realized that here was an Appleby who had small chance of a room for the night he snapped him up at once and with alacrity as a fresh possibility. And—once more—the surprise and consternation of the rest of you when I was introduced was demonstrably greater than could be caused by a mere coincidence of names, Everard, you felt, had taken the bit between his teeth and was proposing some new and pre-cipitate move."

"Hardly that." Everard Raven puffed at a cigar and seemed to feel that a modest disclaimer was due. "I had nothing clearly formulated in my mind. And subsequent events, my dear John, drove your possibilities quite out of my head."

"No doubt. And it's to the subsequent events that we now come. When Judith and I were separated from the rest of you by the accident at the ford she was left with rather a pretty problem. I was an Appleby—and a Scotland Yard detective. How did I fit in? Was I spying upon the whole plan, or was I an innocent instrument of Everard's? She chose to pump me full of the Ranulph mystery—and so was more communicative about her family than such a well-bred young person would naturally be. It was odd."

"I'm not a well-bred young person!" Judith was indignant. "You might be speaking of one of Lady Farmer's beastly dogs."

"Judith," said Clarissa severely, "if your manners made an

adequate impression upon this young man that is surely one satisfactory aspect of this deplorable affair. And never forget, child, that even an artist may be gentlewoman."

"And now for Heyhoe. The accident had given him a shock and he abandoned Spot—perhaps to Luke, but I am not sure—and wandered off with his bottle of gin in the snow. The rest of you spent some time hunting for the carriage and ourselves down the river and then, so as to have a better chance of contacting us, you separated and each made your way home independently. So the next adventure was Everard's alone. It was a shock to Judith—and later it shocked and puzzled Mark, who was plainly anxious as to what his sister made of it until he had an opportunity to slip out and discuss it with her. And I think, indeed, that Everard kept his own counsel for the rest of the night.

"He came upon Heyhoe, stone dead. And again he improvised. I would say at a guess that his action can best be explained by heredity—for might one not except a macabre streak to emerge in Ranulph Raven's son? Anyway, here was Heyhoe's body, and a great deal of snow, and the sudden recollection of an unpublished tale of Ranulph's based on the story of a gentleman who used to take earth baths in his spinney." Appleby paused. "It had been an exciting evening: first the acquiring of an Appleby and then the accident at the ford. It must have thrown Everard a bit off his balance, for this of Heyhoe was altogether an error of judgment—extremely dangerous, and almost certain to lead to trouble."

"Oh dear, oh dear!" Everard Raven looked excessively dejected. "It was not very decent, either, I fear. Smith, you will not like this; you will not like it at all."

Mr. Smith said nothing, but exercised a friend's privilege to pick up the poker and stir the fire. Robert Raven came forward to help him. "Everard," said Robert, "has always been of a sanguine disposition, with some genius for making the best of things. He was proposing to make the best of poor old Heyhoe."

"No doubt. And now you plan was fairly launched indeed. Within twelve hours it was showing every sign of presently becoming a national sensation. Unfortunately, this ghost of Ranulph's that you had summoned from the grave was likely to prove a very Frankenstein. And the reason for this lay in the family circumstances which Mutlow and I became possessed of this afternoon."

With something of Everard's obstinate hopefulness, Clarissa peered into an empty coffee-pot. "This is most disturbing," she said. "Let us hear the worst. What can these mysterious family circumstances be?"

"I can explain them in a very few words." Appleby turned again to Everard. "This business of living off Ranulph apart, it is your family habit to speak or think little of him. He is not really among the more reputable of the Ravens, I fear it must be said. For one thing his writings are a little too crude and popular in manner for your rather sophisticated family taste. But also—and more importantly—he was a man of most irregular life. He had numerous illegitimate children. Heyhoe was your half-brother—just as he was a sort of half-uncle to Mark and Judith, and a cousin to Miss Clarissa. Now, early on, and when I was considering the possibilities of some such case as Mutlow eventually fell for, you may remember my asking if Heyhoe was older than the rest of you. And you declared that he was. The point of the question you will realize at once if I ask you another: are you really certain that Heyhoe *was* illegitimate?

"Heyhoe's mother became—or thought she became—a Mrs. Grope. But I am afraid we shall find that Ranulph Raven—whether through mere indiscretion or from some eccentric delight in the possible consequences that might result long after—had contracted a previous legal marriage with her. And this means that Heyhoe was your father's only legitimate child. When you remember, therefore, that this same old Mrs. Grope met her death some little time ago in a manner which, although in fact purely accidental, could well be given a sinister interpretation, you will see what danger Everard was in when he fell to playing tricks with Heyhoe's body. But that's not all."

"Not all!" Everard Raven had let his cigar go out and had given himself over to frank dismay.

"Most unfortunately not. For just as Heyhoe was *your father's* legitimate son so is the half-wit boy whom you involved in your Tiffin Place plan *Heyhoe's* legitimate son. For before the woman who is now known as Hannah Hoobin went through a form of marriage with her present reputed husband she had married Heyhoe. Or at least it seems probable it was so."

"Heyhoe certainly lived with her." It was Robert Raven who spoke. "I don't remember quite when, but he was already an elderly man. He had left us for a while, and we were rather doubtful about taking him back. But are not all these family circumstances, as you called them, purely conjectural?"

Appleby nodded. "As far as I am concerned they are so. But from the very vigorous diversionary action which Mr. Smith has thought it expedient to take this afternoon and evening I think he probably possesses some certainty in the matter—enough to have convinced him that your elaborate prank was in dire danger of the most dreadful misinterpretation."

"That was precisely the position." Mr. Smith was affectionately pulling Hodge's tail. "But before I explain it I should like to know, Mr. Appleby, how you came so readily to distinguish my part in the affair?"

Appleby laughed. "I was never in any doubt about its being yourself who made away with Mrs. Ulstrup's cake. For, as it happened, I was aware of the association of ideas which suddenly prompted you to feel that an immediate outbreak of witchcraft and sorcery in the district would afford a desirable diversion from your friend's affairs. You had seen the possible case against them, you were wondering what could be done; and you happened to mention—though in another connection —the Tchambuli."

"To be sure!"

"They are a culture much given to sorcery—and a few seconds later Mrs. Ulstrup's cake had gone. Clearly it was the Tchambuli who had put the idea into your head. And, equally clearly, if the thing were to be done effectively, Mrs. Ulstrup's cake must be only the beginning of a swift and concentrated campaign."

"I take some credit for the speed with which it developed. But now I must explain that for a long time I have known that the old man, Heyhoe, had been married to Mrs. Hoobin, and that the boy was their legitimate child. The marriage took place some seventeen years ago at Yatter. On the possible marriage of your father to the woman who became Mrs. Grope I possess no certainty. I have, however, picked up a story to the effect that Mrs. Grope when a young woman ran away with a gentleman to Scotland. And so I fear that the marriage is only too likely. Having this information, I very readily came to see the extreme danger of the position. I knew very well that it was incredible that any of you should commit homicide; at the same time I saw the conclusion to which the police might very readily come. A little clouding of the issue, I thought, might give us time to see where we were. As it happens, my intervention was scarcely necessary as far as the police investigation was concerned since Mr. Appleby had ample ability not only to arrive at the true state of affairs but to carry his local colleague a good distance beyond! But it is something, perhaps, to have headed off the newspapers successfully. Very soon your family affairs will be completely forgotten, and can be quietly adjusted in whatever fashion is proper."

"Adjusted?" Everard Raven was frowning into the fire. "If I understand these revelations aright they mean that young Hoobin is the rightful owner of Dream."

"Would that not depend upon the terms of your father's will?"

Decisively—a thing rare with him—Everard shook his head. "We must not shuffle. The legitimate male heir has inherited here since the sixteenth century. He must continue to do so, even if there is little left to inherit. Both Luke and Robert will agree with me." Everard paused. "Good heavens!" he said. "Two generations of rightful owners excluded. It's exactly like one of our father's romances. John, didn't somebody say something about poetic justice?"

"It is certainly rather striking. The machinery you set in motion in order to make something out of Ranulph is operating to deprive you of the little he actually left you."

"This Hannah Hoobin's boy." Judith broke a long silence. "What's he like? John, you've seen him."

Appleby smiled. "I should call him perfectly charming. Is he not a Raven, after all?"

Mr. Smith, who had been accommodated with a second

rummer of brandy, nodded over it approvingly. "Capital," he said. "How much in this degenerate century one relishes a compliment well turned."

"Capital," repeated Mark. "The Ravens—or some of them —are charming. But, equally, the Ravens—and all of them— are broke. Indeed, they are about to be turned out into the snow. John, I don't suppose you happen to be wealthy?"

"I can buy Judith her barn."

Mark sighed. "But at least you are efficient—extremely so. Everard and you together will no doubt do the best you can for us all. I suggest a small villa in some provincial town, with an attic that can be turned into a scriptorium."

"I should like," said Luke, "to be let take away Theodore's Genius guarding the Secret of the Tomb."

"I hope," said Judith, "that the charming boy won't greatly mind what I've done to some of Theodore's marbles."

"We must ask the Farmers," said Robert, "to return the pig and the cow and the dog and the waxwork. Though explanations will be a trifle difficult."

"The other day," said Everard, "I had a letter asking me if I would undertake a Dictionary of Universal Biography in forty volumes. I had better write at once and accept."

"I understand," said Clarissa, "that all this turns upon the supposed marriages of Ranulph and of the man Heyhoe?"

Mr. Smith nodded. "That is so."

"Then we may desist from this nonsensical talk and go to bed."

"I beg your pardon?"

"Except Judith and—um—John. They may remain chatting by the fire. I suggest that they consider taking the Hall farm. That will be most convenient, I think. On Sundays we will expect them to take luncheon with us at Dream. I must remember to tell Rainbird."

"Clarissa," said Everard gently, "possibly you are overtired. I suggest—"

"I understood you to say"—Clarissa had turned, unheeding, to Mr. Smith—"that the man Heyhoe had married the woman now called Mrs. Hoobin some seventeen years ago?"

"There can be no doubt of it."

"There can be every doubt, sir. No legal marriage can then have taken place."

"May I ask why?"

"Mr. Smith, I fear that you may. Forty-one years ago tomorrow I married the man Heyhoe myself. It is true that I had reason to think better of it a few days later, and paid him to be silent. But Everard, Robert, Luke—you need not stare so." And Clarissa tilted her chin and looked at Appleby. "Was he not a Raven, after all?"